The Bods

Spike Greening

First Edition
Published By House Of Loki
Professor Teldersstraat 372
Vlaardingen, Nederland
KVK : 93090900

This is a work of fiction. Similarities to real people, places, or events are entirely coincidental.

The Bods
Written By
Spike Greening
ISBN: 978-90-834214-0-7
Cover Design by
Spike Greening
Formatted by
Callum Pearce & Spike Greening
Edited by
Callum Pearce
Copyright © 2024 Spike Greening

This story is for

Spinach

it's been his all along really

Don't listen to the older Generations,

we don't know what we are doing

My library
Was dukedom large enough

The Tempest, Act I, Sc. II

A Note on the pronunciation of names:

Pronounce them however you like,

they don't mind.

"Hwæt!"

The Bods

Chapter One

This time, Aethelred was ready. He dimmed the glow lamp on top of his staff and scratched his long pointed ear, trying to work out how long he had been cramped into the tiny space – it seemed like forever, but Red (as most other Bods called him) knew it could only have been a short time at the most. He had carefully hidden inside a gap in the topmost bookshelf in Duke Humphrey's Library. It sat majestically at the westernmost end of the Bodleian Library, as dawn slowly poured over the golden city of Oxford. The hiding place was perfect, the books on either side were large and - for now at least – quiet, calm and rested. It helped that he was only about as tall as a normal paperback book, which wasn't too short for a Bod. Sometimes, Red got quite annoyed about his height. Red sometimes got quite annoyed about a lot of things that didn't really matter. This morning he was glad that he was one of the smaller of his Carrel; these were the loose groups or guilds that each Bod joined when they had made up their minds as to which path they wanted to take through their lives in The Library. His height meant that who or whatever he was waiting for would have to be looking out for him too in order to see him at all. He hadn't told anyone what he had planned, not even his best friends Aedelberga or Aethelstan.

It had taken him an hour or so to climb this particular bookcase. Red had spied the hiding place a few evenings before from lower down on one of the longer stacks. He had been trying to coax a particularly grumpy Latin textbook back into its own section, but he had never climbed this particular case before. He was glad he had decided to kit up with his best climbing gear: carefully crafted carabiners and quickdraws, ropes and ascenders all adjusted and tweaked by Red over hours and days and months of climbing. Most Bods customised their bookcase climbing kit to some extent. They added and changed bits as they gained in confidence or more often than not, in total indifference to how dangerous it was. Climbing up and over a home that was made up of mile after mile of bookcases, stacks, piles, boxes, and tread ways. The whole Library was, to the Bods, a vast dominion made up of much more than just books and shelves. It contained workshops, chambers, corridors and bridges. There were hundreds of walkways and secret passages. The small inhabitants could use these to travel to any part of their amazing homeland.

Some Bods specialised in swinging, others preferred to climb and winch across the great chasms of the Library. Red had heard stories lately that a few of the more adventurous Bods (probably from the Shackleton Carrel they were renowned as the craziest of all the groups) had begun experimenting with gliders and balloon flights in the grand halls of the ancient Bodleian. Red just loved the climb for itself. He still held the Carrel record for the quickest free climb up to the highest point on the Tower of the Five Orders, right up to the Dawn Supper room right at the top. The dare earned him a severe scolding from several of the older Bods, especially Madam Brunda. Red didn't mind, he was used to being thought of as a troublemaker.

The climb had gained him great admiration from many more, especially those in his own Bandinel Carrel. The other Carrels had pretended not to be too impressed, many of the Bods stuck within their own group. Red didn't care where anyone was based if they were his friend, that was all that really mattered. The Carrels had existed forever, and you could join any one of the many that rose and fell within the society that the Bods had created for themselves. Their society grew Bod by Bod as the Bodleian grew stone by stone into the magical fabric of the city. It was important to their feelings of belonging that the Bods stand up for their own Carrel. Sometimes, small quarrels and battles burst to the surface making them pull tighter together. Much more often, it was through feats of ridiculous daring such as Red's climb, or amazing new engineered creations that Aedelberga came up with again and again that a Carrel celebrated its own place in The Library.

***

Red checked all of his gear twice over again, just to make sure. His breath steamed out in the freezing cold air of the dawning day. The dimmed glow lamp of his staff gave off no heat. They were carefully designed and built by the engineers and artificers of Craster Carrel so as not to cause any danger of fire within The Library. That was the thing the Bods feared above all. Red was so mindful of being seen by those he hid in wait for that it gave off almost no light either. Red was grateful for his thick, long coat and leather and wool fingerless gloves. He made sure no one had come in, and carefully stood up on the edge of the shelf stretching to relieve the cramp that had begun to creep into his legs. Rubbing his eyes, he surveyed the grand room along its length. He should have asked Berga for a pair of her dark goggles, they could see in the dark almost as if there was full moonlight. From his vantage point atop the last of the bookcases, he could see most of the other cases on either side of the aisle that ran the length of Duke Humphrey's Library.

The Duke was a legendary figure in the myths and stories of the Bods. It was to The Duke that the littlest of the Bods wrote their wishing letters as The Midwinter feast approached. It was thought by some Bods that it was The Duke who came in the night to take those oldest of Bods off beyond the world when their days were done after the Great Goodbye. Red didn't like to think about that part of their stories, he rubbed his eyes again and peered further into the gloom.

From the Seldon End of The Library behind him (its great window still steeped in darkness as the day slowly awoke) his small black bead-like eyes scanned along to the doorway at the Arts End. He could just make out the lights across the Schools' quadrangle to the Tower of The Five Orders where most of his fellow Bods would be gathering for Dawn Supper. Few of the Bods went about The Library in the daylight hours, compared to their nighttime travels. Their presence tended to confuse the students even more than the poor humans were confounded by the world already.

Red settled back down to wait. He knew that someone or something had managed to breach the careful wards and protections that were spun around The Library almost continuously by the strange Hyde Carrel of Bods known politely as "The Guardians", and somewhat less politely by most as "The Weirdies". Something had got in and Red was sure that it or they were attacking books. It seemed to have been happening at random in different parts of The Library, so no one else appeared to have noticed. It was so unheard of that some of the older Bods (especially Offa, who had developed a sharp dislike of Red and his friends) had openly laughed at him when he had tried to explain his worries at the last Moot. After a week's planning and a near sighting of some intruder only a few nights ago in the Divinity School, Red was certain that he had worked out a vague pattern as to how they had gotten in and where they would come next. The fact that someone was attacking his homemade Red seethed with anger. How could anything or anyone want to bring harm to this most wondrous of places?

Red loved these buildings! He had after all spent all of his short life in and around them. He knew, deep down in his bones, that being a Bod was something special. the Bods had, it seemed to Red, always been here. Summoned by Sir Thomas Bodley himself and given their charter to protect the books and keep the great Library from danger. Some whispered that the old half-mad teacher Erasmus was old enough to have met Sir Thomas in the Beginning Days. Erasmus had been banished from the Library by the Grand Council, in case any of his crazy ideas should infect the minds of the younger Bods. Almost all of the Bods thought this highly unlikely as that would make Erasmus over five hundred years old. This seemed a bit steep to most. Red wasn't so certain. Sir Thomas' Covenant was the sacred pledge each Bod took when they chose their own Carrel and took to the halls and bookshelves in their own right as the protectors and guardians of The Library. There had of course been earlier guardians in the more ancient parts, known now as The Humphs. These had passed into the bedtime stories and legends along with The Duke. Tales that were told to tired little Bods as they drifted to sleep in their cots between the ancient manuscripts and old journals, the smell of old paper and ancient wood floating into their dreams. Hundreds of generations of Bods had grown up within the mighty walls of The Bodleian. Each was as equal as the next as Sir Thomas' Charter made clear. All were born into The Republic of Lettered Men. Some of the grumpier old male Bods had thought to use this as a way of stopping the girl Bods from getting their fair share. the Bods weren't ever falling for that nonsense, all were equal and that was that. the Bods were so very proud of their place in the wondrous city.

Even though the Bods, on the whole, did not venture from The Library. It was large enough that they could spend their whole lives exploring it for new areas, indeed that was what the Shakleton Carrel did all the time. the Bods knew that they were just a part of the strange and wondrous collection of creatures and beings that made what was known as the Oxford Arcanum. From the quarrelsome gargoyles and grotesques that look after the upper parts of the city, to the wonderfully confused Old Gods (they wander the city, under their own covenants and protections), through to the great, but very self-important Trolls beneath their Thames bridges, always plotting, always squabbling. Through all of these and all the others in The Arcanum (including the strange peoples and denizens of UnderOxford – who were better left to their own devices), the Bods knew they did something special. They protected the books. They looked after the stories. The Library was their pride and their joy.

Each Bod found their own place and way in the Library. They found what they were good at and did it (in the case of Aethelstan, Red's best friend, this appeared to be mainly eating and sleeping). Those who had no desire to climb and explore the stacks became guardians, teachers or poets and artists. There were makers of all things within The Republic. Cooks, dreamers, gardeners and musicians, mapmakers and healers all found their own way. Each gave what they could to the whole of the community, accepting from it what they needed to have a good and comfortable life. the Bods grew to know the Library and learn its ways, all of its rooms, its moods and needs. Many Bods could track volumes across the entire Library and knew where to find any book, even when that book might have decided that it didn't want to be found. As they grew, the younger Bods learned all the lore and skills which would help them as they chose their place within The Library. They learned how to avoid being seen by the students that insisted on wandering about the place. They got to know which of The Library's human (and not so human) staff would talk to you and which would jump up on a chair and try to bash your brains out with a newspaper ten times bigger than you. A Bod learned it all. Then, when they thought they were ready, the young Bod would take the Oath beneath the arches of the Divinity school. The glow light bounced shadows across the beautiful ceiling as their solemn agreement echoed into the air. Each would then roll up their sleep cloth and take their new gear and staff with its glowlamp. They headed off into the Library and the adventure that was the rest of their lives.

Red enjoyed himself inside this life (though truly he had known no other). There was always time to sit and read. Admittedly, trying to read books that were considerably bigger than you could be a bit of a problem. Red really did try his best to look after the books, even the grumpy ungrateful ones that wandered high into dark corners and had to be coaxed out with calm words and chocolate biscuits. When he wanted some company and friendly voices he would travel over to Midnight Feast or Dawn Supper. There he would sit and chat about the latest mad climbs or which Carrel was fighting all the others at the moment. There was always plenty of bread, soup, chocolate and chatter in the halls when the Bods met up. Almost every night there were games across the roofs of the New Bodleian and long nights sitting in the high places of the Radcliffe Camera.

This was one of the most forbidden places, off limits to the younger Bods for many years. Stories had grown, as they will, about what lived in the upper shadows of the dome. Many said that the exiled Erasmus, oldest and maddest of those who dwelt in The Library, was imprisoned there. Locked away, shrieking and cackling to himself, spinning ancient curses on any young Bod who was foolish enough to trespass up amongst the forbidden pathways. This of course meant that Red spent as much time up there as he could. It wasn't easy to get up to the tiny rooms high in the uppermost reaches of the Camera. Red had to be sneaky and full of cunning, which luckily, he was. When he had finally managed to get into the dusty chamber at the very top of the dome (where did all the dust come from? Red was sure there hadn't always been so much) he had found no insane wizard. No evil curse came crashing down upon him. Red had simply left chocolate on the table outside the inner wooden door, which seemed to be bolted from the inside. After several weeks, the empty cloth bag where the chocolate had been began to be returned holding biscuits. So each visit Red would leave chocolate and then return many hours later, to find biscuits. This seemed like a perfectly good exchange to him. On the night that Red had run from the Moot, one of the large meetings with all the other Bods, his cheeks ablaze with embarrassment and eyes full of angry tears, he had fled up to the tiny door to find a small scrap of paper on the table. Scrawled on it in tiny spidery handwriting were the words "I believe you".

Red sat, nibbling on a chunk of cheese and swigging his flask of dandelion and burdock, waiting for those who would cause harm to the Library to finally reveal themselves. His cheeks again burned as he remembered how the other Bods had laughed at him at that last Moot

"Is this one of your foolish tales again Aethelred?" Offa's booming voice filled the grand chamber of the Convocation House, bouncing off the fan-vaulted ceiling. Many of the other Bods laughed. Red scowled at the floor, biting his top lip to stop it from quivering. Madam Brunda swept into the centre of the Moot and raised her hand, the Moot fell silent. Most, if not all, had been nursed and cared for by the old Bod. She had pulled them through so many colds, sicknesses, nightmares and thunderstorms in her long, long life.

"We are all equal here," her voice was quieter than Offa's but no less powerful for that.

"We are all of the Republic of Lettered Men. Young Red's thoughts are equal to all other opinions." She turned slightly and smiled at him, winking her one good eye. Stories told how she had lost the other many years before in a terrible battle. Fighting some faceless being from the darker reaches of UnderOxford that had somehow found its way into the Library's domains. Red blushed and stared even more intently at his scuffed brass toe-capped shoes.

"If Red says something is coming, then I for one believe him!" Brunda stepped back from the centre, she moved slowly these days, her glow light dim atop her staff. Many of the younger Bods called out in agreement, the oldest Bodshout of them all;

"All equal! All equal!"

Brunda held up her hand and they fell silent once more, "And yet some feel they are more equal than others, eh Offa?" She stopped in front of the larger Bod. His height had always been impressive but now his waist was almost its equal. His once magnificent, walrus-like moustache now tipped with grey, his thinning hair hidden beneath an elaborately decorated pill box cap.

"Madam Brunda is of course a wise counsellor," Offa muttered through obviously gritted teeth. However, it is still the case that Aethelred has often come flying into a Moot with farfetched tales of some terrible scheme or other!"

Red span around to look Offa in the eye. The difference in their height, their stature and their experience had never been more obvious. "They are not farfetched!" Red felt his cheeks burning and tears welling in his eyes. "I watch things, I read things. I see patterns. And the dust! I think Erasmus..."

A great groan went up from the Moot. Offa stared at the vaulted ceiling, flinging his huge arms up into the air. The tips of his moustache quivered with rage.

"Of course! Erasmus, Erasmus!" Many of the Moot laughed a little, others shook their heads.

"The great Erasmus has chosen to ignore us. Erasmus has attended no Moot in years!" Offa swung his vast belly around, addressing the whole chamber. "Erasmus is a mad old fool. Hidden away, writing works no one wants to read; spouting nonsense and drivel into the minds of young fools like YOU!" Offa span back to point straight at Aethelred.

Red had already stormed from the Convocation House by one of the myriad of tiny doorways that were scattered throughout the skirting boards and wainscotings of the Library. The one he had chosen was almost invisible, directly in the base of the Vice Chancellor's Throne.

***

In the slowly growing dawn light, atop the bookcase, Red finished off the flask of dandelion and burdock and bit down hard on the wedge of cheese.

"I'll show them," he thought. "I know something is going

on, even if I don't know what it is."

At that moment, a door opened some way off at the east-end entrance of Duke Humphrey's Library. Red sat upright and lightly tapped his staff to extinguish the glow. At first, he thought it was Richelieu, the Library cat. He realised quickly that it was the vast shape of a human. What were they doing in the Library at this hour? Red rose nervously as he realised that he didn't recognise them at all.

the Bods got to know the humans who worked in the Library quite well. Many had been working within the venerable walls for most of their lives. Some of the younger Librarians were often skittish if they spotted a Bod. This wasn't often, the Bods were small and extremely good at hiding and disappearing if they need to. The older humans in the library got used to the little guardians of the books. Some of the researchers who had been coming to the Library for years even left small gifts for them. Chocolate was a popular one. Some things were highly prized and quickly taken to the Artificers of Craster Carrel. They would turn them into climbing gear or even more weird and wonderful items. They would be swiftly put to use.

Most humans didn't notice the Bods at all, which was just how the Bods liked it. the Bods got good at recognising the different regulars within their domain, This one, Red was sure, wasn't a regular at all.

His hair was white-blond and very curly, though they were always giant to any Bod, he was tall even in human terms. He walked along the Library, actually, he strutted, as though he thought himself very important. His slightly worried glances around the room suggested he also knew that he really shouldn't be here at all. What was he doing? Red packed up his gear and decided he needed a closer look. It was clear to Red that this was something to do with the trouble he had been looking for. Many of the books close to the human had become agitated and were rattling about, seemingly unhappy to be anywhere near him. Even the older, wiser volumes were on edge and their pages rustled in annoyance. Red tried to comfort them as he rummaged in his backpack finding then pulling out a brass clip. He attached it to his belt without even a glance. He scooped his flask into his bag and the last piece of cheese into his mouth. Red then stepped, without any hesitation at all, off the top of the bookcase and plunged down into the darkness. The air whistled past his ears, the flaps of his hat quivering as he dropped with absolute confidence towards the floor of The Library. His long coat fluttered about him as he plunged. Halfway down the bookcase, the mechanism on his belt snapped into place and connected with one of several carefully positioned rope pullies strung out across the Library. This caused Red to swiftly and knowingly change direction and shoot across the next bookcase with one pure, fluid movement. the Bods had been building these ropeways for centuries and they got better at it with each generation. Most of the humans didn't even notice the crisscross of ropes and pullies, those that did either thought them cobwebs in the upper vaults of the chambers or knew them for the engineering marvels that they were. They simply left the Bods to their strange and curious ways. Red hit the next bookcase right on the corner, picking up speed and spinning slightly as he used the added momentum to swing to a higher shelf. He changed at a set of brass points buried into the oak of the shelf with only the slightest shudder of his gear. After a moment's climb, he slowed and landed with as little noise as possible.

Red unhooked his gear from the web of ropes and checked his new position. From this vantage point, he could clearly see the human that he had spotted entering the room. He seemed to be speaking to someone else now, though Red couldn't tell what or who was there. They seemed to be deep in the recess of the bookcase opposite. Red fumbled in his backpack, the gloom of the dawn light was seeping in through the glorious windows of Duke Humphrey's Library. Red didn't want to risk igniting his glowlamp and drawing attention from who or whatever was down there. After some time furkling about, Red found the device he was looking for.

***

It had taken Red quite some time (and a fair few mint humbugs) to convince Aedelberga to build the device for him. She often made elaborate climbing equipment for her friends. Her legs might not work, but her hands and her mind were more than a match for any of the other Bod inventors, artificers or blacksmiths. Aedelberga rarely left the Bods' workshops in the lower chambers of The Library as it tired her to take too long a journey on her crutches. This meant that she was always eager to hear the latest of Red's madcap schemes or strange stories about what was afoot in the larger domains of The Library.

She had looked at the badly scribbled plans Red had sketched out. They were on scraps of paper he had unscrunched from one of his long coat's many pockets.

"So what you want me to build, is a sort of ear trumpet?" She turned the plans round and around, trying to work out which way up the contraption was meant to go.

"Exactly!" Red tried to say. He wiped his mouth. It was full of a cube of chocolate one of the Divinity Professors had left for him in the main reading area. "Come on Berga, this should be easy for you!"

Berga lifted herself up on her crutches and moved over to her workbench. "It is Red, but I just don't see the point, that's all. So I create this thing and you can hear what's going on a long way away, so what?"

Red sat down on the floor and crossed his legs. He picked up a small lead box and stared into it through the small glass porthole-like door in the side.

"What's this?" He rattled it next to his ear.

Berga scowled.

"Careful with that. It's a Jericho Ember, very rare, if not unique. I swapped it with one of the Exeter Gargoyles for some work on his piping a few weeks ago." She prodded him with her crutch and he flinched out of the way. He knew very well how much those crutches could hurt if Berga caught you just right.

"I'm certain something's going on in the Library, I just can't seem to pinpoint what it is. So I thought, if I could hear better, I might work out what they were up to."

He tilted his head and smiled his biggest smile at her, which usually worked. She raised her eyebrows at him and caught the paper bag of mint humbugs that he had hurriedly pulled from his pocket and thrown to her.

"Okay. Come back tomorrow and I'll have the thing sorted."

Red grinned, ducking as the crutch just missed his head.

***

Red sat in the growing dawn light with a brass curved cone on top of his head and small earphones made of wood and tin in his ears. He was feeling rather foolish and hoping that Berga had known what she was doing. He held a dark wood box in his hand (it was connected to the cone by some thick cord from an old telephone), while carefully turning brass dials on its top. With seemingly nothing at all happening, Red was beginning to feel incredibly stupid and was glad none of his friends were here to see him. He'd get Berga for this. He bet that she was sitting right now with Stan and the others, telling them about how she had got the better of stupid Red and made him sit in the dark with a cone on his head. He was just starting to think up various cruel and unusual things to do to Berga in revenge when he heard a voice right next to him.

"I've been waiting rather a long time you know."

Red nearly toppled over, the cone came loose as he twisted

and turned to see who had got up here without him noticing. After a few panicked moments, Red realised that the cone was, in fact, working perfectly and the voice was coming from down below in one of the alcoves. Berga was a genius!

"I must make myself perfectly clear," the voice was a man's, but incredibly whiney.

"I want all of this sorted and finished by the end of the month. Your... people, or whatever they are, need to get things moving. I want this over and done with!" he sounded quite agitated.

Red turned the dials back and forth, but he couldn't quite catch what the hidden one was saying. It was some kind of rasping whispery voice, just out of range, but Red felt it rather than heard it, like nails down a blackboard. They must have said something, because the man then almost shouted, Red had to turn the noise dial down.

"I have given you two off your list. It is by no means simple to get things out of this place you know!" The speaker stepped backwards then, into the dim light that was slowly growing in Duke Humphrey's Library. His white-blond hair almost glowed in the dawn.

The hidden one cackled a nasty little laugh, the very sound of a sneer. Red only just heard it, but even so, it made his spine shiver. The speaker said something and the human nodded, moving backwards as the other shuffled forwards into the pool of light forming on the Library floor. Their movements echoed how the day pushed morning into the ancient halls from the windows at the eastward end of the chambers. The books in their old cases fluttered slightly as the coldness of the dark left them. It seemed to Red that a different kind of coldness had entered the hall, and was coming into his eye line right then and there.

The thing that shuffled into view seemed not a great

deal larger than Red himself. It was difficult to tell for it was swathed in layers of old, seemingly mouldy layers of rag-like coats and jackets. Even though it seemed much smaller than the human, in fact not much bigger than a Bod, this did not prevent the larger of the two from retreating backwards. He seemed half repelled and yet also half scared of the thing now hunched before him. Red moved silently forwards to the edge of the bookcase and peered over, adjusting the cone and moving the dials as he did so. If it was a Bod, then Red had never seen any like it before. Its filthy, cloak-like clothes were covered in dust and appeared to be stained and damp. Even the most ancient of the books in this section of the Library seemed terribly agitated by its presence. This unnerved Red, as the oldest books had seen almost everything in their time. Something must be wrong for them to get this upset.

The creature cackled again, then coughed and gurgled before spitting a great ball of thick phlegm onto the floor of The Library. As soon as it hit, the spot on the floor blistered and began to bubble with acidic smoke. The human stepped swiftly backwards. The small being raised its encrusted arms and pushed the hood from its oversized head. Red did all he could to stop himself from gasping. Its skin was a greyish green and one eye was shut tight with scabs, dripping pus like yellow tears. The other eye was huge and seemed to swivel of its own accord within the great warty lids that sat above and below it. These scabrous lids barely contained it, as the piercing yellow orb took in its surroundings. The thing's nose was no more than a stub with two slits in the middle swell of its face, both of which dripped more noxious gloop down onto the floor.

The great warty eye swivelled round and for one heart-stopping moment, Red thought that the awful creature had seen him. Thankfully, after a moment, it tilted its head back towards the human. Red almost wished that the cone had stopped working when he finally heard the creature speak clearly. It cleared its throat by once again spitting onto the Library floor, adding to the smouldering slop that blistered the tiles.

"My dear Mr Simper," spittle fell from its mouth, which seemed more like a mere slash in the bottom half of its face. Only there to separate the nostrils from the scarred and blotched chins below. "You should not concern your good self with my humble part in this little enterprise."

"I assure you (cough) that my loyal troops will be perfectly ready to begin their duties (spit) by this time on the 'morrow," phlegm oozed down its chins and stained the stains already present on one of its layers of coats.

It looked to the ceiling of Duke Humphrey's Library, seemingly lost for a moment in its hatred of the place. It smirked and waved a long-fingered hand in the air, turning its eye once again on Mr Simper. He cowered even further back from this beast of a thing that was far smaller than he and yet infinitely more terrifying.

"Simply (cough) bring me the items that I have so humbly requested of you (Spit), and we are able to proceed with our delicious adventure."

Spittle dripped and slid from its mouth in thin shiny strands to its hand as the creature licked its filthy fingers and then waved Mr Simper away. Mr Simper bowed slightly.

"Well, erm, very well. I shall meet you at the same hour tomorrow in the New Bodleian across the way."

Mr Simper scuttled backwards and virtually ran from The Library, no sign now of his earlier strutting.

Red looked back to where the revolting creature had stooped, but it had vanished. The blistered tiles and vile pool of spittle with its nasty smell was the only sign it had been there at all. The nearest books were all agitated

and rattled in their cases, sending spiralling dust patterns into the air. The dust glinted as the morning sun flooded into the Library. After descending quickly to the ground, Red soothed the books as best he could. He was careful to avoid the fetid patch of goo on the floor. He packed up his gear and began climbing the nearest stack as the light gushed through the stained glass windows and brought in the new day.

***

Red made his way from the Old Bodleian to the Radcliffe Camera via one of the many underground tunnels that crisscross this area of the city. Some were manmade, used to transport any of the millions of books and manuscripts from one part of the Library to another. Others, the Bods had made themselves or had been carved out in the mists of history by those that came before the Bods. There were many stories in Bod lore which tried to make sense of the Bods' version of Oxford. Some of the deeper tunnels were best avoided. More than one lonely, lost Bod had delved too far and never returned from UnderOxford. Many strange beings dwelt down there and most Bods, Red included, tried to keep to the higher tunnels, nearer the surface.

Several books had got loose and were flapping around the book store buffeting along the tightly packed shelves. A pair of Bods that Red knew from his own Bandinel Carrel swung from their harnesses above, trying to get the great leather tomes to go back to their shelves. the Bods yelped and giggled as the books flew around them, taking disgruntled swipes as they span and flipped to avoid any nasty paper cuts. One of them spotted Red and waved. Red waved back as the books finally capitulated and began to allow themselves to be herded towards their own sections. Red was still half watching them as he crashed into the older Bod who was coming from the opposite direction.

"Aethelred, look where you are going!"

Red staggered backwards a little, regaining his balance by jamming his glow staff into a crack in the floor. The grand old Bod looked sternly at him,

"And just where do you think you are off to young man?"

"Oh, er, sorry Madam Brunda. Just, er you know..." He tried his cutest smile and then stared at the floor.

"If, Master Aethelred, you are going up to see old Erasmus..."

Red stared even more carefully at the floor.

"Which of course you are not, as it is forbidden. I would suggest that you take extra care. He is being particularly..." She seemed to be searching her mind for the right word, "...curious, these past few days."

Red stared up at the great Lady before him. "Have you been to see him?"

She looked away and seemed to be watching a speck of dust somewhere in the distance.

"Certainly not my young man. As you know, Erasmus does not see anyone!"

She patted him on the head and winked at him. The Lady Brunda bent towards him and whispered in his ear. "Take care boy," with this, she gathered up her ample robes and carried on towards the Towers and a decent Dawn Supper like a particularly hungry and determined galleon.

Red carried on into the lower parts of the Radcliffe Camera. The outside of this building and the square around it was Red's favourite part of Oxford. The haughty Trolls could bluster on about their beautiful bridges. The Grotesques and Gargoyles chattered on relentlessly as to which college was the most magnificent, but Red knew in his heart that Radcliffe Square beat them all, hands down.

He made his way up through the bookstores and into the Lower Camera. Several of the Radcliffe Bods were trying to convince a rather grand Theology book to come down from the ceiling and get back into its proper stack. It seemed intent on staying where it was and having a good long sulk. Two of the more adventurous Bods had harnessed themselves and were swinging to and fro with a large net, whilst a third (Red recognised his friend, Cynwise) had resorted to trying to tempt the book down with peanut butter spread. This tactic seemed to be slightly more successful than the net.

"Hello Red!" Cynwise carried on waving the peanut butter in the air as Red wandered over.

"You look really tired, have you been out all night?"

Red took off his hat and rubbed his head. The other two Bods lowered themselves down to the floor when they saw Cynwise talking to him. They all shared some cheese and bread and a little dandelion and burdock as Red explained what he had seen in Duke Humphrey's Library. The other three's eyes widened as they listened to the details of Red's tale. Cynwise nodded as Red finished.

"There is definitely something going on Red. We've all heard whispers at the supper tables over the past few weeks." The other two Bods looked at each other and nodded.

Red had known these three for most of his life. The two brothers, Oswyn and Osric, never spoke, not that Red had ever heard, but they were great Bookherders. They both wiggled their fingers in a small wave, to say hello.

Red waved back, even though they were only a few steps apart.

"They overheard some of the elder Bods the other night. They were talking to Offa about some of the older books that seemed to have gone missing."

"Offa?" Red looked at the brothers, they both nodded.
Cynwise waved the jar back up at the floating book, which seemed to have taken offence at being ignored and had begun to slowly drift downwards to find out what was going on. "They overheard Offa telling the others not to mention it to anyone!"
"I knew he was in this somewhere" Red stamped his foot on the floor, which sent the book fluttering back up into the dark. "Oh, sorry."
The brothers Oswyn and Osric smiled and shrugged their shoulders.
Cynwise put her hand on Red's shoulder and grinned.
"Take care Red, call on us if you need any help," the brothers nodded again.
"Thanks, Cynwise. Oswyn, Osric," he put his hat back on after bowing the traditional Bod goodbye and headed off into the tunnel.

**

Red slowly climbed his way up the various ladders and climbing holes that were fixed into the spiral staircase that wound its way upwards to the ground floor of the Camera. He always thought it slightly odd that the students who used the Camera as a study space and reading room never seemed to notice their work. The network of ladders, pullies, walkways and tiny bridges that the Bods had installed over the years in order to make getting around the vast human buildings of the Library much easier. The bridges, ladders, ropeways and tunnels stretched far beneath and beyond the buildings on the surface. Old stories told of Bods venturing far and wide below. Wandering into the shadows and darkness and finding themselves in UnderOxford. The chambers, tunnels, halls and pathways below the wondrous city are all connected.

Just As Red's Carrel, Bandinel, took it upon themselves to herd the books and keep them safe, the Shakleton Carrel were wanderers and explorers. These Bods ventured far out beneath and around The Library and they used the lesser-known walkways and rope lines more than anyone. Red knew how much effort they put in, because one of his best friends, Alric, had, on the same Choosing Day as Red, decided to be a wanderer and explorer, Red had chosen Bandinel. Alric had spent many nights sitting with Red atop a high bookcase, sharing bread and sharing stories, poring over maps and spinning tales of the shadow places of the Library.

"Look, Red! I was given this old map by... Well, it doesn't matter who gave it to me, but it clearly marks a set of tunnels off to the North and Northeast. And something about a Sunken Cathedral!" Alric tended to get excited over new discoveries. Red smiled and nodded. Alric had a habit of disappearing for a while, into the deeper sections of The Library, forever in search of new chambers or, more properly, long-forgotten ones. Red swallowed a chunk of bread.

"Do you think that some of The Library can move about Al?" His legs dangled off the bookcase, the brass toe caps of his thick boots glinting in the light from their glow staffs. His friend looked out across the long room, most of whose books were quiet and resting. Some rustled and chafed at the chains that stopped them from wandering.

"I'm sure they could Red. The Library is more mysterious and powerful than we could even imagine. It has ways to defend and look after itself, of that I'm certain," he unrolled another chart, this time of a series of halls and tunnels unfamiliar to Red.

"This is where I'm heading next I think, further than I've been before. Who knows what I will find?"

Alric had headed off into the deeper tunnels to try and map an unknown set of lower chambers. He had not returned. Red missed him terribly; Alric would know what to do with all of this mystery.

Red finally made it to the top of the highest bookcase on the gallery floor of the Camera, just below the beautiful dome. He pulled his harness and carabiners from his bag and clipped his crampons to his boots. He was just buckling on his ropes when he noticed a small paperback book – The History of Byzantium –floating up near the zenith of the dome. Red quickly rummaged through his pack, shuffling the various scribbled maps and notebooks out of the way. Before the intruders had caught his interest, Red had been working on an idea that some of the rooms and tunnels in the Library were capable of moving around or disappearing when they wanted to. The other Bods to whom he had told this theory just laughed at him, as usual. He finally got to the bottom of his bag and found what he was looking for. Red gently put the small brass flute to his lips and blew. He couldn't hear the note that came from the tiny exquisitely crafted instrument, but the small paperback book on the history of Byzantium could. As could all the other books nearby. They began to rattle and shuffle on their shelves, some gently swaying whilst others seemed to be rattling with barely controlled glee. Even some of the Art History books and periodicals on the floor below moved about a little as Red continued the carefully chosen tune from his book flute.

Red wasn't paying any attention to the other books. He was concentrating on the paperback up in the dome which was now gently circling down towards him. Looping across the beautiful Rococo patterns as it came closer. Its open pages flapped up and down as it flew by. As soon as it came within range of his grasp, Red leapt across at it, only just managing to sit astride its spine as it took another swoop up into the dome. Red fidgeted a little in order to get comfortable and patted the book lightly, stroking its cover.

"There there, calm down now," he whispered to it as circled higher above the gallery. "I am most grateful for your assistance. That would have taken me a great deal more time to get this high if not for your kind help," Red was one of the best book whisperers in the whole of The Library. "I most humbly request that we travel a very small distance higher to visit a certain gentleman who lives above us here in the attic tower of your most magnificent Camera."

The book flicked several of its pages to and fro, spelling out the words to its question.

Who. Are. You. Visiting?

Red pulled himself closer to the book's spine, his mouth almost touching the binding. He could smell the wondrous fug of old print as he whispered a single word with a smile,

"Erasmus."

Chapter Two

Aethelstan was considering whether it was time for a light snack as he made his way across the great expanse of The Library's shop. He felt that it had been quite long enough since Dawn Supper and altogether too long to wait until his usual snack time, sometime soon. Stan liked the shop. He would finish drawing up the terrible scribble that Shakleton Carrel called maps into something resembling a proper piece of cartography, something that he, as a member of the Cartographers and Scriveners Carrel, Fysher was satisfied with. Then, he would come and sit on one of the glass cases and look down onto the beautiful bookends made to look like the Radcliffe Camera. Stan dreamed that he was looking down at the top of the real Camera – its mighty dome glinting in the sunshine across the square. He could sit like that for an age, or at least until his belly told him to have another snack.

This morning's snack was a good piece of dark chocolate, left for any Bod who cared to find it, by one of the secretaries in the Claringdon building across the way. Stan wiped the ink stains from his hands and munched on the chocolate as he made his way through one of the Bod doors in the skirting board of the shop and down a series of passageways and rope bridges to Aedelberga's workshop. Stan was sure the passageways were getting narrower, he almost got stuck twice.

"Hello Berga, how're things?"

Berga turned off the tiny blow torch and took off the welding goggles. She had been working most of the night on a large contraption Stan could not even begin to fathom out a use for.

"I'm good Stan. How's you?" Berga yawned and stretched before turning on her swivel seat to crank a brass lever.

This set into motion a series of connected devices around the workshop which almost always culminated in the brewing of a nice cup of tea. Stan walked across the room, ducking as a chain and wheel section clicked round and deposited tea leaves into a brass chute. "
All good, all good. I've been trying to make sense of some of the corridors nearer to Deepdown on the latest plans. You know, the ones where Alric was last sighted. I'm not entirely sure, but I think that some of them have moved."
"Moved? Is that very likely?"
Stan nibbled a bit more chocolate, then handed a chunk to Berga as she set the machine in motion again, handing Stan the first cup of tea.

"Oh, thank you. Not likely, no. I've heard stories and rumours for ages about missing rooms and lost corridors in The Library though."
Berga raised her eyebrow,
"That's all they are Stan, stories."
"Don't forget... oh, good tea Berga... don't forget that this old place is built on stories. It's formed out of knowledge and ideas just as much as bricks and stones. Ideas move around all the time!"
"You're starting to sound like Red," Berga chuckled and sipped her tea, after stirring it with a small screwdriver.
Stan furkled about in his backpack to see if he had any more snacks, sighed slightly and began casting an experienced eye around Berga's workshop for any food that may be lying about.
"I know Red has talked quite a considerable load of rubbish in the past, but this time I think he's really onto something. The Library doesn't feel right, even some of the more ancient books seem nervous. Oswyn and Osric have noticed it too," he calmly wandered across the workshop and picked up a piece of cheese from under an oily cloth. It was covering a brass and glass machine

that seemed to possibly be designed to transport goldfish through space and time (most of Berga's contraptions completely confounded her friends).
"Be careful around that – it's not quite finished." Berga saw Stan's blank look as he nibbled – uninvited - on the cheese,
"It's part of the Trollomicus – you know, the machine the Great Trolls use to stop bits of Oxford wandering off. Madam Brunda has some agreement with the big Troll Himself, Folly. I'm just making some alterations for her."
Stan gulped down the last piece of cheese and cast his eyes around further,
"The Trolls freak me out a little. They're so HUGE and quite crazy."
Berga took up a small spanner and began adjusting the cogs on the device in front of her,
"I know what you mean. Folly was as mad as a Christchurch Don. Madam Brunda says they seem strange because the Trolls are seeing all of the weirdness of Oxford, all of the time."
Stan thought he had spotted a digestive biscuit amongst some clock parts behind Berga. "How does that work?" He started to move around Berga, she slapped his hand back.
"I have absolutely no idea. Are you here just to clear me out of food Stan, or was there something else I could help you with?" It was obvious by Berga's folded arms and scowl that Stan's chances of getting to the biscuit (or any other food from the workshop) were reducing to nothing. He sighed and smiled his best smile, something he had watched Red do many times to get out of a tricky situation. It never seemed to work quite as well for Stan.
"I just thought I'd keep you company but if you have run out of... I mean, if you are very busy, I'll be off. I want to check on a few of the older book stacks. I'm certain that a few of them have moved, or something has been taken.

See you soon Berga!"
Berga put her goggles back on and fired up the blow torch,
"Bye Stan, see you later," she hadn't noticed him swipe the biscuit as she bent down to pick up her tools.
Oswyn and Osric finished off their snack sitting on the roof above the Supper Room at the top of the Tower of Five Orders. Most of the Bods' food came from the hard work of Creswick Carrel, the cooks and brewers of The Library. Although, some was indeed left by friendly humans, especially the chocolate and cheese which were favourites among the younger Bods. The kitchens and store chambers were quite away from the main Library due to the use of heat and fire in the cooking. Creswick's army of bakers and cooks, brewers and servers always managed to get plenty of mouth-watering meals out to all of the Bods across the Library. Most managed to make it up to the Supper Room for their major feast every now and again.
Oswyn smiled and rubbed his belly. Osric grinned and nodded – they were both happily full. At exactly the same time they got up from the roof and picked up their gear, heading down the long series of ladders and walkways towards the ground and The Old School Quadrangle far below. As they were both making their way down the back of the great statue of Stuart Jim, Oswyn stopped and turned his head to listen. His brother did the same as voices could be heard whispering just below, near one of the two great stone lions, holding their grand shields. The voices floated up to the two small brothers,
"I'm sure some of the younger ones are starting to suspect something," this voice was quite high and had a sing-song sort of quality to it. "We must take care of what information is leaking out."
"I am perfectly aware of how to control my part in all of

this thank you!" There was no mistaking that voice.
Oswyn and Osric looked at each other with eyes wide as they recognised one of the elder Bods, Offa. If that was Offa the other voice had to be Wuffa. Wuffa was a sneaky Bod who followed Offa everywhere and seemed to do whatever the bigger, older Bod told him to do. Very few of the younger Bods liked Wuffa even though he was thought to be one of the best of the Hyde Carrel, the Bods who created the wards and bindings that protect The Library.
Oswyn tugged at his brother's arm and looked confused. Osric shrugged his shoulders and gestured that they should carry on listening.
Offa's voice carried up from the stone lions towards Oswyn and Osric as clearly as if he was standing right next to the brothers, both of whom were extremely glad that he was not.
"Most of the older Bods will carry on and ignore that which does not fit comfortably into their way of seeing things, it has always been so. It is the younger Bods we must keep an eye on; Especially Aethelred and his annoying little gang," Oswyn's eyebrows shot up when he heard this. What were the elder Bods up to? He looked to his brother, but Osric was crouching lower now, to hear Wuffa's whispering voice down below.
"I have checked the wards and bindings, Offa, they are all as you have requested. Some of the younger of my Hyde Carrel are more loyal to me than they are friendly to the other Bods of their age. I will instruct them as to what we wish them to do in order to keep that little group of troublemakers in check"
Oswyn stuck his tongue out and waggled his fingers from the end of his nose in the direction he thought the older Bods were, just below their hiding place. His brother smiled at this, but carefully carried on listening. Offa

seemed to be moving away now,
"Good. See to your end of things Wuffa. I want this to go as I have planned. Nothing must disrupt our course of action."
Wuffa answered again, but the two voices drifted away as they seemed to disappear back into the Tower's main body, leaving the two young brothers to think about what they had overheard.
Oswyn looked to his brother with his shoulders hunched and his arms outstretched, he had no idea what to do. As usual, they made up their minds together. They picked up their packs and glow staffs. Osric signed to his brother by

flicking his lower lip downwards with one finger. Oswyn smiled and nodded; they needed to find the others.

***

Red stepped off the book as it ascended through to the upper light well, onto the small ledge around the uppermost point of the dome of the Radcliffe Camera. He patted the book and stroked its binding slightly which made its pages flutter in appreciation. The History of Byzantium floated downwards into the grand space above the reading room far below and drifted away into the morning light, spotted with dust motes. Red thought the dust was swirling together a little more than usual lately. He pulled himself up and swung expertly through into the small corridor behind it. The corridor curved around the inside of the uppermost tower. Red made his way along the highest of many walkways. The whole of the upper domes of the camera were riddled with corridors, pathways and bridges. They extended all around the gap between the inner ornamental dome and the outer wooden, lead-covered outer dome.

Red had listened to the stories from the Old Guard, those Bods who had fought in battles long gone and half-forgotten. Stories of many cold nights during the Great Noisy Big War, when the Bods stood guard in the great circular air vents of the outer dome. They had watched for the fire in the sky that threatened to rain down on their magical city, but thankfully never came. In other cities, other Libraries had not been so fortunate. The humans had their own ideas as to why Oxford had been spared. the Bods knew it had been a grand alliance of the Oxford Arcanum. The Sorcerers and magi of the University span protecting wards and glyphs, while the Trolls hid the most vulnerable areas, hiding them in the Mist lanes, far from

war. The Gargoyles and Grotesques patrolled the skies, watching for enemies. the Bods themselves had poured out from The Library, a very rare event indeed. They had taken messages and instructions from the Office of Empirical Curiosities in Holywell Street, where the magical defences of their city were co-ordinated.
Many evenings, Red had sat at the feet of the Old Guard Bods, listening to the tales of long ago. He had a strange feeling that he and his friends would have their own curious tales to tell soon enough. Something was coming, something the other Bods had not noticed yet.

He had to watch his footing here and there, as no repairs had been made for some time high up here inside the Camera. Red himself had patched up a few of the rope bridges that made the way up towards the topmost tower but he was no master builder. He was extremely careful as he made his way up. He finally came to the ladder that led up to the very topmost small dome of the Camera. He pushed open the trap door and heaved himself through into the small room with the old wooden table. It stood just to the side of an ancient, oak door with a tarnished brass doorknob. On the table, where Red usually left chocolate and found biscuits was simply another piece of parchment. This time it had a different message scrawled upon it 'Come in Aethelred'. Red stood and stared at it for several moments before an ancient voice floated out from the room within.
"Don't just stand there boy, eh? Yes, hehe, come in for The Duke's sake! The kettle has boiled and I cannot seem to find the spoons. Damn it, damn it. Spoons damn it!"
Red nervously grasped the doorknob, twisted it and pushed the door open. At first, he thought that he had walked into some terrible accident or a battle fought with the use of paper and mugs of herb troll tea. Most Bods

tended to live in a kind of chaotic comfort and many of the mealtimes descended into playful food fights. This was an entirely different level of untidiness altogether. The room was circular, being as it was, at the very top of the uppermost dome of the Camera. Its ceiling tapered to a point giving the impression of being inside an upturned bowl. From the centre of the ceiling hung many glow-globes, on differing lengths of ropes, chains, string and strips of leather. Several of them seemed to have given out or if not, then gently gave out only the slightest light. It appeared that when an older glow-globe went dim, another one had simply been added. Many more were at full glow so as to throw a variety of shadows around the room. These danced and flicked across piles and heaps and towers of papers and smaller books. Some of the books were, of course, still nearly as big as Red himself.

The great hills of parchment and paper seemed to be almost growing out of themselves. Upon every pile that was relatively flat on top were cups and small glasses, wooden dishes and knives with ancient clumps of butter or what might have once been honey. The glow-globes gave out all of the room's light as there were no windows. As Red's small eyes adjusted, he could see the walls were covered in patterns. In the steady light of the globes Red at first thought that they had some sort of incredibly intricate wallpaper covering their entire surface. As he looked longer and his gaze glided around the room, he realised that the whole was actually covered in hundreds of maps and plans of many sizes and shapes. They all seemed to be at once very familiar but at the same moment utterly mysterious. Red thought he recognised the buildings on the maps, the rooms within those buildings, but they were all wrong, or at the very least, differently right. He slowly understood that all of the maps were of the same set of buildings, tunnels and surrounding streets, but still, the exact meaning or location was beyond him. He was just thinking that one of the towers on a small circular piece of parchment looked very familiar indeed when a voice behind him suddenly said –

"Hmmm, it is rather like a goldfish looking at a picture of the goldfish bowl I think. Yes, isn't it? Yes, it is."

Red span around, utterly startled, and nearly stumbled over a particularly large pile of books and scrolls topped off with a yellow and blue spotted teapot. This pot slowly toppled from the pile and made its own way rather rapidly down various piles of paper. Red moved like lightning and caught the teapot just before it made its allotted meeting with the floor. He stood back up and found himself gazing into two tiny reflections of his own face in a rather deep and curious shade of green. The perfectly round spectacles dipped slightly to reveal a pair of tiny, beady eyes.

"Good catch young Aethelred, Wasn't it? Yes, it was, yes," the small, ancient-looking individual in front of Red glanced around with an expression as if he had possibly never seen the room before in his life. He gently placed the teapot on top of another stack of papers and maps, notes and wedges of ancient notebooks. The teapot gently slid across the heap, taking the top several sheets with it, down the side of the rapidly collapsing pile and rolled off under what may or may not have been a small cupboard. It was difficult to tell as it was entirely covered in maps and sketchbooks. The old teacher giggled slightly and shrugged

"No tea today then. Would you like some dandelion and burdock? It's here... somewhere? Anywhere? Possibly. Yes."

He wore what appeared to be a succession of long cardigans, down through layer upon layer, eventually culminating in a curiously chequered waistcoat. He seemed to be wearing carpet slippers, but the wrappings around his trousers (cloth? ancient strips of paper?) almost enveloped them, so it was difficult to tell. His brown and green scarf matched his fingerless gloves in colour, It matched his bushy, unkempt moustache in length. His fingers twiddled with or darted from it, seemingly forever tapping and sketching shapes in the air. Red attempted to step backwards but was thwarted by the various stacks and humps of books surrounding him.

"Good day Sir. I am Red. Or rather, I mean to say, I am Aethelred," he bowed his lowest and most respectful Bod greeting. His hat fell off and landed on his boots. Both bods stood there for some moments looking at the cloth and leather cap as if it may, at any moment, perform a series of tricks or perhaps a comical routine. It did neither of these things.

"Yes. Master Aethelred. That is exactly who you are. You are the chocolate delivery service and the biscuit thieving company all in the same set of coat and ..." He waved at Red's feet, "and Hat. Yes? Yes," he smiled and carefully picked up the cap and reached up to put it inexpertly on Red's head. "You are a troublemaker and rabble-rouser my young Bod. You frighten the tiny ones with your tales of fear and things in the shadows. Stories of lost books and things that go Spoon in the night!"

"Spoon Sir?" Red adjusted his hat and pulled it tight onto his head. Perhaps he had made a terrible error coming here. Perhaps the old teacher was mad.

"Spoon, Bump, either, or. It matters not. All that matters Aethelred, all that really matters is that you are awfully and horribly correct."

It took a moment for Red to realise what had been said, "Correct Sir?"

"Yes, boy. And stop calling me Sir, I am ..." His ancient eyes glazed over slightly and he scratched his nose as if trying to remember something of immense importance.

"Do you have a sandwich in one of those bags of yours? Mmm? Do you? Yes? I'm very hungry. Time to talk young Aethelred, time to tell what you know."

Red was utterly bewildered, but he rummaged through his smaller bag and produced a wax paper-wrapped marmite sandwich. The old Bod smiled and took it gently from his hands.

"So... sit Aethelred. Sit and tell me what you have seen. What is menacing our great and wonderful Library, eh?"

Red sat cross-legged in a small gap between the papers and notes and told the old teacher what he had seen in Duke Humphrey's Library. He told of the human and the... the thing. He explained what Cynwise had noticed and the worries of Oswyn and Osric. All the while the old teacher listened intently. Only once did he interrupt.

"Erasmus! That's it. Spiffing! I am named Erasmus now, of course! Carry on boy, I'm listening."

When Red had told all he could tell, Erasmus nodded and stroked his whitened moustache, seemingly lost in thought.

"Yes, this is a great worry, my boy. I recognise something of this evil thing of which you have spoken, but I cannot quite place it in my mind. The Library has had to defend itself many times throughout its long, long history. This is... different. This is a danger as old as The Library itself, maybe older. There are patterns here in what you have said, images and thoughts that sit wrongly in our little world. I cannot quite place it all together."

Red sat up and rubbed his eyes,

"I can find out more. I can gather my friends. We can work this out, I'm certain!"

Erasmus nodded again,

"Yes, Aethelred. Do these things. Scour The Library. Go high and go low. I fear what is coming boy. Something is already amongst us, and to defeat it, we must know all we can of it. Knowledge is our power here, it is the engine of The Library. I believe the old place has already begun to defend itself. Oh yes? Yes," Erasmus turned this way and that, looking at the many maps and plans, charts and scrawled notes covering all of the walls. He pointed at this one, shook his hands at that one, all the time spinning his fingers into intricate shapes in the air. Red followed his gaze.

"What are all these? I seem to know them but..."
"Do you see what the maps are, Master Aethelred? Hmmm? Can the goldfish recognise the bowl? Can He? Yes?"
Red tried to steady his mind in the middle of all this confusion. He looked again at all of the differing plans.
"They seem so very familiar..."
"So they should boy. Think! Think outside your normal way of seeing things!" Erasmus absentmindedly stuck his arm down behind a nearby hill of papers and grabbed out a cork-stoppered bottle of dandelion and burdock. This seemed to please and surprise him in equal measure. He stared at it over the top of his green-tinted glasses. "Spiffing!"
Red continued to grasp for some kind of meaning. Then he saw a plan that he recognised totally. It was of tunnels and corridors, deep places and dark passageways. He remembered the first time he had seen it. He had been sitting talking to the very person who had drawn it – Alric.
Alric had laughed a little and pushed Red as they sat looking at the latest mapping of the bit of UnderOxford that he had been exploring. "
"It's not all that scary down there my man. Really, it isn't any scarier than what you do, swooping about and climbing to the top of The Library all of the time."
Red smiled. He knew that many of the Shakleton Carrel were frightened of the heights within The Library, just

as much as most of Red's Carrel were extremely wary of the tunnels and chambers down below. Of course, not the Library's main underground vaults and rooms, the ones beneath those.

"I just think it's mad to go wandering off into places that seem to never end. What if you get lost?"

Alric grinned.

"You can't get lost if you don't mind where you are going Red. That's the whole point," he pulled out a chunk of corned beef that he had traded with another Bod of Shakleton Brec earlier in the morning and shared it with Red.

"And besides, it's exciting! Finding new ways, new paths that no one has ever gone down before or at least nothing that we would recognise as a someone. And you always find something weird that you didn't know about before. Look at this new bit I've just added," Alric pointed to a rough drawn section on the scroll of brown paper he was still working on. "I know that last Feast Day, that lower room of The Library was near the UnderThames, I could hear it through the walls. But when I went back a few nights ago, the whole thing had... I dunno... shifted, wandered off."

Red stopped chewing on the corned beef and looked at his friend with raised brows.

"Wandered off?!" He tried not to laugh out loud.

"I know it sounds mad, but I'm certain of it. And one or two of the other lower rooms, the ones that contain the rarest and most secret of The Library's books and manuscripts, I'm absolutely sure they've started disappearing!"

Red stood up, dusted off the few crumbs of corned beef and tapped his glow staff into brightness.

"If you say so Al. I'll keep an eye out and snoop around a bit, see what I can find out about it."

"Cheers Red. I need to visit someone to give them the

latest plans, then I'm heading back into the UnderOxford for a while. I want to check on these further passageways. I'm sure I can hear Cathedral bells down there, way off to the North West. I'll see you soon," Alric jumped up and gathered up his pack and glow staff. He waved to Red as he wandered down a spiral staircase cut into the brick and dirt down here an age ago. Red hadn't seen him since.
Erasmus handed Red a small cup of dandelion and burdock.
"Oh, er, thank you. Alric gave you this map didn't he?" Red gulped the burdock down. He hadn't realised how thirsty he had become, too much dust lately, he thought to himself.
Erasmus smiled and his moustache twitched at the ends. Red thought that this made him look menacing and ridiculous at the same time.
"Alric? The young wanderer, yes. Alric? Really? Oh well," Erasmus smiled again. "Has the goldfish recognised the goldfish bowl yet? Mmm?" he waved his arm around to point at all of the maps and charts and plans all at once, whilst also managing to spill most of his drink onto the surrounding piles of paper.
"Look Aethelred. Really look. Use your mind and your knowledge, you know what these are!" He took a swig from his cup and was slightly confused to find it empty. He looked around for the bottle before giving up with a shrug.
Red's eyes suddenly widened. He looked again at all of the walls. The building plans, street maps. The tunnels were scrawled in charcoal, pen, ink and paint...
"They are all The Library! But different," he pointed to two maps that were stuck next to each other. "See here! There is a room on this one that isn't on this one! And again here. And here!" He span around. Once he had seen it, it became more and more obvious. The rooms are...

what?"

Erasmus sat down on a large mound of notebooks and immediately slid off onto the floor, where he stayed for a short while.

"What? Yes, what? I haven't the faintest idea! Hehe!" Red was beginning to see why they had put Erasmus up here in the first place.

"So is someone...?" Red then remembered the terrible creature in Duke Humphrey's Library from earlier, "...Or something, trying to steal The Library itself or destroy it? Not just the books? I don't understand..."

"Then go and find out my boy, go and find out. Bring me knowledge. That is the greatest weapon of all. You are the Bods. This is your time of guardianship. Bring me knowledge and together we may have a chance against... Well, against whatever is happening here." Erasmus leaned back on a first-edition Orwell and twiddled with his moustache.

"I still don't understand," Red felt he was losing the little idea he had gleaned of what was going on.

"The Library isn't just a place boy, it's a person all of and in itself. I have been here... well let us just say that I have been here a very long time. Sometimes the Library is attacked from the outside, sometimes from the inside. Sometimes it finds rather peculiar ways of defending itself. I once heard a very old Humph tell of a book that sometimes really does contain the whole Library..." Erasmus suddenly crawled across the room and pulled out the missing dandelion and burdock bottle from under a stack of Mr Men books. "Oh, marvellous! I've found the bottle! Would you like some more? No, of course you wouldn't. You have things to do! Come on young Aethelred, time to go and work things out!" Erasmus took Red by the arm and bustled him towards the door. "See you soon my boy. Come back when you have something, anything interesting to say. Yes? Mmm? Yes." With this he bundled Red out and closed the door tight, locking it from the inside.

Red stood there for a few moments, trying to work out exactly what had just happened. After a short while, he gave up. Life was getting very strange but at least it was getting interesting!

***

Berga finished wrapping the leather cord around the end of a particularly complicated piece of equipment she had been working on for a while and took off her magnifying goggles. She startled slightly as there was a cough behind her. Oswyn smiled as Osric waved from near the door of her workshop.

"Oh, hello you two, how's things?" The two brothers looked at each other and then nodded to Berga. The three of them had been found in the same corner of the lower reading room only hours before they were due to hatch. They had spent their early days together in the nursery and often met up, as did many Bods after they had chosen different Carrels and gone their own way in The Library.

"What can I do for you?" Oswyn scribbled on a piece of discarded note paper. 'Red'. Berga shook her head.

"I haven't seen him in a while. He's probably off on one of his mad missions again. Sometimes I think that he convinces himself of all of these plots just so he has something to do!" Osric shook his head quite fiercely. Berga frowned.

"You think he's right this time? Gosh," she heaved herself up and took one of her crutches from next to the nearest workbench. Oswyn passed her the other crutch from down on the floor where it lay on top of a huge pile

of canvas and ropes all folded next to two brass canisters and a woven wicker basket. "Thanks. Red seems to think something is attacking The Library. He keeps going on about books going missing. I'm not so sure. The books all seem to wander around of their own accord. How can you tell if they are missing?" Oswyn tapped the side of his head and Osric nodded.

"I get it. You herders would know I suppose." Osric and his brother smiled and both nodded. Berga laughed. "Fair enough. I suppose we should find Red and see what we can work out between us. You two get some of the others who you think will listen. I'll find Red."

Oswyn grinned and stuck his thumb up. The two brothers bowed and left Berga in order to round up the others. Berga sighed to herself. "I hope you are wrong Red," she said to no one in particular, "This is all starting to get a little weird if you ask me."

She picked up her pack and made sure her crutches were secure, before setting off to find her friend.

Chapter Three

There shouldn't be this much blood, he was fairly sure of that. He thought he had been running forever, but it was probably only a short time really. He had no idea which tunnel he was in now. His pack had fallen some way back when the thing had first smashed into him and its razor-like teeth tore into his arm. Everything was swimming in his mind and he was sure he had blacked out a little just then. He could hear his heart beating faster than it had ever done before, then he heard the other noise, the dry shuffling noise that he had been trying to get as far away from as possible. It was right behind him. Scrambling forward, he tried to move against the wall of the tunnel. How far down was he now? He really had no idea, but it was deeper under the City than he had ever been, he thought. He just wanted to lie down and sleep but the thing was getting closer. The air was clogged up with dust. Where was all the dust coming from down here? Was the thing covered in the stuff?
His mind raced through too many questions as his bruised and battered hands scrambled to get hold of something, anything to steady his aching body. He stopped and leaned against the wet wall as the grunting and shuffling grew louder. He started to cry a little now. He could hear the thing's teeth click-clacking together, sharpening each other as they gnashed the air just around the corner. The corridor was getting thick with dust. He could hardly breathe at all and his goggles were slowly losing their oily covering which let him see in the darkest places. He pulled out a short rod of brass from his belt and weighed it between his hands, summoning the tiny bit of strength he had left. He wasn't going to die alone in the dark, not if he could hurt whatever this thing was before it took

him. This thing that had seemed
to form out of nothing, here in the cold and very lonely tunnels deep below the City he loved so very much.
The thing shuffled around the corner sniffing the air (did it even have a nose?). With the last oil failing on the goggles, he saw its great lumpen body almost flow towards him. It was covered in dust. No, it was dust... and grime, and filth, oozing and mixing around and back, forming into a squat but tall shape with great powerful arms and thick shambling legs. Dark patches sat deep in hollows where its eyes ought to be and the teeth, oh, the teeth: Shiny little razors click-clacking, and a black bulbous tongue seemed to form out of the shadows of its throat. The tongue flicked forward right in front of the Bod's frightened face, tasting the air. Spittle flew and joined the dust and dirt to make the thing even bigger as it hunched over him.
He could just see the thing now, here in the dark. Here under The Library where he had explored, played, mapped and wandered for most of his short life. He grasped the brass rod even tighter and pulled together every bit of his remaining strength 'All this blood really should be on the inside,' his mind said to itself. He stood as tall as he could, coughed back the thick grimy air and shouted loud and clear;
"I am a Bod of The Republic of Lettered Men! My Name is Alric, and I am not frightened of you! So, come and have a go if you think you're hard enough!"
In the utter darkness, deep below The Library, where usually silence reigned, a brass rod hit a thing of grime and filth and dust. Sharp, evil teeth tore into his arm and shoulder. A great cry went out that echoed down and up and around tunnels and chambers and long dark passageways. A terrified cry, then silence once more. This lasted only a moment until a light carefree voice from

somewhere in the darkness said
"Well, really. I think that is quite enough of that, don't you Derek?"
Alric awoke in a round chamber, which seemed to have been carved out of silk, or perhaps he was in a giant ball of twine, with the centre hollowed out. His head hurt and not a great deal of his thoughts made very much sense. He tried to sit up and realised that he was tied up, almost completely with the same white twine that made up his surroundings. His arm and shoulder ached but did not seem to hurt very much anymore, which was strange. He was about to try and roll over to see what else was nearby when a voice above him said,
"It seems to be alive and awake in that order Marjorie."
"Ooh, marvellous. I'm rather pleased it isn't dead, Derek. That would have been an inconvenience too far I feel."
"Quite so my dear, quite so."
Alric's eyes slowly began to focus in the soft white light of the chamber. He thought there was some kind of huge white canopy stretched over him until the whole thing suddenly moved and its poles turned out to be eight long thin legs as the huge eyes of a giant white spider swung down in front of his face.
"Hello, my dear fellow. And what, pray, are you?"
"You know very well that it's a Bod Derek. Stop teasing it."
"Sorry Dear, I was trying to be enigmatic."
"Well don't. It simply makes us look eccentric, and that won't do at all," the owner of this voice, a great white spider even larger than the other loomed into Alric's view. It gracefully stepped around him and swung upside down so that its face was very close to his indeed.
"Would you like a mint humbug?"
Alric wondered if he had died and this was where The Duke sent idiot Bods who were murdered by extremely

ferocious lumps of dust.

"Or a cherry bonbon perhaps?"

The slightly smaller spider moved a little closer and began dismantling the webbing from around Alric.

"Are you... are you going to eat me?" He mumbled. He wasn't sure if this was a better or worse situation than fighting the thing. Where was the thing?

"Good gracious no! This is to heal you boy. What was that dreadful beast that was attacking you? Horrid mess it was if you ask me. I think standards are slipping down here. It wasn't like this in Grandmama's day I should say..."

"Oh do shut up Derek!" The larger Spider nudged the other out of the way and delicately undid the rest of the webbing, lightly prodding his shoulder to check that it was healed.

"All better little Bod. Now, what on earth were you doing so far Below? Do tell!"

Alric sat in the warm nest and told Marjorie and Derek how he had visited Erasmus

"Ooh, how is the old duffer? Haven't seen him in an age?!" Derek Interrupted.

Alric ignored the interruption and continued talking about how some of the rooms of the Library seemed to have shifted, or disappeared altogether.

"Gosh it must be worried, it hasn't done that in a while!" Derek began again.

"Shush Derek, let him speak, this is all too, too fascinating!" Alric went on explaining how he had returned to UnderOxford to try and find out what was going on. But somewhere near the Sunken Bridges, he had seen a strange creature covered in mouldy layers of rag-like coats and jackets. It cackled and spat, pacing to and fro muttering to itself in angry little barks.

"No manners, that's the trouble these days" Derek mumbled, he was rewarded for his contribution by an irritated glance from Marjorie.

Alric told them how it had suddenly turned and fixed him with a terrible stare from one huge eye, while its other was scabbed over and squeezed almost closed. Puss was dripping from it, mixing with the spit to splat on the floor of the bridge and sizzle and fester. It had let out a horrible screech and pointed out a bony long finger at Alric, then spun its hand around and around. The spittle and ooze from the floor seemed to dance to the motions of the thing's fingers until it rose up and span, weaving itself into a great heaving thing with dark pits that seemed to glare straight through Alric. Glinting razors of teeth formed out of nothing and split into a weird, fiendishly wide grin which quickly turned into a grimace. Click clack they went as the thing lurched forward. Alric, almost too late, had turned and blindly fled into the tunnels.

The two great, white Spiders looked at each other for a small time before Marjorie tapped the floor thoughtfully with one of her long powerful legs.

"Well you don't have to worry too much about the thing anymore, Master Alric, Derek here bit its head off, didn't you dear?"

"Oh, most certainly. Damned thing tasted of dust. Horrid business."

Alric was beginning to feel much better. The Spiders had given him camomile tea and a piece of fruit cake. Alric wasn't entirely certain where they had got these things from, but he felt it would be impolite to ask. They had wandered a small distance away and were whispering and nodding to each other. After a time, Marjorie gracefully wandered back over.

"If what you say is true Master Alric, and we have no reason to disbelieve you, no reason whatsoever, then it would appear that the thing that attacked you was a Mor'n. A horrid and thoughtless creature conjured out of ignorance, dirt, stupidity and dust. Foul beasts that destroy knowledge and breed idiocy."

Derek came over, somewhat less gracefully.

"We have not seen their kind in UnderOxford for centuries. If they are back, then that means that something very powerful and rather unpleasant has summoned them."

Alric put his cup down. He wondered where giant, white spiders managed to get fine crockery. Maybe Boswell's old department store does a special deal.

"The terrible creature I saw on the bridge!"

"Indeed. And Derek and I are a little concerned that we recognise your description rather too well. We spiders are the keeper of tales, the spinners of stories, and we have heard this one, or ones like it before. If it is who we think it is, then The Library is in grave danger indeed."

Alric felt the hairs on the back of his neck stiffen and suddenly the chamber seemed a great deal colder than it had done earlier.

"What is it?"

"We fear dear boy, that it is someone that was lost long ago. We had all thought it just a tale, or something vanished into the long history of the beginnings of The Library." Derek's legs braced as he moved down to come face to face with the frightened Bod. "Our tales tell of The One Who Was Left Behind. Forgotten at the dawn of The Library, locked away because it wanted all the knowledge and tales for itself. Sealed in the very first library room as a warning to those who came after, that the books were for everyone."

Marjorie bowed down to be level with the other great white spider and Alric.

"It has escaped, little Bod. The Gloob is free."

Derek shuddered slightly.

"Horrid little thing, but very powerful and extremely dangerous. It knows the old ways, Master Alric. And it is

very vengeful indeed I should imagine."
"Why, why is it vengeful?"
"Well, I'd be fairly annoyed if someone bricked me up for nearly seven hundred years!" Derek continued.
"But what do we do?" Alric stood up straight and dusted himself off. He wasn't too keen on having any dust around him at the moment. "We have to do something."
Marjorie stretched herself up to a mightily impressive height as Derek flicked Alric up onto his back.
"We shall do what any sensible person does in a moment of great danger and crisis. We shall call a meeting!"

Chapter Four

Red took the long way down through the Radcliffe Camera, he had a lot to think about. So many times before, he had shouted and argued about some danger or trouble within The Library. So many times, the rest of the Bods had laughed at him or, even worse, ignored him. This time it was all real. This time Brunda actually believed him and Erasmus believed him. Admittedly, Red wasn't entirely sure Erasmus was very good at working out what might be real or not. All that Red had to do now was convince everyone else. Something was attacking The Library. Something was already inside this amazing, magical place and Red needed to find out what it was. He headed down passageways and across bridges, through low corridors and along bookshelves. He finally came to the long tunnel which connected The Camera to The Library. There were always Bods wandering the tunnel, small groups often gathered here in the vast space to chat or just to sit and rest. It was often warmer in here due to The Library's heating ducts and pipes which ran the whole length from the lower bookstores under the Camera right into the depths of The Library.

Red was making his way along one of the warm pipes when he spotted a familiar shape in the distance, apparently attempting (with some considerable success) to talk a couple of younger Bods into giving him a large lump of cheese and a bottle cap full of marmite. This had probably been left by one of the Library workers on the pipe for any passing Bod to find.

Red made his way over just as Stan was explaining that he was much more in need of the cheese than they, as he had just come back from a long and arduous journey through the far tunnels of St. Gile's. The younger Bods

were listening with ever-widening eyes and stretching out their cheese to the great adventurer when Red smacked him on the back of the head.

"Leave them alone Stan. They found the stuff, so it's theirs. Anyway, you're a cartographer, a map maker of the Fysher Carrel, you've never been further than the edges of The Square in your life."

Stan grinned at his friend and watched with a little disappointment as the other Bods scowled and moved their bounty out of his reach.

"That may very well be true Master Aethelred, but my mind, ah my mighty mind, wanders further every day, off into the far beyond, deep into UnderOxford and sores high with the Gargoyles and Grotesques. Only yesterday I..." At this point, Red stood on tiptoes and smacked him across the head again. "Oh do shut up you fool. Have you seen the others?"

"I've seen Berga, she was most unkind to me Red, most unnecessarily unkind!" The smaller Bods giggled as Stan pressed his large hand to his chest and pretended to be hurt deep within his soul.

Red laughed,

"Did she refuse to give you biscuits again? You really are the greediest Bod I have ever known Stan." The larger Bod looked shocked,

"Not the greediest Red, not at all. The hungriest! And she did refuse me biscuits. I had to steal them Red, like a common thief! A most shoddy state of affairs!"

Again the little Bods sniggered as Stan took a piece of cloth from one of the many pockets in his coat and wiped nonexistent tears from his eyes.

Red shook his head, "Terrible Stan, terrible. We have to talk, but not here. I don't want to frighten anyone, it gets me in trouble."

Stan laughed, "You need no excuse to get into trouble Red, no excuse at all."

Red nodded his head then looked up in all seriousness,

"Something is afoot!" The two friends strode off with a new sense of urgency as Stan waved at the younger Bods, who took several moments to realise that he had somehow not only managed to swipe their cheese but the marmite as well.

Stan put his arm around his friend as they walked. Red looked up and frowned slightly,

"There is definitely something going on Stan. We need to get the mob together and start working this out. I have a dreadful feeling that we haven't much time."

Stan began to frown himself.

"I have a dreadful feeling that we shall miss supper!"

Chapter Five

Mr Simper sat at his small table in the small attic room in which he lived above the Tuck Shop on Holywell Street. Through the grimy little window, he could see the lights of the History Faculty across the street outside of which he had, that morning, had yet another meeting with the terrifying little beast all full of spite and spit, in order to hand over another of the items on the list.

It had been a curious day when Mr Simper had discovered the thing. He had been doing some more research on his masterpiece. He was writing the definitive book on Radcliffe Square and The Library. The tiny room where his research had taken him would once have been above the old Congregation Room. It had once been the first University Library founded by Thomas De Cobham in the University Church of St. Mary. Now it was simply a storeroom for the Church. Mr Simper had been moving a stack of chairs to get a better look at the original shape and size of the room. He tried to do this with incredible quietness as he wasn't strictly supposed to be in here, but that kind of thing never really bothered Mr Simper. He had moved several boxes when he noticed that some of the most ancient parts of the wall right at the back were covered in tiny lettering, shapes, circles and symbols. He had taken out his carefully ironed, perfectly white handkerchief and wiped the wall to get a better look. The plaster was extremely old and as Mr Simper wiped, it began to flake away, destroying a whole section of the pattern.

All at once, there was a strange hiss and then a sigh and gurgling sound emitted from the wall, as the very plaster and stones themselves seemed to dissolve in a small patch near the floor, almost as if something was burning itself out from the inside (which, unfortunately, was exactly what was happening). After a few moments the stained area of the wall oozed out and a large glob of dirty, jelly-like goo spewed out from the stain onto the floor at Mr Simper's feet. It took several moments as it darkened and hardened before it twisted and grew into some kind of weird creature, all large head and slimy little body. Mr Simper felt rather ill but also transfixed by what was forming in front of him. It was very small, yet seemed to pulse vengeful hatred as it snapped its body into form, its bones clicking into place, its putrid skin tightening across its back. The thing sneered as it curled around to take in its surroundings. One of its newly emerged eyes had been almost sealed shut, but the other was large and bulbous and blinked its way into seeing. Mr Simper, sitting at his small table shuddered at the memory of it and gripped his teacup a little tighter. This poisoned orb had ripped itself open and stared around, finally glaring at Mr Simper and spitting a vast glob of spittle and ooze out of its nasty little mouth. It had pulled its mouth into being by ripping one of its razor-like fingers across its jaw; Slicing a jagged flap from which a swollen tongue flicked and tasted the air around it.

The glaring orb stared straight at the giant human in front of it. Mr Simper, who disliked mess and horrid fluids at the best of times, had shot backwards in horror. The small, beastly thing had hissed at him and suddenly scurried off behind boxes and chairs along the floor of the room, like some malformed badly burned doll. Mr Simper had hurriedly wiped the goo off of his shoes and trouser leg with his handkerchief and fled the church room out into the clear air of Radcliffe Square. He disposed of the stained and quickly rotting handkerchief as quickly as he could.

Sitting in his shadowy, cold room, he shuddered once

again at the thought of the first sighting of the nasty little thing. He got up from his table and walked (or rather stepped, for the room that was his home wasn't the largest place in the world) over to the small stove and lit the gas in order to boil the stainless steel kettle atop the hob. Once a fresh cup of Earl Grey tea had been precisely made, Mr Simper sat and shook his head at the thought of his next encounter with the creature.

He had been sitting in Holywell cemetery on a crisp, not overly warm morning, eating a cauliflower and pickle sandwich. It had been a Tuesday, so therefore it was, of course, cauliflower and pickle. The secluded cemetery was a favourite of Mr Simper's as few people ever bothered to wander in and he was happiest with as few people around him as possible. The second and final sandwich had been carefully consumed when there was a peculiar hissing from behind a nearby gravestone. Mr Simper had looked around but could see no one. He rose from the bench upon which he had been sitting and cautiously glimpsed behind the ancient-looking stone. Down amongst the ivy and slightly damp grass was the creature from the church storeroom. It seemed to Mr Simper that it had grown slightly, it had certainly acquired a selection of several coats and other clothing: Extremely small coats and waistcoats, a grubby shirt and scarves. Mr Simper wondered slightly where it had found such things, but this was Oxford after all. It was unmistakably the horrid little being though, Mr Simper could tell from the great bulbous eye that turned upon him and the gobs of spittle and goodness knew what else that oozed from its rip of a mouth. It had sneered at him and then shuffled inexpertly around so it was now in front of the stone. The thing began whispering and rasping so that Mr Simper had, against his better judgement, to kneel down to listen to what the creature was saying. It said an awful lot.

Mr Simper sat back down in his room and thought over that long conversation in the Churchyard. It had, he thought, not begun well. It seemed that the creature had forgotten, or indeed never knew, how to talk to others, and often its concentration wandered off. It had prattled on to itself until Mr Simper had to remind it they were in the middle of a discussion. The nasty, little, brutish thing was horrid, but Mr Simper (kettle on again for the next of his evening cups of tea) had to concede that the chat in the churchyard had changed his life. Before then, he had only thought of his magnificent book and how the whole University would congratulate him and welcome him back (not like last time, oh no). After the churchyard, Mr Simper knew that if he helped the creature he would not just be allowed back into the Library, but it would be his own private playground. The creature would have control of the place of course, but Mr Simper didn't care. As long as he could come and go whenever he pleased and take, yes take, whatever he pleased, the creature could do what it liked. Mr Simper sat and smiled a tight self-important little smile and stirred his cup of Earl Grey precisely. He washed up his cup in the small sink by the door and placed it on the shelf, handle out and second place in, as it was the Evening Teacup. Then he gathered up his bag and torch, the all-important stolen keys and the larger of the two towels which he owned. Next to this in his leather case, he placed a small jar of mint humbugs, his little treat to himself for later. Mr Simper checked his tie was straight in the small mirror above the sink and gathered his things together. He locked his room behind him and carefully made his way down the stairs and gingerly over to the Old Bodleian. He was glad he had brought his long coat as it started to rain when he locked the small door which led onto the street. He checked the inner pocket of his suit to make sure he had the creature's strange list of items from the library. Several of them had already been obtained and were therefore crossed off. He smiled to himself and double-checked that he had his stolen keys, ready to begin another evening of burglary and theft.

***

Red and Stan made their way up to the ground floor of The Library and through Duke Humphrey's Library, where Red had made his startling discovery the evening before. They talked little as they walked the long path through their home. Red was thinking about the enormity of the danger that he was sure lay ahead of them. Stan was thinking about the enormity of the pie he was going to eat as soon as they reached the Supper Room.
The walk up through the Tower of the five Orders can take a Bod quite a while, but built into the North West corner of the tower is a series of spiral stairs and ladders which mean that a hungry Bod could navigate the tower much quicker than they would normally be able to do. the Bods' steps spun ever higher, past the offices of the University Archives. Up past the upper rooms that have, in their time housed powder and Shot, and even been an observatory for The Library. At the very top, above all of this is the Bods' Supper Room. Originally created simply to make sure all the Bods had enough to eat while going about their work to protect and care for The Library. It slowly become the place where most of the different groups, factions, Carrels and gangs met to talk, argue and hold gatherings. Red and Stan entered the hall which was full of Bods from across the Library and indeed from the Law Library, Oriental and Chinese Libraries, The New Bodleian and Japanese Library. Those from The Science Library and Hook Library sat and chatted to their fellows from Rhodes and the quiet thoughtful Bods of

the Philosophy Library down on Merton Street. All of the Bods made sure they came to The Supper Room as often as they could make it. This was where they got their news and gossip. The Congregation House may have been where the Grand Council met, and all Bods could discuss their lives or their work and vote on what should be done. It was here in the Supper Room where everything really got sorted out. The squabbles and the gang rivalries; the petty wars between differing Carrels. The feuds between the older, more influential Bods such as Madam Brunda and Offa would spill over through their younger followers. It all happened here.

The room was busy as midnight approached, the usual time for many of the Bods from all of the different Carrels to come together to eat and see friends. A large group of the Hyde Carrel were sitting together discussing which of the wards, scribbles, glyphs and complicated protective seals needed renewing. Stan waved to a few of them as he homed in on the large pot of stew, bubbling away at the end of the room. Several of Red's own Carrel,

Bandinel – the Bookherders, was sitting in the corner swapping new techniques for swinging and climbing, they waved as he passed. He noticed that Osric and Oswyn weren't there, neither was Cynwise. Red stopped to talk with two Bods from the Craster Carrel, the builders and crafters, to ask if Berga was about. One of them pointed to a far corner where Red finally spotted his friend sitting deep in thought in the corner. She was scribbling yet another intricate and curious design for some outlandish contraption into her notebook. He collected some cheese and bread from one of the tables and made his way over, having to negotiate a way around a group of four or five of the Shackleton Carrel – this Carrel was notorious within The Library. They were the explorers and adventurers, Alric's crew, who wandered deeper and farther than any others and returned, or sometimes did not, with tales of strange beasts or beings, old gods and new sorcery. This unfortunately took quite a toll on their minds. Many of the other Bods avoided their company and were always wary around them. Of course that had long ago meant that Red sought them out and spent time with them as often as possible. Stan only got interested when they brought back fruit cake or chocolate ňclairs. Red shook hands with those he knew and bowed to the others who were deep in discussion about how much dust and grime seemed to be welling up from the tunnels deep below.

Finally, Red sat down next to Berga. They sprawled cross-legged on the floor and had spread out a small picnic dinner.

"Good Midnight Red, how's things?" Red bit off a chunk of cheese, gratefully accepting a cup of dandelion and burdock from Berga. "

"Not good, Berg, not good at all. All this stuff I've been shouting about, I'm certain I'm right" Red explained,

Berga snorted slightly. "
You are always certain that you're right Red!" She smiled but urged her friend to continue, he scowled at her.
"Well, yes. But this time I'm certainly certain. Something is attacking The Library. Madam Brunda believes me, so does old Erasmus! He's got Alric's map, the one I saw him with the last time we met. Is he back yet, I'm starting to get worried?" He said all this in one breath as the other Bod shook her head at him rattling out his news. Berga leaned back and massaged her legs slightly.
"You've seen Erasmus? Red, you know how that annoys the older Bods. There's something mad and bad about him!"
Red shook his head angrily.
"That's just what they want you to think! You haven't met him. You're just repeating what they've told you!" Red was getting angrier and louder.
"Okay, okay, so you're saying that he isn't mad?" Berga asked.
"Well, not as such. He is rather... peculiar," his friend smiled again, which only made Red angry. "But Alric had been there! I think he was making maps for Erasmus. He seems to think that The Library is protecting itself. Alric was certain that rooms are trying to move or hide, trying to protect certain books or manuscripts. Something's going on!" He shouted the last bit so loud that a group of Hudson Carrel, the Astronomers, stopped their chatting and all stared at Red. It was not unusual however for Red to start shouting when people disagreed with him, so they quickly carried on pouring over their sky charts and arguing amongst themselves over some apparent shifts in the night skies.
Stan loved this room for all its chaos, the hats and coats piled high in a corner, news sheets printed by Coxe Carrel strewn everywhere proclaiming the latest ideas as spouted

by old Offa. Offa thought of himself as the undeclared Lord Protector of the Bods, everyone else thought of him as a loud bully. Music instruments like mandolins were restrung and old Bod tunes played, while others of Rouse Carrel joined in with wooden and brass flutes and drums. Those Bods who weren't too musically inclined, just clapped and sang along, the songs falling into one another. Verses were changing and being reinvented as ideas flowed through The Republic of Lettered Men.

Stan had made his way over to the others, carrying, with some difficulty, several chunks of bread, a selection of cheeses and three large bowls of stew. Berga laughed at her friend as he tried to sit down without spilling or dropping any of his prized dinners.

"You should have gotten a tray, Stan," he finally sat down and began choosing his first cheese, a nice bit of Port Salut. Stan grinned.

"A tray was of no use! I had too much to carry already! Budge over Red, what's all the shouting about?" Berga laughed and Red scowled.

"Red is right about everything, and we are wrong about everything."

Stan chewed on some bread.

"Ah – the usual then. But I fear that this time our dear friend and self-appointed, unelected leader is right. Something is going on here. The stars are out of kilter, The Library feels – wrong." He dunked some more bread in his stew. It was Parsnip, one of his favourites. Red sat up triumphantly. Berga rolled her eyes at Stan, Red's friends liked him least of all when he was being triumphant,

"You see! I..."

The door in the other corner of the skirting board slammed open and Osric burst through, his eyes were wide and scared. He was covered in bite marks and bruises, cuts and scrapes. The whole room stopped as every one of the

Bods moved to help him. Berga grabbed her crutches and swung over to him, knocking others out of the way as Osric collapsed to the floor.
"What's happened Oz? What did this?" then a creeping realisation hit her and she stared at her hurt and frightened friend,
"Where's Oswyn?" Red grabbed the nearest Bod and shook them. "Go and find Brunda, find Madam Brunda now!"
One of the Myres Carrel who dealt with the Bod's illnesses and wounds had got some hot water from by the food stacks and was wiping Osric's face, trying to clear some of the blood. The weak, little Bod flicked his hands and fingers in quick succession, everyone turned to Burga and Stan for the translation.
Stan wiped his mouth and thought for a moment.
"He says they've found a nest of un-hatched Bods, but - I can't make it out. Something's happened, something has attacked them." A startled murmur went through the room. New hatchings were quite rare, but for something to have attacked them was unheard of by any of the Bods in the hall.
Red pushed through to Osric.
"Can you take us there?" The smaller Bod nodded meekly. Red grabbed his things. Stan grabbed his cheese, stopped for a moment and gulped down as much of his stew as he could manage. Berga just stared at him and shook her head.
Red turned to the Bod who had been tending Osric's wounds.
"Tell Madam Brunda to follow us. I'll spin a thread," he took a ball of almost invisible twine from his bag and attached one end to the doorknob. He and his friends ran (or in Osric's case, staggered) from the hall. The thread unravelled along as they made their way through the tiny

walkways and corridors down through the Tower of Five Orders and into the main Library. They followed the still weak Osric as he headed determinedly back towards his brother.

Chapter Six

Mr Simper was glad to be in the dry, the rain had become quite heavy as he had crossed the road and made his way to the Library. He thought there may be a storm on the way. He had managed to steal the keys from a nice lady who worked in the Library Collections Service. She had stopped to help him pick up a book he had, quite on purpose, dropped outside Blackwell's Bookshop and he had carefully liberated them from her bag. It was but a few minutes' work to discover which door they fitted and he was finally able to get back into the halls from where he had been so cruelly banished. Tonight, as the rain began to hurtle itself against the long windows, Mr Simper made his way through The Library and down towards the bookstalls. All the while, he kept a careful lookout for the security guards, or those infernal little annoyances, the Bods. Goodness, how he hated those little creatures. What gave them the right to claim that The Library was theirs? He would show them when it was truly his to command. They would do his bidding then. He would be their true master. He grinned to himself, he liked the idea of that.

Mr Simper finally got to the door behind which was the section of periodicals he was looking for and took out the list given to him by the hateful creature. Scrawled onto paper that was very old indeed, the writing was almost unreadable. Mr Simper had (with some small amount of personal satisfaction) managed to work out the scribbles and sort out which books and manuscripts the thing wanted. The list had made little sense as a group to Mr Simper and truth be told, he still could find no real rhyme nor reason for the connection between them all.

He had already collected most of the list and delivered

them to the beast in the tiny back room at the church; now for another one. In theory, it would have been simpler to swoop in and take them all in one go, but in practice, the whole procedure was much more complicated. For one thing, it would have been difficult to move through The Library with so many stolen items without being detected. For another, the books put up a damnable good fight. The last, a vellum roll titled 'The Forme of Cury' had taken him three hours to liberate. It was a simple matter to unchain the box from its allotted place, but quite another to get it into the towel. This, Mr Simper, had discovered, calmed the damned things down considerably, rather like putting a cloth over a caged bird. The vellum roll had flipped and swooped around the library attacking and retreating in equal measure. Mr Simper thought he had noticed that as he collected each of the items on the list, The Library became more agitated, more defensive. Indeed he was quite sure that The Library had even somehow managed to move a few of the rooms that he had been searching for. The things seemed to put up more of a struggle as each one was collected. He hoped the nasty little creature appreciated all this work, though he doubted it. The thing seemed full of only bile and malice.

He tutted away to himself as he pushed open the storeroom door. Each of the supposedly secure rooms that had contained the items on the list so far had been miraculously unlocked when he had got to them. Nasty spittle and ooze being the telltale mark of the individual who had seemingly been there before him and somehow managed to open the doors. Mr Simper didn't like to get too close to the locks but had noticed the tiny scrawled writing of the creature, in patterns and arcane swirls around each lock, now open and shattered. As he entered the room, the thunder from way above resonated downwards and the whole place seemed to shake and shudder. He flicked on his torch and checked the list once more. Periodicals in their boxes in here bristled as he entered. He had on several occasions attempted to mimic the Bods. He had watched them whispering to the books, getting them to behave exactly as they wished. He had never managed it, which only made his hatred of the little people even stronger.

Mr Simper ran his fingers along the boxes. He wanted them so much not, of course for their value in money, money had, conveniently, never interested Mr Simper. He wanted simply to own them. It meant so much to him that soon he, and only he, would be able to touch them, stroke them. His eyes followed the torch beam across the titles and labels on the boxes. Finally, he saw the one he was bidden to retrieve. A small snip opened the box and he retrieved, after double checking his list, the copy of Detective Comics number 27 from its storage place. Mr Simper teased it out and flicked it open. It tried to flap itself shut but he grasped it tightly. The boxes nearest to it became restless and began to shake and turn in an even more agitated state. Another thunderclap rolled through The Library and even the torch dimmed for a moment. The comic shook in his hands then flipped itself open and fluttered its pages faster and faster. The edges caught Mr Simper's fingers and blood welled up out of the cuts as he dropped the torch and the comic and squealed slightly in the darkened room. As he bent to the floor he followed the light beam into the corner of the room. There in the furthest corner, near the back under the bottommost shelves, was a Bod. It seemed to be asleep, or, judging by the blood on the floor around it, possibly even dead. Mr Simper had never seen one so close up. They seemed to always have shunned him for some reason. He stretched out his arm and reached under the shelves. His thin long fingers closed around the tiny body, which, much to the man's surprise groaned slightly in a tiny, pained way. Mr Simper knelt there on the floor of the storeroom. Much to his immediate annoyance, the comic had evaded him for the moment and fluttered up to the ceiling, out of reach. The Bod now in his hand had been lying amongst several pods or fungus balls. Not quite as big as the little thing, they were slightly yellow-brown, almost parchment coloured, with blotches of reddish brown forming a varied selection of spots. Mr Simper had no idea what they were but imagined that many of the lower rooms and chambers of The Library probably contained mushrooms and other curious growing things in the darker corners. If it could be the home of the Bods, who knew what else lived in its environs?

The little thing slumped in his hand stirred slightly and its tiny bead-like eyes flickered open. The blood which had dried on the side of its face made things difficult for the Bod to see. Mr Simper smiled his most winning smile (which was not that winning at all).

"Hello, little man. You are going to help me get that wretched book down from the ceiling are you not?" He hoped this was his most soothing voice, but it was actually just weird. Oswyn recoiled slightly, trying to get his sluggish mind to work faster and figure out a way out of this mess.

He remembered their excitement at finding the nest of new, un-hatched Bods; he remembered his brother (Osric? Where was Osric?) being very excited. He remembered shouting to Cynwise, who was still at the top of the shelves to come down and see what they had found. Then the things came crashing in, all dirt and dust and spittle, teeth click-clacking in the dark. He remembered he and his brother fighting for their lives and the terrible creature shambling into the room from behind the great human door. Its head seemed as large as its body, with one great swivelling eye glaring around. It had seen the Bods and screeched a terrifying sound from the depths of its ragged throat. Pointing at him, it had moved slowly forward manipulating the air in front of its long bony fingers. The air in Oswyn's mouth and throat had tightened and seemed to fill with dust and slime. One of the other creatures had caught him off guard and lunged at him tearing at his arms as he tried in vain to block it with his glow staff. The evil, bulbous-eyed creature was upon him in an instant with a strong hand around his throat. It brought its face right up to Oswyn's and its breath stank of rot and foulness, hatred and disgust. Its spittle dripped from Oswyn's cheek as it whispered into his ear.

"I am The Gloob little creature, and this is My Library now. I was here before your kind were even dreamed of. I will be here long after my Mor'ns here have ground you all into the dirt. (Spit) If I cannot have this place, no one will. I will bring it down and all you pointless little beings with it." The spit was hot on Oswyn's face and burned as it dripped down his cheek. The Gloob had thrown him to the floor and he scrambled further under the lower shelf, as the evil creature glared at the pods against the wall. He spat onto the floor and grinned, gesturing to one of his beasts. "Destroy them!"

Oswyn had begun to cry, then lost consciousness in the dark. Now he had woken and the human had him. Oswyn wasn't sure if this was better or worse.

Mr Simper prodded the little thing as his patience grew thin.

"Do that thing you do. Whisper the comic down for me and I'll let you go," He remembered himself and turned the sneer into a smile. Oswyn leaned up slightly and, using all of his strength, he bit the human's finger hard. At that very moment, Cynwise came swinging down from the top of the shelves on her line slamming her tiny body straight into the side of the human's head. He squealed and dropped Oswyn, who hit the floor hard, but managed to roll back under the bottommost shelf from where he watched, broken and exhausted, his friend high above. The collision meant that Cynwise had no momentum to carry on, so simply hung there, kicking the human in his ear as hard as she was able. He thrashed around shouting and screaming, as now the comic had come down from the ceiling and was swooping down on him, its pages fluttering at such a speed, cutting his face and across his nose with hundreds of tiny cuts. Finally, the Human grasped outwards and pinned it to the wall. The other boxes in the room were rattling and rocking to be free. Mr Simper was most glad that they were not. After shoving the comic, now safely wrapped in one of the two towels which he owned, into his bag, he grabbed his torch and glared around the room. The tiny swooping Bod was desperately trying to winch up to the top of the shelves to safety. Mr Simper was too tall and simply plucked her from out of the air.

She struggled and tried to bite him, but he was wise to this trick now, grasping the torch under his arm, flicked her head hard with his long finger. Cynwise's head shot backwards and she slumped unconscious in his hand. Quickly, Mr Simper grasped the jar of humbugs out of his bag and emptied them on the floor. He stuffed the little monster into the jar and shut the lid on it. If there was enough air, all well and good. If not, never mind. With the book now in his bag and the extra prize of a (possibly) live Bod, he fled the room. He quickly made his way from the Library into the storm raging through the City and up the stairs to his safe, almost warm room.

Outside the storeroom, a bulbous watery eye blinked and a jagged slit of a mouth grinned to itself. It had shrunken

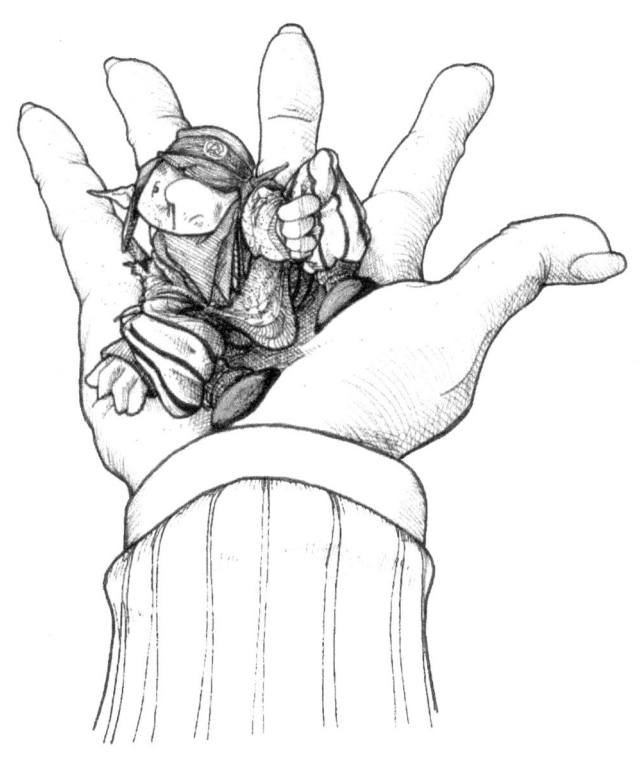

into the shadows to weave another of its creatures from the dirt and spittle, phlegm and dust, now it was weak with the strain of creation. Still, it managed to giggle, happy that all of its long-held plans were moving towards its goal. The dusty slimy creatures surrounding it click-clacked their teeth in joy that their master was happy.
"Another of The Nine gone, soon The Library will have no choice but to protect itself. It will think itself safe, but it will be at its most defenceless (spit). I will destroy it once and for all," he giggled slightly and the things around him guffawed mindlessly in the dark.

It heard talking as a group of Bods came towards the Storeroom, and shrank back into the darkness of the shadows. Even with the three Mor'ns, The Gloob was unsure it could take on several Bods at once. It needed to save its strength and one of the Bods looked too large for his loyal creatures to attack and destroy without help. If its plans were going to come to aught, it would need a little more time and many more Mor'ns. All it needed was to trick the Library into panicking into its last means of defence. The Gloob had had many centuries to consider its revenge. Once The Library had hidden itself, The Gloob knew it could be imprisoned or, even more satisfying, destroyed. The voices got closer, the big one spoke/
"Osric says they were in here when they were attacked."

***

They found Oswyn where he had crawled, beaten and frightened. He had curled into a ball deep beneath the lowest shelves. His brother flew over to him when the light of Red's glow staff finally illuminated the spot. Osric cradled him in his arms and kissed his head. Berga took ointment from her bag and began tending to their friend's wounds. He awoke a little and smiled at his brother who patted his face gently, hugging him closer. Stan decided at that moment to start getting very deliberately angry with whoever had done this to his friend. They were, to his mind, allowed to squabble and, yes, sometimes fight with each other, but no one was allowed to attack them from the outside. The Mob stuck together, The Mob looked after each other.

Red broke the silence. He was staring at the lock, high above in the human door and at the stains on the floor near the edge of the shelves.

"It's been here. The thing I saw in The Duke's Library. It did this."

Stan looked over at his friend and glared around him. "
"Then we find it, and we kill it."

The friends spent a little time making sure that Oswyn was comfortable, whilst Berga continued to treat his wounds. His brother simply rocked him back and forth while Red and Stan explored the rest of the storeroom. Red stopped dead when he finally reached the top of the shelves and found Cynwise's backpack and extra climbing gear. He followed the rope down to where it dangled and snapped in mid-air halfway down the shelves. Stan had become fascinated by the fact that the floor seemed to be covered in mint humbugs.

"What has happened here Red? What's going on?"

Red scaled down the shelves to meet his friend, showing him the stuff he had found on top.

"I've been trying to tell you all. Something has been attacking The Library, and now it's started attacking us."

"Hey, Oswyn is trying to tell us something," Berga called over to her two friends.

The injured little Bod was carefully moving his hands, trying to talk to his brother. Stan came over and they watched as he traced symbols in the air,

"He says the thing is The Gloom, no, The Gloob. What's

a Gloob?"

A booming voice rang out behind them.

"Don't be foolish boy, The Gloob is a myth, a fairytale to scare the Bods in the nursery," Madam Brunda and two other older Bods swept into the room, one Stan recognised as an elder of his Carrel, his name was Aethelbald. This always made Stan smile, as he was the hairiest Bod Stan had ever met. He had a big bush of hair and an enormous drooping, shaggy moustache, his map work was beautiful. The other was quite short and seemed to be wearing too many jumpers and cardigans. His head was covered by a wide hood and a wide-brimmed hat which seemed a bit excessive to Stan. He didn't recognise this one at all, but Red seemed to be staring open-mouthed at him.

"Close your mouth, Master Aethelred. The dust will get in!"

Madam Brunda stood with hand on hip and surveyed the room with her one excellent eye. The old leather and brass eye patch over the other glinting in the glow from her powerful glow staff. She bent down and looked under the shelves, smiling at the two brothers cowering underneath.

"Come out of there my children, all is safe now," the three young Bods slowly emerged, Berga first, crawling along until there was room for her to wield her crutches. The two brothers came out much more gingerly and full of trepidation. Madam Brunda looked beyond them to the broken pods at the back of the wall. She let out a great cry of despair. The hooded one jumped slightly and Aethelbald moved as quickly as he could to see what all the fuss was about. His two old eyes were still sharp after years of concentrating on maps and charts. They widened as he realised what was under there.

"By The Duke's Hat! Who would do that to a Hatchery?" He sank down slightly. Brunda was making her ungainly way in to inspect the damage. She shone her light into the smashed casings inside were small green lumps, no bigger than a marble. They might, had they had the chance, have hatched out into Bods one day soon. Madam Brunda carefully brought each one out and only realised as she was finishing that four of them were still intact and humming slightly. She took off her grand cloak and gently wrapped them inside it, handing the precious parcel to Aethelbald. "Take these to the nursery, I shall attend to them soon enough."

She turned to the younger Bods and raised herself up to an imposing figure of a Bod, as wide as she was high. All of them had been on the receiving end of her wrath as little Bods, finding their way in The Library and getting into a shelf-load of trouble on the way, Red more than any of them. They all stared at their boots.

"WHAT has happened here?" She boomed. Oswyn whimpered slightly but Stan stepped forward, his cheeks red with fury.

"I will tell you what's happened here Madam Brunda. While you and the other Old Bods have been swanning around making great speeches and acting terribly important, Red here tried to tell all of us that there was danger in The Library. Well, here it is, you old boot. So stop shouting at us and do something about it!" Red stared at his friend and simply thought, oh dear, he's dead.

Madam Brunda glared at him and seemed about to explode when the one in the hood and hat suddenly burst out laughing. This only ended when he couldn't breathe properly and bent over double to catch some air, causing his hat to fall off. He looked up and removed his hood, tears rolling down his face behind small round green glasses, and into his long moustache beneath.

"That told you young Brunda. I imagine no one has spoken to you like that in quite some time!" He started laughing again.

Madam Brunda scowled at him and waved him away with her glow staff.

"Oh, shut up Erasmus you mad old fool!"

"Me, an old fool? When these young ones came to you and tried to tell you what was going on, did you act? Did you fly into righteous fury in defence of our beloved Library, did you? Yes? No. You and your terribly important friends held a few meetings! Had a bit of a discussion! That young lady is foolish, yes? Yes. Now I suggest we get this poor young chap back to the Tower and try and figure out what in The Duke's name is going on around here!"

With this, Erasmus picked up his hat and strode out of the storeroom. Madam Brunda looked around at everyone and banged her glow staff so it shone brighter than ever.

"You heard the old fool, come on then!"

Berga stopped as she was gathering her gear together.

"Wait a minute. Where's Cynwise?"

Red and Stan halted as Red gently tapped Oswyn on the shoulder as he held on to Stan's back, where they had hoisted him.

"Where is she Oswyn? Where's Cynwise?" The tired little Bod raised his head with a pained look, haltingly moving his hands to sign.

"She was taken," relayed Berga to the older Bods and Erasmus. "The human took her."

All the Bods looked at each other then. No words passed between anyone, but they all felt a little colder all of a sudden. Stan shifted his friend on his back to make him more comfortable, he looked at Red, who nodded.

"Then we go and find her," Berga moved over to her friends.

"Sounds good to me chaps. I mean, how much trouble can we possibly get ourselves into?"

Chapter Seven

In all his exploring of UnderOxford, Alric had seen many strange sights. The Great Halls of the Thames Trolls, from the vast baroque chambers of Duke Cornelius at Magdelen Bridge to the equipment-filled halls of Donnington bridge. They were as strange and varied as the Trolls themselves. He had walked the maze-like cloisters of the Silent Brethren, stance beings wandering their domain, hunting for prey, and endlessly searching for the Autumn Bell. This had been stolen from the Brethren by the Pendunculate Guild when the City was young. Just as mysterious were the great grub like Cherubim that called to each other from their deep, dark burrows, culminating in a wall of joyous song.
It would reach its pinnacle each May Morning when the great Peace is observed by all. Many things had surprised and even frightened him, but he had really never seen anything like this.
Alric and the two giant, albino spiders, Marjorie and Derek, had left the spun chamber. They headed at some considerable speed through passages deeper and longer than any Alric had ever travelled before, eventually coming to what Marjorie had called 'The Clubhouse'. It was a huge cavernous hall with great pillars made of hardened spun silk rising high to the vaulted ceiling. From there hung hundreds of crystal chandeliers shining brightly over the whole amazing diorama. The floor was covered in rich, woven carpets of intricate and amazing patterns. Tall single-legged tables, higher than five Bods tall, held crystal glasses full of sparkling wine and other drinks Alric didn't recognise at all. Derek called Jinand Tonic. The arrival of Marjorie and Derek meant there were twelve great spiders in the hall. Several of the others

were sitting seemingly reading newspapers; a few were standing around chatting whilst two were playing cards. Alric simply stared.

Marjorie gently placed Alric on the carpet from Derek's back and began introducing him to the others. He soon got the hang of shaking the deadly clawed tip of a long white spider's leg.

"How do you do?" Asked Cynthia and Clive.

"Charmed," Mumbled Melvin and Petunia

Jennifer and Lydia spoke next.

"Aces High Dear, read 'em and weep! Oh, hello, what a delightful little thing you are!"

Now it was Charles and Portia's turn.

"Good lord aren't you grubby. A pleasure to meet you, I shan't get up, did my back on the thirteenth hole."

Derek handed him a glass of Jinand Tonic that was almost as big as he was.

Major Gattling and Beatrice looked at him.

"Hmm, tiny chap. Good to know you Library lot are still manning the guns eh?"

He was then shown around The Clubhouse. There were grand pictures on the walls of previous illustrious members.

"That's Mufty Fortingbrass, took one for the team in '43. This one here is Florence Crassendale. Wonderful singer, terrible cheat at Bridge," Alric nodded politely, even though all of the portraits looked exactly the same to him. They were all giant, albino spiders.

When Jennifer and Lydia had finished their card game, the group gathered around the vast ornate fireplace. Several of them had somehow gained large glasses of brandy.

Marjorie reared up to a terrifying height and coughed slightly, causing the others to stop their little chats.

"I would like to bring this extraordinary meeting to

order. We have a dilemma Ladies and Gentlemen. A thing our kind thought long gone and dealt with, appears to have returned with dire consequences for The Bodleian above. Our tales tell of a thing called The Gloob," there were a few startled splutters as the name was said. "It has somehow gained freedom and is building an army of Mor'ns, as it did the first time our fables tell of it."
Alric raised his hand and Derek shouted.

"Point of order for the chair!" Alric became slightly more confused as there were no chairs, but he asked his question anyway.

"How do you know what it is and where it came from? I'm sorry, I don't understand."

Major Gattling coughed slightly and rose to his full height, removing his cigar with the claw hook of his front great leg.

"Call yourself an adventurer little Bod, eh? We are The Company of True Spiders. We hold the stories of Oxford together. We bind the tales of this magical, mad city and keep them for everyone. You guard the knowledge little Bod, but we tend the tales," Petunia rose then as Derek shouted again,

"The Major gives the floor!" While the great spider called Clive seemed to be writing down everything everyone was saying on a notepad. Alric hadn't the faintest idea what was going on.

"We roam across Oxford young thing. We pull in the myths and the poems, the tall stories told at bars, around fires, in common rooms and bedsits. We travel far through Upper and UnderOxford finding the canticles and the rumours and spin them all together here," she gestured all around them at the clubhouse with a long elegant white leg, tipped with a vicious hook.

Portia rose to speak.

"As far as we can tell young Bod, The Gloob was one of

the first guardians of the Bodleian – ah, you didn't know there were ones before you did you? But there were others. Before the Bods, came the Humfs and long before those ancient folk, came the Cobs; these things the old tales make quite clear. Of the Cobs, the myths tell that there were five of them only. They were brought into existence using the old ways by Thomas the Bishop, to guard The Library when it was but one single room in the Church. This was hundreds of years even before Radcliffe's great Camera was built to pin the site together. Old Hawksmoor knew what he was doing with the plan, what?. The Cobs were wise little creatures, so the tales tell us. One was also proud, selfish and cruel."

Alric sipped his Jinand Tonic, he liked it rather a lot.

"The Gloob?"

Melvin leaned forward on his huge, thick legs.

"Indeed. That is the name that has come down to us. Our tales do not tell us of the names given to the other Cobs. But The Gloob lives on through his treachery. When it was decided to move The Library, the Humfs were created to take the books and manuscripts, papers and letters to their new home. There were far too many then for just the little room in the church. The Gloob tried to keep them out. It sealed itself inside the room with glyphs and wards and threatened to destroy all of the collection rather than let it go. The Humfs, being newly formed, were too weak to fight it, but the other four Cobs joined together and broke the seal to the room. They fought The Gloob, with hands, sticks and powers of their own. After a long and arduous battle, both The Gloob and the four were terribly hurt and exhausted. Eventually, the four prevailed and sealed The Gloob into a tiny prison, in the walls of the room. They finally sealed it with symbols and wards and incantations."

Alric's little eyes widened at the tale.

"And now this thing is free? That is the terrible creature I saw on the Sunken Bridges?"

The Major rose again to speak.

"It would seem that it may well be young Bod, it may well be. I for one think it may be time to act!"

Marjorie banged a small wooden hammer.

"Order! As I was saying... If this is The Gloob, we have little time to lose. We must gather the troops. We must span out across UnderOxford and issue a declaration of war against this pernicious, nasty foe. Ladies and Gentlemen spread out from our dear Club and take word to others within our great City. We must gather. We must prevail!"

Marjorie stared triumphantly around the meeting but they all just coughed a little in embarrassment, while Clive (still taking the minutes) looked up.

"Sorry I missed most of the last bit, shall I just say we're going?"

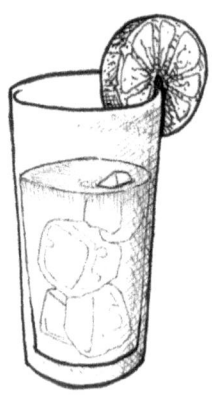

***

The floor of The Congregation House was filled with Bods from all over The Library and beyond. Word had spread quickly to all of the parts of their domain of the attack on the Unhatched and that Cynwise was captured. The different Carrels were roughly massing into their groups. The Shackletons had already decided to declare war and invade... somewhere. Craster Carrel, the builders and architects, seemed to be pouring over the maps from Erasmus' study, unsure of how they had got down here. Offa, as usual, was trying to tell everyone what to do from the base of the Vice Chancellor's throne, with very little success. Aerlene, one of the elders of the James Carrel, the collectors and keepers, was arguing quite loudly with Aethelbald. The whole thing was a sea of chaos. The Mob sat in the middle of it all, a little shell-shocked. Oswyn and Osric both had their hands tightly clasped over their ears, which Red thought might not be a bad idea. Stan was looking around whilst chewing on a piece of Brie he had acquired somewhere along the way.

Madam Brunda was huddled with a group from the Nursery Carrel, Jolliffe, discussing the recent events. Their faces were a mixture of horror and anger. The ongoing noise from all of the different groups was almost deafening until one solitary note began to hum above the throng. It grew into a base note then flared into a fanfare blast like that of a regiment of trumpeters. Every Bod in the hall quietened and turned to see where it had come from. Slowly they all began to move back from the middle of the room where Berga stood, holding a small box, with a brass handle. As she turned it, it seemed to be the origin of the amazing sound. Next to her, with his old, frail hand on her shoulder and his ancient frame leaning heavily on his stick, was Erasmus. Offa glared at him and prepared to boom out his mighty voice.

"Oh shut your cake hole young Offa!" shouted Erasmus, surprisingly loudly. From somewhere nearby, Stan spoke. "Did I hear a mention of cake?" Some of the youngest Bods giggled. Offa carried on glaring but said nothing.

Erasmus looked around the hall, the tassel of his pillbox flopping this way and that as he took in all of the Bods. They all knew of mad, old Erasmus, locked in his tower. Crazy Erasmus, banished for his own good many years before most of those in Congregation House were even hatched. He stared at them all over the top of his green glass spectacles. He raised his hand and the last murmurs around the hall died away.

"Hello to all of you, I say. You all know who I am I think. I was old and foolish long before your kind came to The Library. Something else very old, but much less foolish seems to have made its way into our home as well. Madam Brunda here has raised most of you since you hatched, and she has frightened you many times with bedtime stories of The Gloob I'm sure." Some of the Young Bods giggled, most of the youngest Bods tried to hide behind the others. "The Gloob who will eat you all up if you're not well-behaved, yes? Yes. Well..." He turned slowly, gazing at all of them. "The Gloob is not a fairy story to frighten the little ones. The Gloob is a monster that wishes to steal all the books, and he's not coming soon. He's here!"

Erasmus banged his walking stick on the floor and everyone jumped slightly. Brunda swept into the centre and stood next to Erasmus.

"This is true my dear Bods. There is a monster in our home and he is raising an army. We must find a way to defeat him before all is lost. Gather into your Carrels, for we must act swiftly. Begin your planning my children. A battle is coming that we must not lose!"

The great Bod shout swelled up then and all joined in.

"All Equal! All Equal! All Equal!"

As the shout died down and the various groups began to huddle and plot and plan. Red saw Wuffa, Offa's sidekick and bully, slide over to Offa's side and whisper something

in his ear. Offa nodded and whispered back. The two older Bods looked at each other and Offa nodded again. They glanced around and slunk back into the shadows, quietly heading out of the hall through one of the Bod doors at the back. Red turned to Stan.
"Did you see that?" Stan turned to his friend licking crumbs of brie from his lips.
"I did, Red, I most certainly did. Now, who do you reckon has the cake the old gent mentioned?"

***

Red and the rest of the Mob did not split off and join their separate Carrels. They moved to one of the quieter corners to decide what to do. Red initially wanted to go straight after Offa and Wuffa. Especially when Berga had explained what Oswyn and Osric had overheard near Jim Stuart's Statue on the Tower. Berga pointed out the rather more important fact that Cynwise was missing, seemingly captured by the human and now, well, who knew where? Red realised that Offa and Wuffa would have to wait.
"How do we find out where she was taken?" Red hated it when he didn't have the answers or didn't quite know what to do. Burga thought for a few moments.
"Wait here," she span off on her crutches into the throng of other Bods, all planning what their groups would try to do to help The Library. Soon she stuck her head up over a particular group and waved at the others to come over.
"This is Rheda, she's with Creswick Carrel and was on watch duty over at the Clarendon building a little earlier on. Tell them what you saw Rheda. I need to get something. I'll meet you at the front steps."
The young Bod smiled at the others who bowed in the usual Bod greeting.

"I was just watching the folk of Oxford wander by when I noticed a human rushing from The Library. Not from one of the main doors either, one of the side doors that should be locked at this time of night. He was holding a package and carrying a bag."

"What hair did he have?" Red interrupted. She thought for a moment then smiled.

"It was yellowish in the great lamps, but it was definitely really light, curly and long. It stuck out rather than hanging down."

Red clenched his fist.

"That's the one I saw in The Dukes Library, talking to The Gloob!"

Oswyn signed frantically and Stan stopped eating a piece of toffee he had found in an inner pocket.

, "He says that it's definitely the human who grabbed him and then took Cynwise."

Rheda thought some more. "I watched him cross the road over towards the King's Arms and along Holywell Street a little before going in through a door." Stan looked a little confused.

"Isn't that where The Office of Imperial Curiosities is, the black door next to the Tuck Shop?" Rheda nodded,

"Yes, but above there. I watched the lights go on up at the top, the room in the... what do the humans call it? The attic!"

Stan clenched his teeth a little.

"Now we know where he is, let's go and get our friend back."

They all looked at each other and nodded, Red picked up his backpack.

"This is going to be dangerous you know." He grinned at Stan and the brothers. Stan grinned back.

"Good. I quite like dangerous. It's much more fun."

Chapter Eight

Rheda led them along the quickest route through the Bod tunnels and passageways over to The Clarendon Building. The pathway came out into the Vice Chancellor's robing room. None of them, save Rheda, had been into this area of The Library before. It was only just dawning on Red that they were about to leave the environs of The Library altogether, he was now wondering where had Berga suddenly disappeared off to. It would be the first time any of them had done so. Most of the Bods lived their whole lives within the buildings and grounds of The Library. Only Alric's Shackleton Carrel ventured further out, usually into UnderOxford. Only the Fellow Travellers, those Bods who decided to leave for good and explore libraries further afield ever dared the outside world. Those Bods were rarely seen again. Even Stan was looking slightly nervous as they made their way across the floor of the robing room, filled as it was with Napoleonic helmets, swords and goodness knows what else. Finally, they opened a sliding slab in the base of the wall and felt the cold fresh air hit their faces. Thankfully, the storm had calmed, rolling further down the Thames Valley to the south. They all moved across to the base of one of the gigantic pillars that loomed up to the vast expanse of The Clarendon Building's roof. They stared at the vast steps that led down to the long, wide cobbles and pavement in front, then across the vast tract of tarmac road and up to the giant front of The King's Arms Pub. There along Holywell Street, further along the hodgepodge collection of buildings and attics squashed together behind the grand building of the pub, a light could be seen shining from a grimy attic window. Stan gulped as humans wandered past in all their hugeness.

"I don't believe we have quite thought this through."
Red slapped him on the back.
"When have we ever thought anything through, Stan?"
Stan laughed and even Osric smiled.

"Sorry to bother you, but I thought this might come in useful," Berga came through the doors with two other Bods from her Carrel.
They struggled from inside with a large section of carved, wooden plank connected to some long brass poles. These in turn had triangles of leather attached to them with tiny rings. The other side of the wooden base seemed to be a collection of gears and levers, several lengths of rope. There were three fairly large wheels, one at the thin end and two at the fat end. Stan stared at it.
"Thank goodness you've brought it with you, I was just thinking that we may require one of those!"
Berga raised an eyebrow at him.
"Do you even know what this is, Stan?"
Stan rubbed his chin and gave the whole thing an approving look,
"I have absolutely no idea."
Berga shook her head then turned and thanked her comrades who ran back to join in with all the planning in Congregation House. She stood in front of the contraption and waved a hand, bowing with a flourish,
"Gentlemen, may I introduce a small invention of mine. It is a Land Barge."
Stan stared at it.
"You have your words mangled, Berga. I believe that it is pronounced 'death trap'."
"How does this thing work Berg?" Red laughed.
Berga scowled at Stan and set the thing down on its wheels. She tugged expertly on a few of the levers and the brass poles were pulled upright with the leather sails

tightened and tacked in the wind. Berga jumped on.
"Come on!"
The other four looked unconvinced for a moment but Oswyn sprang up and sat behind his friend. His brother leapfrogged Stan to get up at the back. Red took Berga's hand and pulled himself on board. This only left Stan who stood alone staring at the thing. He then shrugged his shoulders and clambered up.
"You do realise this is madness, don't you?" He complained.
Oswyn and Osric both nodded and Red smiled the widest smile.
"Oh yes."
Stan grinned at his friends.
"Well then, here we are. Let us go from this place to another place. Onwards!"
Berga grabbed a leaver and the whole thing tilted forwards, wobbled on the top step and stayed there for a moment or two. Stan then decided to lean forward to see what was actually happening, and at that moment gravity took control. The bits of wood, leather, rope and brass that had, under the genius of Berga become a Land Barge, hurtled down the great steps of the Clarendon Building and shot with increasing velocity across the pavement. It sped between the legs of two Essex College students arguing about the existential nature of kebabs. It narrowly missed the signpost and sent the Bods rattling up and down as it crossed the cobbles onto the road.
Berga leaned to her right and yanked one of the ropes, this caused the barge to tilt slightly and Stan to go green, almost regretting the last piece of toffee.
Stan craned his head around and stared up at the vast picture of one of the Oxford Bridge Trolls spread across the entire surface of the great sail as it billowed out and pulled the barge further and faster.
"What the hell is that!?"

Berga pulled hard at a lever causing something to creak ominously below near the wheels. She cupped her other hand against her ear.
"WHAT!?"
Stan pointed furiously with a sandwich that had somehow appeared from within his jumper, "The Troll. Why is there a Troll on the sail?"
"It's a tea towel - they sell them in the Library Shop. It's quite a good likeness of Donnington really!" Berga replied grinning.
"Why aren't we on tea towels? Why do the Trolls get tea towels?" Stan shook his head and mumbled something else which was completely lost in the racing wind. This was not helped by the fact he had shoved what was left of the bread into his mouth.
Red stared ahead of them and shouted something into the wind that was unintelligible but almost certainly incredibly unacceptable in polite company. Oswyn and Osric both closed their eyes and covered their faces at exactly the same time. Stan barely had time to find another cheese sandwich before Red pushed him down into the body of the craft as it hurtled straight at the wall in front of them. The vast cliff face of bricks loomed high above and seemed to stretch on and over them forever into what Berga realised was the arch of Hertford College Bridge. The wheels under them thundered towards the brickwork. They all braced for what they thought might very well be the last thing they would feel as their whole world and minds filled with the idea of brick. Red truly believed for a moment that the very last words he would ever hear would be Stan's...
"Oh, I thought there would be more pickles"
There was utter darkness for a while. Red had the sensation that his whole being had been pushed through solid brick, his head was thick and his ears were ringing. Slowly he

could make out dim, warm lights far off above him, and the sound of gentle humming. He sat up and realised that his friends were all sitting around him, shaking their own heads and checking each other for broken bones and bruised egos. He was about to ask them if they were all okay when a vast shadow loomed over them, bigger than anything Red had ever encountered before. It seemed to form into the shape of a huge, round face nestled in and surrounded by a great silk ruff. It reminded him of the humans in the Elizabethan pictures all over the University, but it was much much bigger.

Red took off his hat and bowed low, which was easy being so very close to the floor in the first place.

"Excuse us Sir, but we were travelling to find our friends and seem to have... well, we seem to have died, I guess. Are you Duke Humphrey? He pulled and twisted at the hat in his hands as he began to realise that they had truly failed after all.

The voice, when it came, after a long pause, seemed to be incredibly gentle and boom at exactly the same time. Filling the space they were in even as it carried off into the endless darkness.

"Hmmmm..... I do not believe that I am a Duke. No, not a Duke. Never that, I'm sure. And you have Died? Died of what and why I am wondering? You were there, now you are here, and I am thinking to myself, for whom else would I consider addressing here inside my Bridge, eh? I am thinking that you might require a little amount of tea. Yes. Tea I think, is the answer to all of this. Yes."

Berga sat up. Her eyes widened and she paused from checking that her crutches weren't broken.

"You... You are a Troll! An actual Oxford Bridge Troll!"

Stan stopped trying to find his sandwich and stood up. He made a vague effort to dust himself down and looked up, up, and up at the huge being in front of him. The individual was enormous. It was at least three times as tall and as wide as any humans Stan had seen in the Library. His boots alone were twice as high as Stan, great battered, red, leather things with rope-like laces and huge domes of brass across the toecaps. The rest of the Troll's clothing seemed lost in a long and flowing dressing gown of velvet curtain-like material. It was covered in swirls and arcane symbols, like a sorcerer's cloak, only with a greater variety of pockets and attendant handkerchieves. They billowed from out of small pockets and large, every conceivable pattern and texture. It was as if there had been an explosion in a Morris Dancers Factory. The vast ruff, made of old parchment covered in scribbles sat beneath a huge gnarly head. The head was covered in swirls and knots that could have been scars or could just as equally have been tattoos. the Bods couldn't tell as it loomed so far above, disappearing behind the disc of the ruff as the Troll busied itself in the shadows cast by huge candles and oil lamps. It fussed over a long, brass teapot on a stove top high above them. The Troll's long, ornate horns glinted as he expertly ducked and dived around the vaulted room to add a spoon of this and a pinch of that to the mixture brewing in the pot. A quill pen bobbed to and fro, perched behind his ear as he hummed and muttered to himself. Every now and then, he would stroke his perfectly trimmed beard, or flick the long quiff of his carefully combed hair away from his eyes. He had several rings pierced through both his long, gnarled, pointed ears, all glinting as he stirred the increasingly pungent contents of the pot. He tasted it every now and again from the long, thin, copper spoon he wielded as if a duelling sword or a conductor's baton.

Stan had always wanted to meet a Troll and had thought very long and extremely hard about what he would say to one of the most important members of the Oxford

Arcanum should he ever be lucky enough to talk to one.
"Are there any biscuits to go with the tea?"
Berga began to look around as her eyes adjusted to the shadows and dark cavernous corners for it was, after all, not so different from the half-light of the Library. Except here, instead of shelf upon shelf of ancient, beautiful, grumpy books, there were desks covered in scrolls and maps, stuck to the walls. They lay like rugs across each other on the dark, oak-beamed floor, piled upon other older, stranger parchments. They all seemed to be maps of Oxford, or at least some version of Oxford, a house changed there, a park different there, a college gone altogether on another. Between and around these curious cartographic wonders were incredible, complicated, crazy devices made of hoops of brass, rules of wood, long copper pipes and glass domes. They were all connected and buzzing, clicking or whirring like a group of hens who have somehow decided to do impersonations of arguing robots. It was the most wonderful place Berga had ever seen.
Oswyn and Osric nodded in thanks as the great Troll handed them thimbles full of dark, steaming Troll Tea. Red had accepted his tea and was sitting on a pile of leatherbound notebooks at the thick base of one of the huge desks that were scattered across the enormous room. He sipped the tea and whinged slightly. It was very hot and very strong. Red was fairly certain that if he drank it all he would be very, very drunk very, very quickly. Stan had finished his and was pestering the Troll for another. The Troll spooned some more into Stan's cup and smiled down at them all.
"Now, yes. Yes, I think, I really do think that it is certainly the time to understand why you are sitting in my study drinking my tea. Yes. Hertford College has its own Library and therefore its own Fellow travellers, whereas I, Rialto

of Hertford College Bridge am an Oxford Troll, and have no need of Bods, yes? Yes. So then, we must think about what has brought you to my Bridge and what I am to do about it?"

Red put his cup down carefully on a space between maps on the floor and stood up as tall as he could, which in the presence of the Troll wasn't very high, not very high at all.

"We are trying to get to the Human offices in Holywell Street Sir Rialto, we went a bit wrong as we aren't very good at steering yet. We will be though, one day, we'll be the best and beat all of the other Carrels in a great race and they will all sing songs about how good we are!"

Berga coughed loudly and stared at her friend, rolling her eyes as he stopped talking and scowled at her. "So, well, Sir... We need to get up there because a Human has taken one of our friends and we need to rescue him. We think we need to be near the Offices of Empirical Curiosities, up by the roof."

Rialto nodded as Red explained what had happened and how their friendship was now in danger. The Troll pulled various levers and turned dials, moving cogs and measuring tubes, lengths of spiralling copper wire and glass orbs until he slapped his hand on the desk and let out a deep booming answer.

"YES!"

the Bods all jumped slightly and looked at each other as the Troll cleared away a pile of books from against the wall. They revealed a panel of Oakwood with a large crack in it. The crack seemed to be moving slightly, curving and twisting, but Red couldn't be sure if this was just because he'd drunk too much Troll Tea. The Troll knelt down, rolling his long dressing gown around his arm out of the way and got low with his face low to the floor.

"This will now take you to the place you need to be, with

only the slightest need to enter the Mist Lanes. Do not linger there. Do not speak to anyone in the Lanes and DO NOT FEED THE CATS!" He thumped the floor and each of the Bods jumped, spilling what was left of their tea. All except for Stan, who had drunk every last drop of his second helping and was actually working on getting another. Red grabbed his arm and pushed him towards the crack.

"Thank you, Sir. We are most grateful. We hope you have a good day, and that people stop calling your Bridge by the wrong name"

 the Bods each climbed through the crack and disappeared from the room, Oswyn waving as he passed through last. Rialto nodded, waved a little wave, and sighed.

Across the road in the doorway of the New Bodleian, The Gloob spat and seethed as it watched the Bods disappear into the Troll Bridge. He was coughing up enough phlegm to build another Mor'n, pulling in the street dirt and dust, spinning his hands in intricate patterns to form the lumbering homunculi in front of him. When it had settled into its lump-like shape, The Gloob gestured to the other three to come out of the shadows. He sniffed the air, sensing them push through the Mist Lanes and into the Humans' Building.

"Come, my boys," he pointed to where the Bods had entered the building over the road, "Let's go (spit) Bod hunting."

Chapter Nine

The Congregation House was still full of noise and action. The different Bod Carrels had begun to merge and split off into different groups that needed many different abilities and expertise. Erasmus sat to one side watching as Madam Brunda moved from group to group. She was encouraging, pushing and cajoling them into better, more, and faster. Some of the older Bods had been in battles before, but none had faced a foe that appeared to be able to fight from within The Library itself. Everyone felt a little unnerved, Erasmus could sense it in the hall. Brunda was doing her best to contain the nervous energy and channel it. Erasmus only hoped it would work.

He beckoned over one of the younger Bods and asked her if she knew of any Bod that might have a list of the books that had gone missing in the last month or so. She bowed and said she would find out, before heading off into the massed crowds. Durwyn, one of the older cartographers from Fysher Carrel came over and bowed deeply, Erasmus smiled. Durwyn had been one of the loudest Bods calling for him to be banished all those years before.

"How can I be of service my good Sir?" He could see that Durwyn was holding several of Erasmus' own collections of maps and charts that had been commandeered from his study, way up at the top of The Radcliffe Camera.

"We have begun to sense patterns in the changes that The Library has been making to itself my Lord. However, we do not fully comprehend what they mean."

"I will come and look at your notes good Durwyn, I have an idea, I think, as to what has been going on."

He hauled himself up and leaned heavily on his stick, hobbling carefully between the groups. Taking most care to avoid the makers and engineers who were putting the

finishing touches to a prototype of a great sling, capable of flinging glow orbs and goodness knows what else. By the time he had made it over to the area strewn with maps and charts, he had been handed a scroll with an almost complete list of missing books.

He stood for some time in contemplation, reading and re-reading the list, staring at this map and that chart. Madam Brunda came over and placed her hand on his shoulder.

"Well, old friend, do you see anything, can you give us any idea what is happening here?"

He carried on staring, his eyes flickering and twitching as the thoughts span through his ancient mind.

Finally, he raised his clasped hands to his lips and tilted his head slightly.

"Two very different things are happening at exactly the same time here," he said stepping across the maps, diagrams, scrolls and sheets of note paper. He stood in the middle of them all pointing first at one then another. "It's like a game of chess but..." He looked at all the different diagrams. "It's as if The Gloob is intentionally doing certain things in a particular way in order that The Library will defend itself."

Madam Brunda scowled slightly.

"I don't understand."

"Each time one of these items was taken," Erasmus brandished the list, "The Library retaliated by removing a part of itself, out of harm's way. Old Library Lore states that when The Library has done all it can to protect itself by moving itself around, it has one course of action that it can take to finally stop itself from being attacked."

Durwyn moved to the front of those listening to Erasmus.

"And what is that my Lord?"

"The Library can turn itself, effectively inside out and hide deep within a very safe and impregnable book. It has only done this once before, in the earliest of its days, when only five of us stood guard over it. On Saint Scholastica's Day, a very long time ago indeed. We called it, as a kind of joke, The Bibliolibrum – the book of books." Erasmus took off his pillbox hat and scratched his head.

"The strange thing is, The Gloob appears to be actively trying to get The Library to turn itself into the Bibliolibrum, but why? If it wishes to attack The Library," he wondered. "Why goad it into becoming the safest thing it possibly can become? I confess. I am at a loss," he leaned heavily on his stick, deep in thought while a younger Bod brought him a cup of tea.

Madam Brunda shooed the others away, so as to give him a little peace and quiet.

"Well, whatever the reason, I fear we shall know soon enough."

***

Red and the Gang kept a hand on each other's shoulders as they walked through what Stan would later describe as 'a weird set of not quite right pathways, with a distinct lack of snacking opportunities. It had seemed to last forever and no time at all, they managed to avoid any of the cats that Rialto had mentioned. They did however have to duck several times in the fog to dodge various enormous bees wearing goggles and singing a variety of Abba songs. They fell out of the Mist Lanes into the hallway of a Human building and realised they would have to climb.

Stan and Berga did remarkably well, considering they weren't really climbers at all and Berga's legs were little or no use for this kind of thing. The other three had cobbled together some tackle for them, and, after some slight mishaps, the Mob had scaled the stairs up to the attic room with few problems. They had crept passed the door to the Office of Empirical Curiosities with a great deal of nervousness. All the Bods knew that The Office looked after the mysteries and ancient beings of Oxford; keeping an eye on the Old Gods and refereeing the various squabbles between the magi of the different colleges, but nobody was really sure what all that actually meant. Red didn't really want to find out at the moment.

They eventually stood outside the plain blue door to an attic bedsit. It was peeling and the doormat was old and threadbare. The base of the door didn't quite meet the floor, allowing a nasty draught through in the winter months and a group of Bods inside any time they liked. Beyond was dark but grubby, thin curtains let the light of the City's lamplight outside shine through. There was a sink and a small stove to one side and a bed and desk in the other corner. On the Bed they could just see, high up, a human lying on top of the sheets, snoring loudly into the pillow. Stan tapped his glowstaff lightly and the shadows leapt around the room as they all froze for a moment. The human just carried on snoring. the Bods moved further inwards, avoiding a large pile of dirty washing in the middle of the floor. The whole place smelled of dampness and onions. Osric frantically patted Red on the shoulder and pointed at a shelf, high up the wall opposite the window. Red's eyes followed Osric's finger and there, jammed between two old dictionaries, was a large jar. In the half-light, they could just make out the slumped shape of Cynwise huddled up in the bottom. It took her a moment to notice the glowstaff and her friends. Then she jumped up and waved smiling but she also kept looking anxiously over at the sleeping human. Berga had noticed a pile of freshly washed and ironed

handkerchiefs on the floor near the bed. She wandered off towards them, furkling around in her bag for a specific pouch of powder.
Oswyn stood on Stan's shoulders and swung his grappling hook around a few times. He launched it up at the shelf, where it stabbed into the wood and held firm. He clicked his gear into place and began winching himself up towards his imprisoned friend, his brother followed. Red carefully padded over to Berga, who was very meticulously smearing some kind of very fine power onto each of the giant sheets of handkerchiefs before placing the back on the pile. He whispered in her ear.
"What are you doing?"
She smiled at him.
"Itching and sneezing powder, just our little present to the nice man." Red grinned,
"How very thoughtful of you Berg. You're a very considerate Bod," they hadn't noticed that the snoring had stopped.

The brothers had made it onto the shelf and climbed on top of the dictionaries, which fluttered slightly when they recognized that the Bods were on them. Osric patted the one under him and calmed it. They lowered a line down to Cynwise who took no time at all to wrap it around her wrist and heave herself out of the jar. The brothers each gave her a great hug and then attached a spare harness over her shoulder, adjusting it as they did so. As speedily as they could, the three winched themselves back down towards the floor. At about halfway down Cynwise waved to Stan. Stan waved back just as the whole room blazed in the light of the single bare bulb hanging from the ceiling. They froze as Mr Simper sat up in bed, with one finger on the light switch next to him,
"Well, well. A prison break!"

Stan stood frozen as the human started to move. Oswyn and Osric frantically worked their gear to try and get the three of them to the floor before he got to them. Mr Simper picked up a large fly swatter from on the desk next to his bed and swung his legs over the edge to get up. He seemed not to have seen Red and Berga directly below him. As he leaned off the bed, Red wrapped himself around his friend, whilst she jammed her elbows in tight and stuck her crutch straight up into the air.

The noise Mr Simper made when his soft barefoot stabbed down on Berga's hard brass crutches was nothing any of the Bods had ever heard before. He jumped back onto the bed, but missed the corner with his hand and crashed down onto the floor. He lay there seething until his eyes began to focus on a tiny thing running straight towards him. Mr Simper totally forgot the pain from his foot because Stan had sunk his teeth deep into the long pointy nose of the human and seemed to have no intention of letting go. Mr Simper squealed an entirely different type of squeal to the one from a few seconds earlier as he leapt up and, with the Bod dangling from his nose and tears streaming from his eyes. He blindly put his head down and ran straight into his front door.

The great human collapsed into a heap as Cynwise and the brothers reached the floor. Stan unclenched his teeth and rolled out from under the howling fury of Mr Simper. Red and Berga, now limping slightly with one slightly bent crutch, joined the others and ran hunched up under the gap in the door. They could hear the chain being taken off on the other side, so Red made a run for the gap under the door opposite, signalling to his friends to do the same. Just in time, they seemed to make it into the unknown room. They caught their breath and were all hugging Cynwise, when, from behind them came the unmistakable voice of Offa...

"What on earth do you think you are doing this time, Master Aethelred?" Red span around and, sure enough, the great bulk of Offa stood glaring at him, with Wuffa sneering at his side. "I shall ask you once more, boy. Why are you here?"

Red could feel the anger welling up inside him.

"We came to get our friend. Why are you two here, as if I don't already know?"

Wuffa strode forward, then scuttled back when Stan took a step towards him.

"Such impertinence from ones so young, we are here to rescue that girl," He pointed at Cynwise. Red looked at Cynwise, who shrugged, then looked back at Offa.

"She has rescued herself, as you can see. You're here to meet up with your human friend, admit it! How else would you come to be cowering in this..." He looked around him at the vast white tiled room, "...bathroom?" Offa was going purple with rage. Stan pointed at him and turned to Berga.

"That's my favourite colour. I've always wanted a waistcoat in that colour."

Berga nodded.

"Oh, lovely. I like waistcoats."

"SHUT UP!" Offa nearly exploded. "The old network of tunnels from The Library leads out to here. We were on our way over to rescue her," he pointed distastefully at Cynwise. This caused Oswyn to bob his tongue out at the older Bod. "You are complicating matters, now follow us and..."

"We will follow you nowhere! We won't fall for any of your traps Offa. Now leave us alone or..." Red barely kept control of himself.

"It upsets me so to see friends quarrelling in the dark (Spit). Why should your last words be ones of anger, eh?" Out of the shadows, from the gap in the wall where Offa

had entered the human room, shuffled The Gloob. Three Mor'ns followed him in, huge and menacing; their razor teeth once again click-clacking at the air. Oswyn and Osric whimpered behind Stan, who tried not to look as petrified as he felt.

Offa and Wuffa span around to face the attacking throng. Offa bashed his glowstaff on the floor lighting the whole room with its powerful shine. He turned and looked at Red, and for the first time in a very long time, he looked kindly at the young Bod, but with sadness in his eyes.

"This is not your battle boy. You must get back to The Library and prepare for the worst." With this, he swung his glowstaff around his head and roared towards The Mor'ns. After a mere moment's hesitation, Wuffa stepped back against the wall of the room. It seemed he was trying to keep out of the way of any trouble and almost grinned as old Offa was surrounded. The Mor'ns sprang forward and soon enveloped the old Bod, who flailed with great fists and staff, ripping and bludgeoning the Mor'ns. The creatures of ignorance and bile just reformed and attacked again. Stan grabbed Red by the shoulders,

"He's right Red, none of us is strong enough right now. We have to go!"

The Gloob shuffled forwards, reaching out towards Oswyn, who cowered behind Berga. She suddenly grabbed the pouch from her bag and threw it at the great bulbous, putrid eye. The Gloob shrieked and shrunk back, just enough for the young Bods to flee between it and the chaotic fight. As they fled down the dark unfamiliar corridors Red heard the booming voice of Offa for one last time,

"Protect my Library, Boy. Keep it safe!" Red ran with tears falling down his face. He hurried them on, fearful of what was behind them.

Chapter Ten

Godwin gave the young messenger some chocolate to keep her strength up and sat and dried his hands on his leather apron. There hadn't been this many Bods in the Supper Room all at the same time for as long as he could remember. Keeping them all fed was proving to be a bit of a challenge. The food supplies were fine, there were fresh things every day left by the librarians, the researchers and the odd student (some of them very odd). There were also great storerooms over at the New Bodleian and the Trolls always made sure that tea was sent to The Library, it was just the sheer numbers. They were sorting it, they always did. The Supper Room had started filling up after Mad, Old Erasmus had spoken to them all down in the Congregation House. All of the Bods had spun off into their different groups and were now mingling with each other to find out who could do the best with which group. The high skirting boards had become impromptu notice boards, with hundreds of messages and requests for things or skills; offers of help and knowledge. Everyone seemed to have the same unspoken thought: This is what they had been created for, to protect The Library. This was their greatest test and every one of them wanted to do their best. They were the Bods and very, very proud of it. Godwin decided that he needed to get some air. The other cooks and bakers of Creswick Carrel bustled around making sure the tables were stocked so that all those pouring over the various plans didn't have to worry about empty stomachs.

He headed through one of the Bod doors in the wall and climbed the old carved steps up and round to the roof of

the Tower of Five Orders.
The clean air hit him as he opened the hatch onto the

copper roof. This had been repaired not so long ago with the help of the humans, and it shone beautifully. The moonlight of the clear sky after the storm reflected off it as Godwin wandered over towards the vast human-arched door. Using one of the many Bod ladders fixed around the roof, he climbed up through to the outer edge and sat down to survey the east of their city. In the moonlight, he could see across the roofs of Hertford College, then New College and off into the darkness. Just to the right was Queen's College and the glittering lights of the High. Oxford was too magical and unique to have a High Street, so it has a High instead. The bells of Magdalen Tower struck the hour and the lights of Headington, Cowley and Iffley twinkled off in the distance.

Godwin usually felt calmer when he sat up here, but things were very strange in The Library at the moment. He would do his bit, he knew that. A shiver went down his spine. Something was coming, something bad, and he didn't mind admitting that he was very scared indeed. He patted the roof of his beloved Library.

"Don't worry my old friend," he whispered into the wind. "We'll look after you, or fall trying." The Library didn't answer, but the cook knew deep down in his being that it was listening.

***

Meghan ran through the Reading room as fast as her young legs would carry her. She grasped the message scroll tight to her side. Her bag was full of her favourite thing in The Library, a big chunk of chocolate. She had always wanted to be needed, to be useful and now her chance had come. The engineers of her Carrel had needed some of the older maps of the Quadrangle. She had volunteered to go and find some of Fysher Carrel and ask for them.

The south range of the Upper Reading Room was still quite dark as she stopped for breath. The Theology books huffed and puffed around her on the shelves, each one was absolutely convinced of its own importance. This was one of Meghan's favourite parts of The Library. Before she had chosen Craster Carrel (Meghan had decided she wanted to be as good a maker as the older Bod, Berga) she had, like all young Bods before they choose, been left to wander The Library. To talk with all the Bods they met; to learn what it was to be a Bod. Only when they themselves decided they were ready, did they make a choice and join a Carrel. One or two, of course, never made the choice and were quietly allowed to carry on wandering. The Shakleton Carrel generally looked after these weird and mystical ones. It was usually one of these that became, over time, Fellow Travellers. They would take up the brass staff and red bowler hat to wander out into the world. They would wander far beyond The Library and its outposts to find their own book collections

to protect.

Meghan looked around her, she could never quite understand why anyone would want to leave The Library. It was her entire world. The City outside was just pulling the light of the day into itself and she could make out the faces on the frieze around the room, stern, old gentlemen gazing out from history. Meghan often thought they were looking after her just as much as she was trying to look after The Library. She ran on, through a Bod door and along a rope bridge. This one needed some work on it; she made a note in the back of her mind to let someone in her Carrel know. The young, eager Bod made her way through a passageway over the southern entrance to The Library. She came out on a balcony overlooking the Exhibition Room. She looked down on the great, white and glass boxes, filled with many of The Library's most amazing things. She shook her head, who would want to hurt all this? The top of one of the glass cases had been turned into a temporary workshop for a group of Fysher Carrel's best cartographers and Readers. These were the Bods who were experts at interpreting what the maps were trying to tell the Bods. The vast sheets of paper and parchment were as individual and sometimes as stubborn as any of the books. A few wanderers from Shakleton Carrel had joined them. The group seemed to be in the middle of a heated discussion over one of the maps. Meghan clipped her winch rope onto the balcony and let herself down slowly, the Craster Carrel weren't quite as good climbers as Bandinel's bookherders, but they came close. She landed calmly on a pile of ancient plans and unhooked her gear. The discussion had become quite loud as the young messenger approached. Meghan took the letter and unfolded it carefully. She tugged the arm of one of the Bods at the edge of the group who smiled at her and read the request. The older Bod wandered off to another part of the makeshift workshop atop the glass case and found the map the message asked for. Meghan thanked her and started her journey back to Congregation House. It was hard going, but she knew she was being useful, and Meghan knew that she would do anything asked of her to defend The Library, whatever it cost her.

***

"I'm simply saying there aren't enough of us. We need more!" The Bod from Shackleton was easily recognisable in his purple hat.
An older Bod leaned across the maps and charts scattered in front of her,
"I understand what you're saying Drefen, but has anyone tried to contact The Spiders? Or the Ashmoles? They might help, they've done so before."
Drefen took his purple cap off and wiped his head, this was turning into a very long night.
"We have some of Shackleton out there Elswyth, as always, but it's difficult to know how many to call back to defend The Library," he explained. "The worst is that our best young wanderer is still missing. We haven't seen him for days."
"Perhaps we need to send the beacon up?" Several of the other Bods around the pile glanced nervously at each other. Drefen rubbed his chin, thinking
"It is a desperate thing to call in all of the Bods from out in the City, the Fellow Travellers won't take kindly to being summoned home for no good reason."
The old cartographer looked up to the old explorer,
"Drefen my friend, I don't think there has ever been a better reason," he nodded and turned to give a young Bod of his Carrel instructions. The boy bowed and gathered

his things together, heading off to find Madam Brunda.

Elswyth sat down and took a drink of dandelion and burdock. She was exhausted, they all were. It all made very little sense, and she had difficulty accepting it was actually happening. Just like all the other Bods, Elswyth had sat in the nursery after she had hatched and listened to stories of The Duke, and of Thomas Bodley; the great legends and thrilling adventures. But the ones that had stuck most firmly in her mind were the terrible tales of The Gloob. Stories told late in the dark of the nasty, selfish creature that wanted to keep the books all to himself and was bricked up in the walls by his friends. 'Be good or The Gloob with get you', 'Eat your Supper or The Gloob will take you away', 'Go to sleep or The Gloob will come!'
Well, he had come. It wasn't a tale to tell naughty little Bods, it was real. The Gloob was a vicious, evil thing and it was building an army. The Gloob was here, inside their precious Library and it wanted revenge. She was old now, and her life had been rich and full. The Library had cared for her and looked after her, and in return, she loved it and defended it without question. She had spent many hours and days, reading the maps and charts held within these walls. Maps of places that even Fellow Travellers had probably never been to. Her life had been full of imagination and beautiful images now it seemed the nasty little thing from her childhood nightmares was coming to pull it all apart. Elswyth wasn't sure they were going to be able to stop it, but they would all do their damndest to try. She looked around the workshop at all the Bods working feverishly together to try and solve the great puzzle. What was The Gloob up to and what did he want? She watched all the young Bods racing around, their minds exploding with new ideas and after a sigh,

she smiled. The smile disappeared quickly and her face darkened. How many, she wondered, how many would be lost in the coming storm? How many of these faces would she lose to The Gloob and his relentless Mor'ns?

"As few as possible, if I can stop you!" She said to the air. If the revolting little creature wanted a fight, it was going to get one.

***

Brec left the Exhibition Room by the main Bod door and headed across the quadrangle towards the Tower of the Five Orders. His instructions from Drefen were quite clear. Find Madam Brunda and tell her that she needed to call The Quire together and have it authorise the release of the Beacon. Brec had heard stories about the beacon since he was in the nursery. It was a great and powerful signal, set off high above The Library in order to summon all of the Fellow Travellers home. There were old, old tales that told of Bods heading as far as Abingdon and Didcot to the south, and Witney in the north, but Brec wasn't sure that any Bods had travelled so far. The Carrel-less Bods who had taken up the brass staff and donned the red bowler were a weird and temperamental bunch, or so the stories said. If The Quire was even thinking of bringing them back, the coming trouble was very bad indeed. Brec had never seen so many Bods in The Quadrangle before. There were groups talking and heading this way and that. Other groups were bringing supplies from deep storerooms and beginning the construction of great slings and trebuchets. He saw one of his own Shackleton Carrel helping heave a length of wood into position. Others bound it with rope to form the crossbeam of some kind of crossbow. A huge, nineteenth-century book on Roman warfare loomed over them as they consulted the diagrams

within. Brec slapped his friend on the shoulder.
"Hello Scead, how's things?" The other Bod pushed the wood a little higher and grinned,
"All good, Brec, all good. This is amazing, isn't it? It's all so exciting! I can't wait for it all to kick off!" Brec raised an eyebrow and the other Bod laughed. "Oh, come on! You can't pretend that you're not enjoying this Brec. At last something fun is happening around the old place. I love it!"
Brec smiled nervously.
"I guess so Scead, You take care, okay," he hurried away as the wood fell into place and the group cheered.
Brec had to admit, despite all of the nervousness, this was certainly different. Wandering the tunnels and old passageways of the Library was fun and the other Bods always looked on the Shakleton Carrel as a bit more adventurous and daring, but this was different. He had been born and grown in The Library. He had pledged to look after it and defend it come what may. Well, he wasn't too sure what was coming, but he wanted to be a part of it. Maybe one day he would sit in the Supper Room and tell the tiny new Bods tales of heroes and battles that he had actually been part of! That would be amazing.
He made his way up through the passageways and the long, long steps and ladders up to the Supper Room. It wasn't difficult to find Madam Brunda: she was like a vast, graceful island at the centre of a huge storm. Bods were running everywhere. Groups approached her for advice and span off to work on a hundred different things at the same time. Brec pushed his way through to her and whispered his message into her magisterial ear. She stared at him and then nodded, quickly scribbling a note on a scrap of paper produced from one of the many pockets inside her voluminous gown. She handed it to Brec and patted him on the head and whispered her

instructions. He nodded and headed into the throng of Bods in the hall. Brec watched as Bods who usually spent their spare time arguing with each other now working together on this project or that. Old Bods who had not spoken in years sat side by side drawing plans on sheets of enormous paper and working out the best defence against a bewildering number of possible attacks. Brec didn't like to own up to himself, but he really was starting to enjoy all of this. He understood what Scead had meant out in the Quadrangle. He pushed his way through a group of Bods who were trying to work out how to defend the huge space of the Divinity School if The Gloob got in there. No one seemed sure when or where it would attack. They didn't know how many Mor'ns he had managed to create, so the different groups were trying to prepare for any eventuality.

Brec dutifully found each Bod on Madam Brunda's list and explained that she humbly requested their presence at a gathering of The Quire. Each bowed to him and headed off immediately. Most were older and important Bods who would never have even noticed him before. Brec felt very important. One of them, Yrre, a short elderly Bod from the Hyde Carrel even talked to him.

"So, young Bod, what do you make of all this, eh?"

Brec gulped slightly. No one ever asked his opinion, certainly not members of The Quire.

"Well, sir. I think, well I think it's all rather exciting really. I can't wait for The Gloob to come and try and hurt The Library. I think we'll beat him pretty swiftly Sir. That's what I think."

Yrre smiled sadly at the small, young Bod in front of him. "Well, I hope you are right my boy. But I fear that we are not prepared for this danger. It is unlike any we have faced for a very long time. Stay safe little Bod. Stay safe." He patted Brec on the arm and slowly made his way over

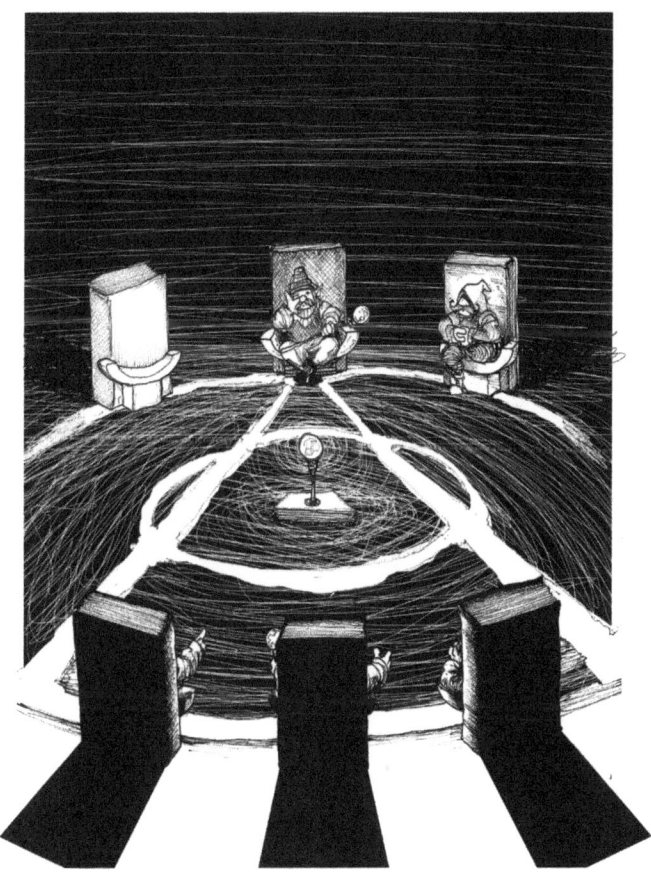

towards The Roundel Room, the chambers where The Quire had to meet since the Bods had been called to look after The Library. Brec didn't understand the attitude of some of the older Bods. It made sense for the younger ones to be a little frightened, but he thought this was all an awfully big adventure. Brec was determined to enjoy it to the end.

Yrre took his seat with the ten other members of The

Quire who had answered the call. here in The Library was Offa? It was just his luck, he thought, to have been called for duty at this time. Any decisions they were called on to make would weigh heavily upon his conscience, of that, he was certain. The eleven sat and discussed the need for the Beacon. One or two argued that they should hold back until they absolutely had to send it up. Yrre banged his staff on the floor.

"We must send it now! Don't you see? They have to come now or it will be too late!" Several others banged their staffs on the floor in agreement. "We have to figure out a way of sending it as high as possible so that the furthest see it. The Fellow Travellers may be as mad as hatters, but we need them. Now, more than ever before!"

Madam Brunda raised her hand to speak.

"I think we all realize that we have no real choice. Erasmus thinks that The Gloob is trying to goad The Library into defending itself, but none of us can quite work out why. Our biggest fear..." She turned and looked each of them in the eye, "Is that if The Library brings the Bibliolibrum into being, it will leave us all dangerously exposed. We can if needs be defend the book, but what will defend us?"

Aedre raised her hand and was more than a little surprised when everyone stopped and turned to listen to her. She was a young Bod, much younger than most of the other members of The Quire. She had been rather panicked to find herself holding the small red marble at the last Great Meet. The other bakers in Creswick Carrel had crowded around her to congratulate her. Aedre had simply stared at the red marble and rather nervously gone with the other eleven to pledge the oath to Think Things Through. Now, here she was in the Roundel Room with as much right to speak and be heard as any of the other of The Quire.

"I think," she gulped, "I think we should imagine that The Library will do anything it can to defend itself and us. I think we should go out and find The Gloob," she shivered slightly at even saying the word."Wherever it is hiding. Before it comes and tries to hurt us."

One or two of the older Bods nodded and whispered to each other. Madam Brunda thought for a moment.

"There may be something in that, Aedre. Word is coming through that a group of Bods have already left The Library on some sort of contraption. Apparently, it was Aethelred and his friends, The Duke alone knows what on earth he is up to, as usual!"

One of the other of The Quire, Eldwin, snorted slightly.

"He has probably fled like a coward in the night." He nodded to himself, but Madam Brunda glared across the Roundel Room at him.

"Aethelred would never flee! Remember it is he and his friends who warned us of this catastrophe and we did not listen. He loves this place with all his heart!"

Eldwin banged his staff upon the stone floor.

"And yet he has gone into the night, and left us to deal with it all!" Brunda scowled at the floor. She knew Red and the others would never abandon The Library. But she had to admit to herself that she hadn't the faintest idea what he was up to.

Yrre stood and leaned on his staff.

"The Quire, the twelve, I mean to say eleven, here," he noted that there was still no sign of the old warhorse, Offa. " have stood against danger to The Library before, but this is different. We have all fought to defend our beloved home, but in small fights, nothing like this. We all know that nothing will be the same after this. Those brave souls out there are plotting, planning, working and building. We know, we absolutely know, that many of them are not going to come through this alive!"

Another of The Quire, Cearo, stood and raised her hand, "Do you think we have not pondered this fact, Yrre? Do you think we are moving towards this battle with joy in our hearts? We must protect The Library. It is our purpose! What else would you have us do?"

Yrre smiled wearily at the floor.

"I think we must go out and prepare for battle. I think we must march straight at this terrible enemy and destroy him before we are destroyed ourselves. I only hope that we can look those young Bods in the eye when all is done and over. Now, let us vote on getting the Beacon up above the city."

The Quire debated for some while longer and then, finally, agreed to send the Beacon up. Cearo, as a member of Craster Carrel, who had after all built the thing long ago, agreed to make the journey to Turl Street and bring the Beacon home.

"But first," she said, "I need something to eat!"

The other members of The Quire sat in silence, each pondering what the coming days would bring. Cearo headed back into the Supper Room. Aedre caught up with her and asked if she could go with the Older Bod. Cearo smiled and said she thought that was a splendid idea. They made their way over to Godwin, who was back piling cheese and bread onto one of the tables. Each bowed to the other as the two Bods of The Quire loaded supplies for the journey ahead. Aedre was quietly excited. She had never been out before. Perhaps this would be a great adventure after all.

***

Leof and Odelyn of the Jolliffe Carrel were doing their best to be in control in the Nursery. Every single Bod had started their time within The Republic of Lettered

Men in this vaulted, safe place. It was tucked away at the furthest edge of the Selden End of Duke Humfrey's Library. The tiny, new Bods were running riot around the place, fighting great imaginary battles with the evil Gloob, trying to climb to the top of Radcliff Camera, built in here out of pillows, to rescue mad old Erasmus. One of the more enterprising ones had found some twine and was attempting to swing across the room to save some books only he could see inside his own imagination. It was chaos. Madam Brunda had left them here and it had taken very little time for them to lose control. Leof looked at his friend and laughed. She scowled back at him "It's not funny! Madam Brunda will skin us alive, or simply throw us to the Mor'ns!" This was taken up as a chant by a few of the small ones nearby and soon the whole room was shouting,
"Throw them to the Mor'ns! Throw them to the Mor'ns!"
Odelyn just put her head in her hands.
"What kind of a chant is that may I ask?" They all stopped in their tracks as Erasmus strode into the hall. He stood over the little ones and glared at them, then, when he could hold it in no longer, he burst out laughing and made his way over to the two forlorn Nursery minders in the middle of the room.
"That is not your chant, tiny Bods. You should be shouting, loud and clear, 'All Equal!' Yes? Yes." They needed no prompting to join in until the hall rang with the Bods' own shout.
"All Equal! All Equal!"
After a small while, Erasmus raised his hand and the hall fell silent. Leof leaned over to Odelyn and whispered.
"We should learn how to do that. It may prove useful," Erasmus turned and winked at them.
"Come around little adventurers. Come and sit and I shall tell you a tale worth listening to." The excitement ebbed

out around the room with the tiny Bod that had been attempting the daring rescue, doing his best to get as close to Erasmus as he could. Within no time they were all sat in a semicircle, waiting for every word from his ancient lips, buried somewhere within the great drooping moustache.

"Far and long ago, The Library was simply one small but strong room filled with a hundred or so books. Old Thomas, the Bishop came and sat here thinking many important thoughts. When he had done this for a good length of time, he summoned to him from the surrounding villages, the best of the wise folk and witches, sorcerers and hedge mages. The greatest five came, from Iffley and South Hinksey, from Boars Hill and Abingdon. Even the Green Witch of Wytham woods, whom almost everyone was fearful of. They came and talked and listened to what Thomas the Bishop wanted to do. They each gave their knowledge and each left a thing which might help him to achieve his goal. Old Thomas spent many days wandering the bookstalls of Catte Street and Schools Street. For, little Bods, this was far and long ago, before Dr Radcliffe had his great Camera built. Thomas the Bishop found books and scrolls to help him. One morning, just after breakfast... because humans are strange folk, who eat and wander about in the daytime, wasting their nights in sleep... Old Thomas used all of the things he had learned and been given and wished. He thought into existence five small beings. These were the Cobs. The Cobs were told to look after the books and defend The Library Room for all time to come."

Even Leof and Odelyn were mesmerised by the tale as it unfolded. Erasmus seemed to be staring far away as if he was remembering the tale in its telling.

"The Cobs worked hard and tended the books, but one of them..."

One of the little Bods stood and also put her hand up for good measure.
"Please, What were their names?" Erasmus thought for a moment, then for a moment longer.
"I don't know. Let's call them Comatus and Panagrellus, Erasmus and Saxaferetto and, erm, Trevor. Anyway..." Several of the small Bods were jumping up and down, one shouted out,
 "But you're Erasmus!" The old storyteller nodded at this. "Indeed, I am named Erasmus, and so was the Cob. Strange indeed, strange indeed," he continued, as they settled down again.
"Now, one of the Cobs liked the books very much. Perhaps a little too much and he started to grumble and complain when anyone wanted to read them... what else are books for, except for sharing and learning from? He began hiding the books and wouldn't let even the other Cobs get near them," he continued. "After some time, Old Thomas went away to where ever the humans go to when they are not here anymore. The Duke came to The Library and let it be known that there were too many books, so a new Library would be built. The books began to be moved but the selfish Cob became quite angry and attacked all who

tried to take the books he had hidden away. Eventually, the other Cobs overpowered him and sealed him away, where he could hurt no one at all. This was a nasty thing to do, but they were frightened of their brother, and fear makes you do bad things sometimes."

The younger Bods were jumping up and down a lot less as the tale unfolded.

"So the selfish Cob stayed bricked up whilst the others went out into the world. All except for one, who stayed to help the new guardians of The Library, the Humfs." The old storyteller smiled then and patted the nearest Bod lightly on the head.

"Well, I must go now, for there is much to be done, and you all probably need a good nap after all your adventures. I will return soon and tell you the rest of your story, I promise," he pulled himself slowly up and nodded to Leof and Odelyn, who bowed deep and low. As he was leaving, Madam Brunda swept into the nursery and was slightly startled to find him there.

"Erasmus. What are you filling their little heads with?"

Erasmus smiled. "Just stories, my dear. Old, old stories."

Chapter Eleven

Wann secured the door as tightly as he could, making sure the bindings and sigils were fixed and intact. This deep, secret chamber, far below The Library had been constructed in the earliest days by Bodley himself and the great John Townsend. Special, hidden rooms, the knowledge of which had been passed down secretly to the Humfs and then to the Bods through Wann's own group, James Carrel. They were the collectors and wardens of The Library's treasures. Not that all the books and manuscripts, maps and artefacts weren't valuable. A number of the things in The Library were so important, so fundamental to the whole, that they were almost part of the Library itself. Offa, the elder of James Carrel, had gathered his most trusted Bods together. This was just after that little know-it-all Aethelred had stood shouting in the Congregation house, getting everybody all hot and bothered. Wann tutted at the memory of it. Offa had brought them together to tell them another secret, the Bods of James Carrel were good at secrets. Offa had sat down in his favourite chair and told them a terrible thing. "Young Aethelred is right," the room had remained silent as this sank in. "There is something that has gotten in and it is attacking The Library. You all here know our solemn vow concerning The Nine. Well, my friends, it seems that our worst fears have been realised." Offa let the startled chatter between them die down before he continued.
"Several of us have noticed... things happening in The Library for some time. Our good friend in Hyde Carrel, Wuffa, has been watching the wards and protective bindings of The Library for me. I have taken the most unusual step of asking him to come here and tell us what he has found."

Offa knew that this would not go well with the others of James Carrel. They were by their very nature a secretive group. Their great vow and hidden knowledge had been added to over the years and a natural reluctance to let outsiders near anything they did, had led to a reputation for secrets and coldness. One of his closest advisers in the Carrel, Arianrod, stood and confronted him.
"We have always accepted that you are the elder here, Offa. But we are as in all things of us Bods, equal." Offa had never seen her so angry.
"You should not have invited another here without talking to us first. I cannot think of any danger so great that the careful guarding of our Carrel should come second."
Wuffa stepped out of the shadows, from behind a curtain at the edge of the room.
"Unfortunately, good Arianrod, the danger is actually worse than any you can think of."
The room descended into shouting and banging of glow staffs on the floor as the rest of the Carrel made plain their outrage at this unprecedented intrusion. Wan had moved across the floor to confront the intruding Bod. Offa took some moments to calm his comrades down.
"Let him speak! I beg you."
Wuffa bowed low to them all.
"Just as you have great secrets that you keep in order that The Library is safe, so I have, of late, been the keeper of dark notions and possibilities. Some of the most powerful wards, bindings, glyphs and protective bonds of The Library have been broken," a murmur of unease ran around the room at this new revelation. "What is more, they have been broken in the easiest of fashions. Whoever has done this, knew perfectly well what to do and how it should be done."
Offa moved to the middle of the group once more.
"It is much worse than that my brothers and sisters. Not

only has something broken our defences, but it seems it has been able to procure the aid of some human agent. This individual has been, very carefully, taking certain items from The Library."

Toland stood, startled.

"Have any of the Nine been taken?"

Offa looked down at the floor, embarrassed. Few of those present, if any, had ever seen Offa embarrassed before.

"Yes. This human has taken three items so far as we know. All three are part of The Nine." This time the room erupted into a storm of rage that even great Offa could not quell.

"How could let this happen and not tell us, Offa!" Arianrod shouted as others shouted their agreement. "The Library must have The Nine. They are the very essence of the place itself."

Offa held his hand to the roof and bellowed above the noise.

"I thought I could stop it. I thought I could bring them back without causing great panic in The Library. Then young Aethelred started poking around..."

Toland banged his staff forcefully on the floor and glared at the older Bod.

"Do not presume to blame the young Bod for your failing Offa. At least he came to all of us when he found that something was wrong!"

Offa calmed down and held his hands up.

"I know, I know. I tried to shame the child into silence, and for that, I am truly sorry. Wuffa and I will find this human. We will return what belongs to The Library. We believe we know where to find him."

Offa had left the Carrel's Hall then, with the Hyde Carrel's Bod trailing after him. Wan had not seen him since, though Arianrod had said she had seen him at the back of Congregation House when Erasmus had appeared with Brunda. It seemed other Carrels held their own set of secrets. Wan secured the door tightly. The Hyde Carrel had tried to keep a close eye on the remaining artefacts that made up The Nine, but since Offa's revelations, another four had been ripped from The Library. Wan was beginning to think that maybe the James Carrel should tell Brunda or Erasmus what they knew. This left only two; The Shakespeare first folio was somewhere far off in The Library with Arianrod and Toland. Wan was proud that his Carrel had given him the task of hiding and securing the copy of the 1887 Beeton's Christmas Annual. This small section of the lower chambers was known to very few of even his own Carrel. Wuffa himself had set the glyphs and bindings in place. Wan thought that this was the best and most secure place of them all. He took some time to replace the pile of old books in front of the door and began spreading dust over them, in order to give the impression that they had not been moved. He had begun patting down his robes when the dust and dirt in front and around him began to spin and swirl around, seemingly forming larger and larger clumps in front of his eyes. They started to suck towards each other with a revolting slurping noise, heaping themselves together, growing and moulding into great, fearsome beings.

"All this trouble and all these secrets Wan, for absolutely nothing," Wan turned and instinctively banged his glowstaff into greater light. Wuffa stood, arms folded and a smile of absolute arrogance on his face. The great lumbering creatures of bile and dust, ignorance and dirt stood next to him, their teeth click-clacking as they slowly advanced. They were terrifying, but the thing that slouched and hobbled from behind Wuffa was far, far worse. It gazed at Wan with a seeping, globular eye, its face full of hate and disgust. The spit from its ragged slash of a mouth dripped onto the floor causing it to fizz

and bubble, dark, nasty stains spreading from the spot.
"It is very naughty to keep secrets little Bod. Did old, dead Offa not tell you that? (cough)". Do not take long here with this one. I must travel much deeper to elicit the help of some old friends. (Spit)." It began to shuffle away, into the gloom.
Wann stared in utter despair at The Gloob. Hatred then began to overrun his face as he glared at Wuffa.
"You!" He lunged at the sneering Bod, but one of the Mor'ns lunged forward and beat him back with one of its great, powerful, claw-like hands. Wan crashed back against the wall and slumped down into the pile of books, groaning slightly. Wuffa strutted over to him.
"Still trying to keep your secrets? Still trying to keep me from my rightful place above all here?" He kicked the injured old Bod, who simply stared up at his former comrade. Wuffa laughed.
"That was the look on Offa's face as I watched them kill him. Did you know some of these chambers wander around Wann? Did Offa let you in on that secret? It's taken my friend here quite a while to pin them down. The damned Library keeps moving them around. Offa wouldn't tell us where they were, even at the end. He tried to order me about, even then! Can you imagine the arrogance, Wann? Well he's not bossing me around anymore, is he? Now all the secrets will be mine!" Wuffa moved back as the Mor'ns moved in on the broken Bod. Wann's scream echoed from the walls, down in the deep, secret chamber, far below The Library.

***

Madam Brunda swept into her own chambers and virtually fell into the old leather chair next to her large desk. The walls were full of paintings and etchings. Sir

Thomas Bodley stared down at her from his portrait in the centre of it all, gripping his sword hilt in his left hand as if willing her on to the battle ahead. One wall was full of scrawls and crayoned pictures made for her over the years by the hundreds and hundreds of Bods who came from under her protection in the Nursery and took their chosen places in The Library. She glanced over them: One was in bright greens and blues, showing books flying this way and that on a background of pink shelves. Another was of a big red Bod holding his staff up high shouting, this one made her smile. Aethelred had painted it whilst he was still tiny. She hoped he was safe, where ever the mad group of friends had shot off to. Yet another showed Brunda herself bashing a great blue mess of a monster on the head with her glow staff. She subconsciously touched her patch as she remembered the reality that had caused that particular story to come into being.

Long ago, when she was not much older than Red and his friends really, The Library had been attacked from far below by a group of wild and strange creatures known as the Ignor'ns. They seemed to feed on knowledge, without any care or understanding of the damage they were doing. Offa had suggested they might have been spun into existence in the Planning Department of the City Council, but no one was sure. The Library had suffered greatly and the Bods had united in battle with the Ashmoles to drive them off. Good friends had been lost, as well as an eye. It all seemed like a lifetime ago and yet only yesterday all at the same time. Brunda poured herself a small glass of dandelion wine and yawned. She had not slept in what felt like days. The Creswick Bods had kept the food and drink in plentiful supply but she had given herself little time for such things. The old Bod sat back down and dared to allow the eyelid on her good eye to close for a moment.

The knock on the door seemed to come almost immediately. She sighed and double-checked her eye patch, coughing slightly and opening the door.

"Our apologies Madam Brunda, but we need to speak with you with some urgency!" Arianrod bustled her way into Brunda's chambers, followed by three others of the James Carrel.

"Good day to you Arianrod; Bawdewyn; Wilda. Please come in," this seemed a little superfluous as they were already there, in the middle of her chambers. All three looked rather apprehensive and nervous.

"What is it? Is there news of Offa?" Brunda was beginning to worry about her old friend.

Wilda looked at the others and stepped forward.

"No Madam Brunda, we have heard nothing from Offa. We are here because we need to tell you something that has been happening, something important that due to our vows within James Carrel, we may not have fully explained before," Wilda looked at the floor. She couldn't quite bring herself to look Madam Brunda in the eye.

Brunda scowled at them, and they all felt much younger than their extensive ages.

"What have you done?" she said this rather more quietly than they might have preferred.

Bawdewyn smiled his most winning smile,

"Oh, Madam Brunda, we have done nothing. It is quite simply that The Nine have been going missing over recent time and we thought you should know," the other two liked the way this sounded and nodded enthusiastically.

"How recent and how many?" Brunda's voice was icy cold. She put her glass down on the table to stop herself from breaking it.

"Oh, only a week or so, Madam Brunda. And... Well at least eight of them, we think... possibly all Nine. Only possibly mind you, we can't seem to get a fix." Bawdewyn ducked just in time as the wine glass hit the wall behind him.

Brunda grabbed her cape and shoved the three of them out of the way. Before she left her Chambers, she turned and pointed at them, her one good eye burning in anger. "If any of James Carrel gets through this alive, it may do you well to keep out of my way for a while, or I might just kill you myself!" The door slammed behind her and Sir Thomas rattled in his frame.

Bawdewyn smiled.

"Well that went better than we expected, didn't it?"

Arianrod simply stared at him for a moment and then clipped him around the back of the head.

Chapter Twelve

Cynwise moved forward as quietly as she could. The others weren't so careful
"Shut up Stan!" Berga threw a pebble which bounced off his head.
"Don't do that please, it's unpleasant behaviour."
She scowled at him.
"Be grateful it wasn't a jar of something!"
He grinned.
"A jar of salsa. I like salsa!" His stomach started to rumble.
"Anyway, I'm simply stating the facts. We are lost."
Red sighed and turned around in the narrow tunnel, his nose pressed against his friend's chin.
"We know we are lost, you buffoon," he walked back a little, sat back down and looked at his small notebook again.
He had kept the little book since he chose Bandinel Carrel. It contained all his ideas and thoughts, all the parts of The Library he had visited and things he had found. There was nothing to give any idea where they were. The main problem was that when they had fled from The Gloob, leaving poor old Offa and Wuffa to face the danger for them. The Mob had run blindly through the old passageways and tunnels. They had simply needed to get as far away as possible from the evil behind them. Cynwise sat quietly between Oswyn and Osric eating the bread Stan had (only a little grudgingly) given up out of his pack.
"It's weird Red, I can't tell how far we are from the Library at all," she nibbled on the crust and looked at their surroundings. It was a brick passageway, with not much more room than three Bods wide (or one and a Stan). This section was long and straight, very long in fact. It almost

seemed to go on forever. Berga was quite sure they hadn't taken too many turns whilst fleeing, but it was difficult to say exactly which direction they had started off in. They could be just about anywhere in UnderOxford.

Stan held his glow staff up to the walls.

"These still look Bod-made, Red. I believe we are closer to The Library than we think," he tapped the wall in front of him and then wandered on a little. "Come and look down here!"

The rest of the Mob joined Stan as he made his way down a side passage which had sparked his curiosity. He had noticed it seemed to have a more ornate floor and ceiling than the long passageway that they had been travelling along up to now. It seemed to be patterned in cream-coloured octagons, separated by small squares and ended, not much further on, in a fine oak door, only a little larger than a Bod. Osric put his ear to it then shrugged and shuck his head.

Red touched it with the palm of his hand.

"Well, we haven't anywhere better to go," he grasped the brass ring in the centre of the door and pushed.

They walked out into a vast hall, still in shadows. Some light spilt in through a huge arched window at the one end to their left and through a great line of windows high in the walls opposite.

The patterns were clearly visible in the expanse of the white marble floor. There were black squares alternating with black diamonds along either edge, flowing off to the left and right. Osric and Oswyn walked slowly out into the middle of the hall and gazed up at the wall from which the Bod door had emerged. Their eyes widened and they pointed upwards. Red joined them.

"Oh," he stared at the vast shelves of books stretching the whole length of the hall and rising up and up to the high ceiling, split by a beautifully carved balcony. "We are in

a Library!"
Berga joined him and glanced all around.
"But not The Library. Where are we Red?"
A voice from the far end of the hall called out.
"You are in the Codrington Library my friends, welcome."
Stan walked towards the voice, which seemed to be coming from a very tall human seated high up on a throne of some kind. He wore flowing robes and a curly, long wig, all were white, as was his pale skin. He seemed to glow in the little light that floated in through the windows. Stan bowed low and removed his cap.
"Hello, Sir. Are you one of the famous mages of Oxford? It is an honour to meet you," Red took his cap off and joined his friend, bowing low. The voice laughed out loud and then called out.
"That's Lord Blackstone you fools, I am down here!" Stan and Red followed the direction of the voice to the base of the marble statue. Out of the shadows came a Bod, she wore a red bowler hat and carried a gleaming brass staff. Red's eyes widened, and both he and Stan bowed even lower than before. Berga came striding over on her crutches. Thankfully, Stan had managed to straighten the warped one out, mostly,
"What are you two doing? Oh my goodness, a Fellow Traveller!" She nearly fell over in her attempts to bow and look at the Bod in front of them at the same time. The Fellow Traveller smiled and bowed back.
"Welcome little Bods. Come and sit with me, I think, perhaps we need to talk."

***

Red had never tasted honey like it. He gulped it down in great handfuls. They were sitting in the centre of the library on a woven rug that had room enough for all of

them. The Fellow Traveller had dragged a hamper from a small chamber beneath the statue of Lord Blackstone and laid out a sort of grand picnic. The young Bods tucked into without being asked twice. Stan was starting to imagine that he had died and been taken by the Duke to the Land of Books and Picnics. This was perfectly fine by him.
"So, what brings you here?"
Red wiped butter from his mouth and tried to finish the fresh bread he was chewing.
"We were lost in the long tunnels from Holywell Street

and found you by accident, my Lady."
The Fellow Traveller held up her hand and smiled, shaking her head.

"My name is simply Codrington, little Bod. Nothing grander belongs to me," Cynwise leaned over Oswyn to get at a piece of red Leicester.

"That's a strange Bod name, if I may say so."

Berga scowled at her friend.

"Cyn, that's a bit rude!"

Codrington laughed and drank a little dandelion wine. Osric slowly drank his way through another bottle of the stuff he had discovered in the hamper.

"When a Fellow Traveller finds their library, however long it may take them, and however far they roam, they forsake their Bod name and take the name of the Library. Hence, once I was Acca, now I am Codrington. It suits me better I think," she spread a little pate on a noggin of bread. "But you have not told me what brought to be in the tunnels from Holywell in the first place."

The Bods sat, in the middle of the beautiful Codrington library, eating the best picnic they had ever tasted, and told the Fellow Traveller of The Gloob; they told of missing books, lost rooms, attacks on un-hatched Bods and the return of Erasmus. Red explained about the evil human and Cynwise's rescue including Offa and Wuffa's sacrifice. She stopped them there. "I knew a young Wuffa once, very sneaky, never trusted him."

Stan asked for more bread to dip in the honey, whilst Osric simply sat, grinning and swaying slightly. Berga wiped her chin.

"Will the Fellow Travellers help us do you think, Codrington?"

She took off her red bowler hat and scratched her head.

"It is difficult to say. If something is attacking libraries, many will be loathe to leave theirs undefended. But if

The Beacon goes up, well, most of us will find it hard to ignore such a summons. We were all Bods at the hatching and we are all Bods at the end, so...." She stared away into the dim light from the great windows of her own dominion. "If you need me, call my name. I will hear it. We're odd like that, us Fellow Travellers," she winked at Osric, who simply hiccupped.

"That is how the beacon works, you see. When we take the coat, hat and staff, we pledge ourselves to the ideals of The Library, and place our name in the heart of the beacon, ready for it to sing out in times of need."

Oswyn nudged Stan and signed.

"He wants to know, has the beacon ever been used, to your knowledge?"

Codrington thought for a moment.

"Not in my time. I don't think it was used even when the Michaelmas Angel came amongst us. But I could be wrong, let us hope we do not need it this time. Eh? Come, finish the picnic and I will show you the way home."

***

She led them across the hall and through some more of the ancient brick passageways. They led through chambers and corridors until finally, they came to a larger chamber that seemed to drop down into the deepest depths of UnderOxford. There were shuffling shapes across the chasm, the only passage across which seemed to be a long rope and wood bridge. It was fairly dark in the chamber. The Bods couldn't quite make out what was over the other side, but the noise carried across very well indeed. Oswyn and Osric whimpered slightly as the click-clacking noise of the vicious, sharp teeth echoed around them. Berga grabbed her dark goggles out of her pack and slid them on.

"Oh. Oh, dear. There seem to be three, no four Mor'ns over the other side. Wait. And something else, something huge," Codrington took a small orb from her backpack and threw it into the air over the chasm. It arched upwards and then burst into light, illuminating the whole chamber as it fizzed and frothed slowly downwards into the hole below. The young Bods gasped at the sight across the bridge. The four large Mor'ns were frightening enough, swaying slightly and lumbering about. The thing behind them was like nothing they had ever seen before. It towered over the Mor'ns. In the sharp light of the flair, its shadows flashed across the roof and walls of the chamber. The great bulky head of the thing had a thick crest of a brow. If it had eyes, they weren't visible, its mouth and lower jaw jutted out in great stubborn ridges. Two thick muscular legs or arms hauled its mighty, armoured body around. It did not seem to have any back legs. It was simply dragging itself this way and that as it moved forwards and back again from the chasm. It was many shades of blue with darker patches across the ridges of its back. Great lumps stuck out all across it, each ending in deadly-looking, thorn-like spines that shone in the dwindling light of the flare. It had a short stumpy tail of sorts as if whatever may have conceived of such a monster had given up halfway down its back. It ended in a fleshy knot that thrashed about as it ponderously rocked to and fro. The noise it made echoed around and around, like someone playing the tuba whilst they had a terrible cough. The two Bod brothers cowered back as the others stared at the way ahead. Stan patted his best friend on the shoulder.

"That sounds just like you snoring that does," Red scowled at him.

"I do not snore!"

Stan looked down in mock amazement.

"Yes, you do! It's terrible, some nights when we're out in

The Library together I have to go and have a snack, just to get away from you!" Cynwise coughed beside them.
"I hate to break this up, but they seem to be moving towards the bridge."
They all watched as the Mor'ns seemed to come to some collective decision and began lumbering forwards.
Codrington stood in front of the other, younger Bods and stretched her arms out protectively. In her left hand, she grasped her Brass Staff, the last light of her flare twinkling along it.
"You go back, I will defend the bridge," she stepped forward towards the edge of the chasm and the swaying bridge. She held her staff aloft and adjusted the tilt of her bowler hat.
"You cannot pass! I am a servant of the..."
Red pushed her on the back.
"Stop that, please! We've had quite enough of leaving people to fight our battles while we run away, thank you!"
Stan took his pack off and hefted his glow staff as he purposefully strode onto the bridge.
"I've certainly had enough of all this hiding and running. Let's cause some trouble."
Berga made some quick, twisting adjustments to her hand grips then touched the two tips of the crutches together. A shock of fierce blue light charged between them for a moment. The brothers stared at her and she grinned back.
"I never leave the workshop totally unprepared. I added more copper and silver to these ones. They've taken rather a long time to charge up though!"
Oswyn and Osric looked at each other and both shrugged and grinned a little. Osric swayed, still slightly drunk from the wine, they had had enough of running away too. They banged their glow staffs on the ground and moved towards the bridge. Cynwise smiled at Codrington

and grasped her staff in both hands.

"Come on then, I don't see why Stan should have all the fun!"

The fellow Traveller shook her head and laughed.

"You're all mad, totally barmy."

They ran to catch up with the big Bod as he carefully but determinedly made his way towards the Mor'ns.

The others were about three-quarters of the way across when Stan made it to the other side. The light of their glow staffs threw shadows all across the chamber making them look, in silhouette at least, like giants. Red didn't feel like a giant, but he was certainly not going to let his friend face the enemies of The Library alone. He leapt the last few paces and got to the other side of the chasm just as Stan took a hefty swing at one of the Mor'ns. The glow staff crashed into the side of its head and knocked the lumbering beast staggering to one side, crashing into another.

"Ha, not so big and nasty with someone nearer your own size, are you?" Stan shouted as he prepared for another swing of the staff.

The Mor'n shook its head or body, both? It was impossible to tell where one started and the other ended. It let out a deep and menacing growl. Stan suddenly didn't feel so certain of himself. Red came flying across and dived at the legs of the growling thing, which Stan thought was an interesting approach to the situation. It toppled over and lay there, thrashing about. It tried to turn its click-clacking teeth towards Red who shouted at his friend.

"Just hit the damned thing will you!"

"Why, certainly old chap," Stan grinned and bashed the prone Mor'n as hard as he could again and again.

The other Mor'ns had begun to clamber towards them as Berga came flying off the bridge. She used her crutches to launch herself at the horrible great creatures. Just as

she got to the Mor'ns, she twisted her hand grips and plunged the crutches together into the dust-filled filthy mass of the nearest one. The two lengths combined and the Mor'n stared at her in utter surprise for the briefest of moments before it exploded in a cloud of sparks and evaporated into the claustrophobic air. It left behind only a handful of metal teeth and the smell of ozone.
Stan hooted in joy.

"They're not invincible!" He laughed as Oswyn and Osric sprinted off the bridge.
"Go for the legs! Go for the legs!" The two brothers grasped either end of one of their climbing lines and ran full tilt at another of the Mor'ns, scything it down. Stan moved over with Red and both began hitting the thing as hard as they could. The last Mor'n had begun to back away. It seemed there was just enough mind in there to suggest it might not win this one but then suddenly there came that snoring booming noise from further back. The vast blue behemoth dragged itself forwards on its two great muscled limbs, dragging itself towards them. Cynwise stopped in her tracks at the edge of the bridge. The other Bods stopped and backed away a little, still brandishing their staffs and crutches. The badly injured Mor'ns simply lay on their backs and tried to work out which way was up.
Codrington gently pushed past Cynwise and moved in front of the others, kicking one of the prone Mor'ns as she went past.
"I'd quite like a turn now, if you lot don't mind," she span her brass staff around in her hands in a bewildering pattern. It seemed to move faster than the other Bods could follow. The blue-mottled creature turned its head slightly and seemed to taste the air with its long, barbed tongue. Codrington stood calmly in front of it the brass staff now still, held in front of her in both hands. She closed her eyes and the other Bods could almost hear her heart beat slower as she waited. The moment seemed to last an age before the great beast lunged forward with a great and mighty roar. Red gasped as it seemed that Codrington had been swallowed into the gaping jaws of the thing. The stench of its breath was almost too much to bear. Cynwise staggered forwards, almost without thinking, to try to help their new friend in some way.

"Wait!"

It was Stan who saw her first. She had somehow leapt onto the thing's back and was forcing the brass staff down hard onto its skull. It seemed to take the beast a moment or two to realise it had not bitten the head off the tiny being in front of it. Another few moments gave it the extreme pain puncturing its mind. It howled at the roof of the chamber. The dreadful noise echoed everywhere. Codrington then seemed to almost fly up then backwards and land in front of it again. She hit the beast forcefully, first on one side of its huge horned head and then the other. The thing lumbered backwards slightly and shook itself, the deep grumbles it made shook the ground. Oswyn hid behind his brother who had seemingly sobered up in all the activity, but his eyes were wide with excitement at what he was watching. The Fellow Traveller raised the staff in front of her to eye level and pointed it at the spot at the centre of the creature's bulky head in between where the eyes might be.

"We are the People of The Republic of Lettered Men. You stand within the dominions of The Library of Sir Thomas Bodley, and you are most unwelcome here!" To emphasise the point she jabbed her brass staff forward with such force that the beast's head seemed to recoil back into its body slightly. It roared at the ceiling again but then backed away into the dark tunnel from where it had emerged and disappeared into the shadows to lick its wounds. Stan looked around, but the Mor'ns had retreated too whilst the Bods were watching Codrington. She turned around and took off her red bowler hat, dusting it off a little.

"Well, that's quite enough of that." She smiled at the young Bods who stood opened-mouthed before her.

Berga shouted first, quickly joined by the others. They cheered, whooped, laughed and jumped up and down. Codrington smiled and simply bowed slightly before replacing her hat.

"It will not have retreated far, and there are almost certainly more Mor'ns that way I should thin," Codrington was packing food and drink into Stan's backpack, much to the evident delight of the bigger, younger Bod. Red smiled and shook his head at his friend. She handed Berga a folded map.

"It would be wise to head back to The Library by a much longer but safer route I think. There is a narrow tunnel, far too narrow for the Mor'ns or that thing and its kind. It leads from here below All Soul's right across to Turl Street."

Red pulled his pack on and almost without needing to think about it, checked his climbing gear.

"What was that thing?"

Codrington rubbed her chin, and thought before answering,

"I'm not entirely certain, but from the descriptions I've read and the tales that are told, I think that was an Ignor'n." Oswyn signed speedily, Stan began to explain, but Codrington held up a hand to stop him,

"Actually I can understand Master Oswyn perfectly well, Stan." She smiled at the little Bod as he continued his question, then she answered.

"Yes, I believe that was one of the creatures that Madam Brunda fought and lost an eye to. She is indeed a formidable woman. I think I would rather confront several Ignor'ns than be told off by her again," they all nodded in agreement with that.

Cynwise stood and shook the Fellow Traveller's hand.

"Will you not come back with us? I think we may need your help. Any help." Codrington shook her head. "

Those things were far too close to my library Cyn. I have a duty to protect it as much as The Library itself. If the beacon goes up, then I will come. We will all come, of that

I am sure," she smiled and clasped Cynwise's hand in hers. "Safe journey my friends. I hope the next time we meet will be much more boring!" They all smiled and took their turn to thank Codrington and shake her hand before bowing low.

With a few glances backwards and waves, they headed off into the narrow, long tunnel towards Turl Street.

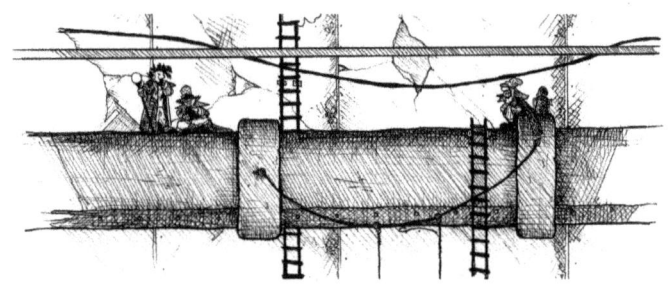

***

Cearo and Aedre checked the map again. They were fairly sure that they were heading in the right direction, but things had become a little confusing. Cearo had recovered the sealed instructions from within the hidden box. This was after a majority of her Carrel had agreed to allow her to retrieve it from their carefully guarded treasury. The Beacon had been hidden amongst the humans long, long ago and the map showed them how to retrieve it. They had walked a great distance and decided to stop for a little while and have something to eat.

Aedre unwrapped the cheese and bread.

"We are going to win this, aren't we?" She spread a little butter and passed the bread to Cearo. The older Bod looked into the distance. They had come such a long way,

she wasn't sure how much further there was to go.
"I hope so. We can only do our best. It's going to be a hard road I fear."
Aedre shook her head at the situation she now found herself in. Not long ago, she had been cooking and readying meals in the Supper Hall. The most exciting parts of her day were inventing new dishes or trying to improve old ones. Now here she was, a member of The Quire, on a quest to retrieve The Beacon, a thing she had only heard of in the tales of the Nursery. Cearo checked the map and its instructions again. She was certain they were heading the right way, towards Turl Street. The two of them gathered up their rations and carried on, making their way through unfamiliar chambers and passageways. Onwards and sometimes up, sometimes down. It was all very disorientating. It was no wonder members of Shakleton Carrel disappeared for an age at a time.
The two Bods forged further into unknown territory until they came to a sharp curve in the length of the corridor they were currently passing through. They heard strange chattering up ahead. Aedre moved forwards slightly and dimmed her glow staff. There was a clicking noise like something sharp tapping on metal or glass. They both looked at each other and tried not to be too fearful. Cearo came to the younger Bod's side and strained to listen. It took all of her concentration not to cough and splutter, the dust in the corridor was quite thick. They seemed to have kicked quite a bit up into the air somehow as they had edged forwards. The click-clacking sound grew louder until a voice shouted from somewhere around the corner, making them both jump.
"For goodness sake Derek, I told you to bring a corkscrew, give it to me!"
"Yes, Marjorie, of course, my dear."
The sight in front of her was one of the strangest things

Cearo had possibly ever seen. Around the curve of the corridor, the whole area opened up, and in the open hall stood three enormous albino spiders. They seemed to be rather preoccupied with trying to get a wine bottle open. In the centre of the group, laughing and shaking his head, was a Bod. Aedre moved forward slightly nervously and coughed.

"Erm, excuse me, would this be of any use?" She produced a small tool from inside her coat which seemed to contain lots of different useful bits, one of which was a corkscrew. Alric turned and grinned at them.

"Good grief, what are Bods doing out here?"

Marjorie knocked him out of the way and elegantly moved towards them, looming down and tapping the corkscrew with the tip of her long, powerful leg.

"My dear, you are an absolute saviour! Come, come and join us. We're having a bit of a break in proceedings to gather our thoughts."

Alric introduced himself and explained that after some rather lengthy discussions and a few more emergency meetings the True Spiders and he had come to a decision. They had spread out across UnderOxford to try and warn the various inhabitants that The Library was under attack and needed help. He became most excited when Aedre asked what kind of people he had met.

"I have seen things you could never believe, things even more strange than our friends the Spiders here,"

"How Rude! Pass the Brie would you Major?"

"We talked to the Sheldonian Theatre herself, I made it all the way to Boswell's and talked to the Store himself! They are alive, those buildings. But the most amazing thing was meeting The AshMoles, They are enormous!"

Cearo accepted a glass of wine from the spider that had introduced himself as Derek.

"Oh, thank you very much, very kind. So you went out as

far as the Ashmolean Museum? Gosh."
Alric grinned.
"I know, I've never travelled so far and so quickly. The True Spiders can really get going when they finally make up their mind to do something."
"I heard that young man, cheeky imp!" Derek teased.
Alric rolled his eyes and carried on.
"The True Spiders move so fast that sometimes you think that you'll end up outside the City itself! But it's also the most amazing thing because when you finally get your breath back, you suddenly look up and lose it all over again."
"But the AshMoles," asked Aedre. "what about the AshMoles?"
Alric sipped his wine and smiled at the other two Bods as they listened to his tale.
They had slowed down to a walk as they approached the chambers nearer The Museum. The travelling group had skirted around the sunken Cathedral of St. Giles, much to Alric's disappointment. At least he would now be able to tell Red where the sound of the bells had come from. Major Gattling explained as they tip-toed through a narrow corridor full of buttresses right next to the great church, that there was a delicate and rather complicated dispute over who held control in this area of UnderOxford. The Silent Brethren held that they alone should be able to claim tithe here, whereas the AshMoles disagreed somewhat with this version of events. It was best not to get involved. They eventually arrived at the vaults beneath The Ashmolean Museum. Alric had always been extremely proud of The Library and its beautiful buildings, but even he had to admit that the Hall of the AshMoles was impressive. The true Spiders and the little Bod had entered through a carved arch at the southern end into a huge chamber crisscrossed with

light and shadows. The whole hall seemed to be centred around a large circular area which was surrounded by vast, tall columns that seemed to stretch on up forever. Great orbs of light floated high between them, casting beams through the pillars. More and more pillars fanned outwards from the centre in ever-increasing circles like a forest of stone. In the very middle, through the steams of light and lengths of shadow, Alric could make out huge shapes, standing together. From somewhere high above organ music was playing.
Marjorie had stopped and turned her head as far as she could to look at him riding the saddle hump on her back. "Now, please consider my dear, that the Ashmoles are a powerful but sensitive people. Think before you speak, I implore you."
Alric nodded and was about to bow his deepest bow when Derek shot forward and shouted.
"Hello, old bean! Terrible mess, need your assistance, spot of bother at the old Bod place you know!"
Marjorie tutted.
"Oh, for goodness sake," she moved forward. Alric looked up from his bow and carried on looking up and up again at the magnificent beings that had been waiting to greet them.
There were eight of them and they were massive. At first, Alric thought they had tiny eyes but soon realised that they were all wearing glasses. They were very similar to the ones Erasmus was wearing when he had delivered the maps to the mad old fool, just as Offa had told him to. They wore leather overalls and huge, steel-toe-capped boots. Some of them wore caps and others had spiky black hair sticking out from their scalps. All of them had massively long whiskers that seemed to smell the air as they towered over the little Bod. All of it was overwhelming, but their digging hands were beyond anything. Huge piles of claws

moved towards him as if they wanted to scoop him away. Instead, the nearest AshMole gently shook his tiny Bod hand. The boom of its voice had almost knocked Alric over.

"True Spider Derek, it is good to see you. There's a Bod here it seems. What goes on?"

The Spider Derek had looked a little bemused then as if he had forgotten why they had come here at all. He seemed to remember and then smiled at Alric, nudging him slightly to respond.

The Bod looked up at the giant and, being a Bod, bowed. The great creature's voice rang out and echoed off into the chamber, the organ music seemed to rise in response.

"What business would the Bods have with The Guardians of Tradescant's Ark? Tell us your needs, boy."

"Please Sir, The Library is in danger and we, The Republic of Lettered Men, need you and your friends' help," Alric stuttered nervously.

The AshMole nodded and wiped its brow. All eight of them seemed to begin humming at the same moment then. The melody in the background joined them and a great swell of music filled the chamber. All of the AshMoles raised their heads and snouts and seemed to breathe in the sound. Marjorie had leant in close to Alric to whisper.

"They are talking to The Ark, little Bod, and it is answering them in return."

The Ashmoles stopped as suddenly as they had begun and another stepped forward towards Alric and bent down slightly in front of him.

"Oh yes, word has been coming little Bod. And the AshMoles are never ones to break an ancient promise. Tell Erasmus we are coming. Tell Erasmus ALL of us are coming, for we have never forgotten that it was he that saved us. Tell him that."

"Will they come?" Aedre whispered as if saying it out loud

would mean she didn't believe him.
"Yes," Alric nodded.
Derek nodded too.
"We believe that the AshMoles will honour their promise if it gets that far."
Cearo and Aedre looked at each other and the older Bod coughed.
"It's already started Alric," Cearo began, "since you've been away, things have gotten much worse. That is why Aedre and I are all the way out here, we are ordered to retrieve The Beacon from its place of safekeeping and bring it to The Library so that the Fellow Travellers can be summoned back." Alric grew slowly more pale as he took this knowledge in. The Spider who had been introduced to them as Major Gattling stopped chewing and raised what may have been the True Spiders' version of an eyebrow.
"My goodness me, things have become a grand pickle. We should get you folks to The Beacon and back to your Library as soon as we can. No time to waste. Come on troops, let's fall in and mobilise immediately. Time to take the battle to the enemy, me thinks!"
It took very little time for the Spiders and Bods to clear up their impromptu lunch. Each Bod was heaved onto the back of one of the True Spiders and they followed Cearo's directions down and on towards their destination in Turl Street.

***

The sun was just rising, though the Jewellery shop on Turl Street was still deep in the shadow of Lincoln College over the road. The Jeweller had come in earlier than usual to check on a delivery of rather beautiful silverware which he had acquired for Duke Cornelius, the great Troll of Magdelen Bridge. The whole business of verifying each piece had taken longer than he had thought, so he decided to treat himself to a cup of tea and a few biscuits. The Jeweller was not a tall man, but what he lacked in height, he made up for in waistcoats. Today's was a majestic riot of silk and gold brocade with a carefully woven design which, almost undetectably, contained a series of wards and glyphs to protect him from harmful curses. The shop itself had its own defences in the form of guarding cantrips inside the swirls of the wallpaper and an innocuous-looking sugar mouse hidden about the room that could, it was rumoured throughout the city, kill a burglar at fifty paces. The Jeweller had just sat down and taken his first sip of tea when the tiny door in the base of the grandfather clock swung open. Three albino spiders ducked through it carrying three Bods on their backs. The Jeweller put his cup down and gestured to the sugar mouse not to cause any bother, as if this was a perfectly normal occurrence.

"Ah, the good folk of The Library, I rather thought you might be paying me a visit sometime soon." He clapped his hands slightly and the light glowed on the beautiful rings on his fingers. Cearo, Aedre and Alric dismounted from the spiders (who took themselves over to the breathtaking displays of silverware in the cabinets along the wall, "Look at that Derek, a solid silver marmite cap, whatever next?"). The three Bods bowed as the Jeweller bent down on one knee so as not to tower over them so much.

"We are grateful, Sir that you have looked after a certain object for us and humbly request that it is returned to this Bod here stood," Cearo smiled nervously as she read from the scroll. "Erm, that is to say, me, Sir. And hope that we find you in good health and spirits at this time of need."

All three Bods then bowed and Cearo handed the scroll

and its oak box to the jeweller. He gently took it and held it up to his eye, examining it through his jeweller's loupe. He nodded slightly and then checked the box for its correct seals and official inlay. He glanced over to the sugar mouse. It had, for reasons known only to it, affixed itself to the Grandfather clock again.

"What do you think, Crespin? I believe it to be the genuine article."

The sugar mouse let out a loud squeal.

"Cod Trumpets! It'll never come out in the wash!"

The Jeweller sighed and shook his head.

"Ignore him, he's having one of his turns again."

He knelt back up and made his way to one of the cabinets towards the front of the shop, which contained a bewilderingly magnificent variety of pearls and amber. After a small moment lost in thought, he clicked his fingers and smiled. He started unlocking the cabinet opposite the front door and reaching towards the back. The Jeweller gently brought out an amber broach set in silver which he placed on the floor in front of the Bods.

"Please, touch the top of the clasp."

Cearo looked at the others, who nodded and gestured her forward. She carefully tapped the silver ball that was bigger than her hand and it clicked open. The Jeweller lifted the amber to reveal a small compartment in the back which contained a brass tube. It was about as high as Cearo's waist and as round as her arm. It was ornately carved with swirls and lettering that the Bods immediately recognised as the work of one of the Hyde Carrel.

They thanked the Jewellerafter he had made sure they were fully supplied with biscuits and a little tea then remounted the Spiders.

"Take care little folk. There is something wrong in the air. Something evil is abroad in Oxford and I fear it's heading for The Library," Alric nodded as they moved towards the front door of the shop, which the jeweller held open for them.

"I think you are right Sir, but I also think that it is already upon us."

The True Spiders scurried out onto the pavement as the Jeweller waved them good luck and went back to his silver and amber and pearls.

Chapter Thirteen

Mr Simper checked the piece of paper again, absent-mindedly tapping the sore bandaged and bloodied nose. This was definitely the correct room, but it didn't look like the kind of door that would have a copy of William Shakespeare's First Folio somewhere behind it. It was a kind of old, storeroom type of door. It even had a mop leaning across it for goodness sake. Then he realised. He thought back over the different places where he had found the other eight things that The Gloob had asked him to retrieve. At first, the instructions led him to the very places you would expect the most important things to be kept. A vault held the handwritten fair copy of Frankenstein. A specially constructed cabinet held Holst's original score for The Planet Suite. After those, he had begun to locate them further afield, in odd places. It had taken him until now, as he stood in front of the unprepossessing door to realise what had been going on. Several times the instructions led to dead ends with Mr Simper having the curious feeling that the relevant room had been there moments before. Of course, that was exactly what had been happening. The library had started to protect itself. There was something about the things he was collecting, something The Gloob had obviously discovered, that was causing The Library to take more drastic and odd measures to try and stop him from succeeding.

"Well," he thought to himself with a nasty little smirk as he turned the handle and opened the door to the cleaning cupboard. "You have all failed and I have triumphed. It will all be mine!"

Mr Simper stepped through into the cupboard and nearly fell over. It wasn't a cleaner's room at all. It was a circular room that seemed to stretch upwards for an unimaginable distance. It made him rather nauseous and giddy to look up too far. Every inch of space was filled with shelves. Every inch of shelves was filled with books, books of every description. Simper smirked again. The Library was trying one last trick to stop him from getting his hands on the First Folio. Well, it wasn't going to work. Mr Simper has figured out a while before that it didn't matter if he got the items on The Gloob's list, it simply mattered that The Library lost them. He checked the pockets of his suit and found what he was looking for. He took out his handkerchief and a small can of lighter fluid. The latter, he liberally poured all over the former and across the nearest books for good measure. He retrieved an engraved lighter from his other pocket and, without a moment's hesitation, lit the soaked cloth. It whooshed into flame he started backwards a little and dropped the ball of heat to the floor. It spread and flared up in a moment. Within a small time, the whole section near him was aflame. Somewhere in here was the First Folio, and at some point, it would go up. And then... well then he would see if The Gloob had been telling the truth about the book of The Library, The Bibliolibrum. He closed the door behind him and wandered off down the corridor, whistling to himself as he went. He would get tea from that nice little place on Broad Street next to the Art Shop, and watch the fun from there.

***

Red blinked in the dawn light as the Mob stood on the cold pavement and tried to get their bearings. Stan shielded his eyes and stared across the street whilst the rest of the Mob dug their scarves and gloves out of their packs. Oswyn shivered and hugged his brother to keep warm.

Cynwise rubbed her hands together and blew into them. Stan looked over to Berga and then back across the street.
"Have I finally gone mad?"
"Yes," Red, Berga and Cynwise all said together.
"Let me finish, please! Have I finally gone mad, or can I actually see Alric and two other Bods riding giant albino spiders along the other side of the street?"
Red stared over the road and let out a great whooping laugh.
"Alric! Over here!" His friend stopped the Spider he was riding and a huge wide smile spread across his face as he waved to them. The three True Spiders chatted to Alric and then headed across the road towards them. They managed to avoid the few humans and their speeding bicycles that were on the Turl at this time of the day. Red hugged his friend as hard as he could, lifting him off the ground.
"Oh, my man! We thought you were lost in UnderOxford, or worse!"
Alric grinned and hugged the others.
"I was nearly done for but the True Spiders saved me," he swung his arms wide to introduce the giant beings. The Bods all bowed and were only a little startled when the great albino spiders moved towards them. They had, after all, seen many terrifying things of late.
"Good morning young man. I am Marjorie, this is Major Gattling, oh and this is Derek," the Spiders each raised one of their powerful legs as they were introduced.
Red shook Marjorie's hook-like tip.
"Pleased to meet you. I'm Red."
"Lovely. And what do you do?"
"Well, I'm a Bod. One of The Republic of Lettered Men, we are all trying to get back to The Library and stop The Gloob."
"Ah yes, well, jolly good."

There was a slightly awkward silence before Berga jumped forward on her crutches and introduced herself, followed by Cynwise and the brothers Oswyn and Osric. Red beamed a wide smile, the whole Mob were back together at last. The Spiders had gathered around the brothers and were inspecting them rather closely.
"The two quiet ones.... how interesting."
"It could be them, we are in the midst of Strange Days."
"One of them is very slightly drunk, how splendid!"
Red moved over protectively in front of the brothers.
"Is there some kind of problem?"
Major Gattling shook his jowls.
"Good grief no my boy. We are the True Spiders, we keep the tales and know the lore of this mad, magical City. The weave spins and catches the stories you see."
Derek turned his attention to Red.
"There a few of our number that are the Blind Weavers, they sit at the centre of the City's web and spin the tales yet to come to pass."
The Major nodded.
"One of the stronger threads tells of The Two Quiet Brothers who save the True Spiders, from something the weave calls The Whispering. We always thought it meant one of the Brethren of the Sunken Cathedral, but, well, who knows?"
Red looked over at his two friends, timidly trying to each hide behind the other. Before all of this, he would have laughed at the suggestion, but now anything seemed possible.
They all made their way down Brasenose Lane towards the Square, chatting and recounting their incredible adventures since they had all last been together. Derek had learned Oswyn and Osric's language remarkably quickly and talked intensely with the brothers, watching their hands closely as they eagerly chatted back. They

rounded the base of the great wall of Exeter College garden when Stan let out a great cry,
"Fire!"
The Square was full of Bods running back and forth. Most of Bandinel Carrel was desperately trying to herd books over to the Radcliffe Camera. Many others were heaving the great defence machines out of the Quadrangle and down the stone steps to safety. Berga shot forward but Cynwise grabbed her arm.
 "What are you doing?"
"My workshop, I have to seal it down!"
"It will be fine Berg, It's way underground. The Library will sort this..."
There was a rumble then. It began in the soles of their boots, each and every Bod felt it. It expanded outwards and became a rolling thunder swirling through, up and around The Library.
Thousands and thousands of books shot out of the doorways, some smashing out of the higher windows with Red's comrades grasping onto them for their lives. They swarmed and swooped like terrified starlings, massing into the sky above The Library. The morning sunlight bounced from their magnificent covers. the Bods who had been inside were spilling out into the square and Catte Street. Huge cracking noises and booming came from all corners of the beautiful old buildings. Red spotted Erasmus being pulled out of one of the Bod doors nearby. He was trying to get back in but Brunda was a lot larger than he, and she almost carried him out. Red and Stan ran over to them. The wind ripped around the square. Many of the smaller Bods were knocked over or grabbed onto the railings to stop themselves from being blown away.
"What's happening?" Red shouted over the cacophony and chaos.

Madam Brunda stared at him and dropped Erasmus, pulling the young Bod to her and hugging him.

"You're alive! Oh Aethelred, you're alive!"

Erasmus got to his feet and wiped his knees.

"They have succeeded in removing the nine things that The Library uses as a sort of barometer to know if it is safe," he had to shout to be heard, his hat flew off and away across the square. It hit a little Bod in the face, causing him to sit down on the cobbles, totally confused.

A great rush of air then suddenly roared through the square and around and around The Library. Faster and faster, the books swarmed into a vast spiral, a great funnel pouring back into the buildings. The New Bodleian began to glow slightly, then the Old Bodleian itself seemed to seep a bright light from its stones. The books surged back into their home. Even the books from the Radcliffe Camera swooped and dived out of the grand entrance and shot over to The Library itself. All those in the square and around huddled down as the great wind of moments before reversed itself and gushed back into the buildings. The Bods shielded their eyes as the light became brighter and brighter. Slowly the choir-like singing from the books started up again, louder and higher as the stones of the buildings themselves glowed and began to separate. They joined all of the millions of books in the great dance, spinning and swooping around and around in an ever-tightening spiral. Red pointed to the base of the terrifying yet beautiful thing.

"Look!"

They shielded their eyes and could make out a dense dark shape forming on the ground beneath the maelstrom above. It thickened and formed in front of them. Bindings appeared and swiftly after, pages. A huge leather cover grew itself out from the spine with brass corners and a mighty clasp. It hovered slightly above the ground and

the singing, or chanting seemed to be coming from within it now, calling all above it inside.The great maelstrom of building and books obeyed. The noise was almost deafening as it surged downwards in its spiral dance disappearing into the book below. Everyone huddled down onto the floor grasping each other or curled into a ball, with arms wrapped around their legs. The song became a mighty roar and then...

Nothing, absolute silence. This was followed by a resounding thud as the book slammed itself shut and hit the ground with a thump that echoed around the Square. the Bods near the Claringdon Building, the other side of where The Library should have been, gazed across the empty expanse of stone slabs.

Red and Berga and all of the others in Radcliffe Square looked across at those in Catte Street and by the Claringdon Building.

It took them all a moment to realise. They began to stand up and stare. The Library, their home and the place they had pledged their lives to look after, was gone.

Chapter Fourteen

It had taken Erasmus quite some time to find his hat. Eventually, it turned up on the railings of the Radcliffe Camera nearest Brasenose College. The old thing had seen better days and the intricate patterns around the edge were fading now. The tassel on the top really had no right to the name at all, being now just a few threads and a frazzled bit of cotton. He dusted it down, blew the bits of dirt off it that had most recently settled there and sat it back on his head at what he hoped was a jaunty angle. The great wave of fear and panic had begun to die down a little and most of the Bods had instinctively begun to group into their Carrels. They gathered around the ornate steps that formed the entrance to the great round building. Madam Brunda had first made sure the smallest and youngest Bods had got out of the nursery with Odelyn and Leof and the others of Jolliffe Carrel. They were all safe and had managed to get the unhatched Bods out as well, which made Madam Brunda very proud of them. They blushed when she told them this. Eventually, she made her way back over to Erasmus.
"I don't understand, why is the Radcliffe still here but The Old and New buildings have gone into the book?"
Erasmus stopped a bottle of dandelion and burdock that was rolling past with his foot.
"He's a stubborn old place is Rad. Besides, I think the Bibliolibrum was thought up by The Library before The Radcliffe was built, and The Library simply sees the new building over on Broad Street as just an extension of itself."
Many of the Bods were staring into the emptiness where The Library used to be. The Radcliffe Building stood like a great island tower with this vast hole surrounding it.

Within minutes, members of the Craster Carrel had slung makeshift rope bridges and swing lines across the gaps so that the Bods could get to the Radcliffe and some kind of safety. No one was sure what would happen next so they instinctively tried to gather together. Cearo made her way over to Erasmus and bowed low.

"We have the Beacon. What should we do now?"

Erasmus scratched his head and thought for a small while.

"We must send it up at once and get it high above the city so that as many Fellow Travellers see it as possible. If we get it to the top of my tower," He pointed to the very highest part of the Radcliffe Camera, "That may just be enough."

Red, Berga and Stan made their way over. Cynwise and the brothers Oswyn and Osric had joined some other Bods in setting up swing lines and slide to get across the great divide. It wasn't as complicated as it seemed.

Berga listened carefully to Erasmus and Cearo before raising her hand to interrupt.

"I think I may have something in my workshop down below that might help us, if any of it survived. Stan, come with me."

Aedre tugged at Berga's sleeve.

"May I come with you, please?" Berga smiled and nodded, a great grin spread across the younger Bod's face. The three of them headed off downwards to try and find what might remain of Berga's workshop.

Red bowed to Erasmus, who smiled and patted him on the arm.

"How does it feel to be right, eh, yes? Yes." Red looked around at the great space where The Library used to be.

"I don't understand why The Gloob wanted The Library to protect itself and make itself safe?"

Erasmus stroked his long moustache,

"Perhaps it couldn't attack The Library when it was so

huge, so used its own cleverness against it?"
Red thought about this and then his eyes widened.
"We have to get the Book, it's still in The Library, We have to protect it!"
Brunda nodded and grabbed the shoulder of a small Bod who was running past.
"Little one, what is your name?"
The girl looked up at the massive expanse of gown and old Bod in front of her and shook back her hood, "Meghan, Madam Brunda, I'm Meghan."
"Well Meghan, pass the word around. Tell everyone you can. Find the Bibliolibrum, find The Book of The Library." The little Bod nodded and ran into the crowds to spread the word.
It took some time before a shout went up that the book was found. It was lying in the middle of Broad Street. Red ran as fast as he could when the word had come and it took Madam Brunda and Erasmus some while longer to make their way over to the Broad. Several younger Bods had giggled as the grand old Bod had made her way over one of the rope bridges in a rather undignified fashion. They quickly stopped when she glared at them, only to burst out laughing when Erasmus took his hat off and shouted.
"It's rather like watching a ship being launched is it not? May the Duke bless her, and all who sail in her!" This made Brunda glare even more.
"Shut up you old fool! If we survive all of this, you are going back in your tower!"
Eventually, they joined Red and a great crowd of Bods around the book. It was a great leather-bound volume. It was still smoking slightly and the hint of a glow seeping from its huge wedge of pages locked into it with the great clasp. Its huge leather bound cover was almost enveloped in dark ink inscriptions beginning 'Do fidem me nullem

librum vel...' - the oath of The Bodleian. The words were spiralling out from the lock clasp and looping all around the huge book. Massive, brass, triangular covers tipped its four corners. Madam Brunda and Erasmus eventually made their way over to Red. She placed her hand on his shoulder,
"So there it is, the Bibliolibrum. I never thought it was real young Aethelred, I thought it just a tale," Red looked up at the old Bod.
"Like The Gloob you mean?" She smiled at him and gently cuffed the back of his head. He turned to Erasmus. "I still don't see how this has helped them, even if he wants to have the book, it's still far too big for The Gloob or his Mor'ns to move."
Erasmus was about to answer when his tiny eyes widened and he pointed over Red's shoulder.
"It is not too large a thing for him though!"
From across the road came a human, tall and thin with a nasty little smirk on his face. He strode through the Bods. They had to run or leap out of his way or be crushed under his perfectly polished shoes.
"I've been looking for that!" Said Mr Simper, covering his bandaged nose, as he bent down to grasp the Bibliolibrum.

***

It took Berga, Stan and Aedre quite some time to find the workshop. It was far from the centre of The Library. It was nowhere near where the books had been, but deeper and further off. This meant that it had escaped the pull when The Library had turned itself into the book. Berga had chosen chambers a good distance from the usual areas for the workshops. Some of her more outlandish creations had the unfortunate habit of exploding or generally breaking everything around them. She was

hugely relieved when they found her room. Everything was still here, even the part of the great Trollomicus that Madam Brunda had brought to her for repair. The worktops were covered with cogs, gears, oily rags and plans for different machines. The walls were covered with notes and blueprints: this one for a Difference Engine, that one for the Land Barge. Another for Red's Listening Device and another for a lunar clock. The whole workshop had an air of organised chaos. Stan immediately got to the task of trying to locate any biscuits that might have survived the night, whilst Berga started cramming pipes and rubber tubing into a large bag. She eventually hit Stan over the head with her crutch.
"Will you stop worrying about your stomach and help me with this!"
"Ouch! What do you want with all that rope and canvas, what use is a big tent?"
Berga shook her head, for someone so clever, her friend could really be a total idiot.
"It isn't a tent you fool, it's a balloon!"
Aedre giggled at the bigger Bod. Stan's eyes widened and a great smile grew across his face. For a brief moment, all thoughts of food left his mind.
"We are going to go up in a balloon!"
Berga laughed.
"Well someone is. If we can get it high enough over the Radcliffe Camera, it means the beacon can be launched even higher. Who knows how far away they might see it?"
Stan grasped the canvas to his chest.
"Oh no! If anyone is going up over the Camera it's me, Berg'. I've dreamt of this my whole life!"
Berga shook her head and smiled.
"Alright Stan, just help me get all the stuff together, okay?"

***

Inside the Radcliffe Camera the Bods had begun to try and get some order restored. Many of the younger ones had been sent out by Godwin to find food and supplies as he bustled about with others from Creswick Carrel, They were building a makeshift kitchen, under the watchful gaze of Dr Radcliffe's statue in the main hall. The little ones had done a good job and a good stack of cheese and bread and chocolate was building up along the wall. Other Bods had pulled some of their defence engines and catapults inside as the chaos had started around the Library. They were fixing minor damage and cranking things into position. Members of the Hyde Carrel were busy scrawling glyphs and wards to protect the place. The engineers of Craster had rescued their plans from the exhibition room and were sprawled out over the reading tables, organising what to do next. The Herders of Bandinel, Red's own Carrel, were at a bit of a loss with no books to cajole and tend to. They tried to make themselves useful by connecting extra rope slides and swings to get the Bods across the great hole to and from Broad Street.

Godwin unpacked one of the great blocks of chocolate and placed it high out of temptations reach on the stack behind him. Elswyth, the cartographer from Craster Carrel wandered over and sat on the corner of the table.

"Good Day Godwin, what do you think this morning will bring?"

"Who knows Elswyth, who knows? I'll be happy just to make sure they all have a full stomach, whatever we send them out to," the old Bod nodded at this.

"There is trouble coming, no doubt about that Godwin. But we should not grumble. We were made by The Library to defend it, and that is exactly what we shall do."

Other Bods came in and were fed, or met up with friends and were relieved that all had survived the monumental events outside. Leof and Odelyn had gathered the tiniest Bods from the Nursery into an alcove around the back of Dr Radcliffe's statue. They were tired, confused and very, very scared. Many of the older Bods had quickly found them coats and blankets. Each little one had been given chocolate and dandelion and burdock. Some of Rouse Carrel, the musicians and players, came and sat with them. They began singing and music making which calmed them all down. Soon, many other of the Bods began to gather around as the troupe started tapping their feet and dancing. The music grew louder and louder until one of them, a big round Bod with a magnificent yellow hat sporting a raven's feather burst into song.

"A holiday, a holiday and the first one of the year..."

In a few small moments, lots Bods had joined in and the panic was almost forgotten. Many danced and jumped around as the song burst into a great jig, the Rutland Reel. Even Godwin and Elswyth were linking arms and spinning as the mandolin and fiddle filled the whole Camera with music. A gruff, wild-haired Bod held the beat with a makeshift set of drums built from discarded boxes. At its end, they all whooped and clapped. "

"More! More!"

The big Bod with the yellow hat and raven's feather held up his hands and quieted the crowd. "Time, me thinks, for a tale or two!" The tiny Bods clapped at this and gathered around him as he sat down cross-legged at the centre of them all.

"My name, for those of you who know me not, is Beadwof, and I sit here to tell you the tale of Catte Street!" The older Bods let out a great 'oooooh!' which had been the proper thing to say at the start of a tale or two, for longer than any of them could remember. Beadwof raised his hand and calmed them.

"Those too nervous to hear the truths I speak should go home now and put their heads in a bucket!" Elswyth shouted out the required response.

"I have no bucket!"

All laughed and a few of the younger Bods clapped as the tale began to take on its familiar form. Beadwof took his hat off and produced from within a bucket that seemed to be larger than the hat that had held it, much to the delight of the little Bods at his feet.

"Here is a bucket for the nervous. The rest must hear the tale and pass it on true." He offered the bucket to all present but, of course, none took it.

"Very well, you have been warned and worried, so I give you the tale of Catte Street."

Many of the smaller Bods cheered at the familiar name and even the elders smiled as the story of the very ground the sat on as they sat and stood in the reading hall of the Radcliffe Camera. Beadwof smiled, and began his telling,

"This is my tale and my tale is a song and the song is as long as it's old. Now, the tale is a tall one although it is short and as real as any I've told. The tale might have happened or possibly not, BUT the tale is as true as the tale can be, never minding how long is the length of my tale or the why or the who or the where or the what. I tell you it now so that you can tell all your friends and the tales and the songs carry on. So listen to this and don't wander off. Take the tale as your own when I'm done!"

Godwin shouted out just as he should at this bit in the storytelling.

"Get on with it!"

"I will and I am and so here it goes!" Beadwof stood up straight and bowed a long and low bow.

"And so I shall begin "

He told the tale of the Book Wyrm that sleeps beneath the Castle Mound and wakes every hundred years to add to his own library. The story of the man who bought The Bridge of Sighs, not realising that there is no such bridge in Oxford. He shouted the yarn of Lyra and the Birds, and the Bods all cheered, for they loved Lyra as much as they loved Alice. The tales tumbled out, one after another. Jack and the Book Tower. Spinning Jenny. The Old Woman and the Trees. Old Tom and his Bell. The Oaken Bark. And on, and more. There were great shouts of excitement as the tales rolled out. Great whoops of laughter went up and every now and again a shriek of fear from the tiny Bods sat around him, and the older ones who began to gather to listen and shield the smaller ones from what was happening all around the hall and beyond. Beadwof took another sip of his dandelion wine and made sure all of their eyes were watching him. Many of the greater war machines were being trundled out towards Broad Street as the wind and rain returned and the storm seemed to be enclosing the City once again, and he did not want his audience to dwell on what was out there, the great trouble that was starting to build beyond their walls.

When the Wyrm had been sent back to sleep, and The Bridge was safe and the Oakenbark had finally found his Hart, all the Bods clapped and cheered and Beadwof swigged down the last of his wine and took a bow. He was the best of the Rouse Carrel of tale-tellers and players, and he had timed his telling so that as the smaller Bods left him, all of the defence engines and older Bods had got the call that the book was taken and they were needed to get it back. The other Bods charged with looking after the little ones could now keep them safe and unaware of the nightmare outside.

Chapter Fifteen

The area of the street outside the Clarendon Building and where the New Bodleian used to be was in absolute chaos. Red and a small group of Bods had tried to climb onto the book as the human had bent to get hold of the great thing but his sheer size had been too much for them. He had simply heaved the huge tome up and shook them all off. They had fallen to the ground, a few of them rolling in agony with broken arms or legs. Other Bods who had found themselves in his path scattered or vainly threw their glow staffs at him as he strutted off, laughing into the growing wind and rain. Madam Brunda was trying to gather the groups together from around Radcliffe Square and into the shelter of The Clarendon Building as the storm flew back into the City. The thunder seemed to rumble all around them as they huddle through into the Vice Chancellor's Robing Room. Some of the engineers from Craster Carrel were already in here stocking new glow staffs from the supplies that the bookherders had managed to retrieve, along with slings and shots. Erasmus was trying to get as many of the Bods back into Clarendon from the other, Broad Street side when the thunder seemed to get even louder. It took them all a while to realise that the noise was coming from deep within the pit which used to hold The Library's book stacks. Cynwise and Oswyn and Osric were the first up and out, terror on their faces. Soon all of the other members of Bandinel Carrel had abandoned their swings and bridges and were fleeing from whatever was coming up out of the hole. The first sight of it was a great, purple and blue arm or leg with massive spines upon it. The rumbling grew to a roar as the beast pulled itself over the rim of the pit and flicked its bulbous tongue, tasting the air for Bods.

The thing's great bulky head and thick crest of a brow hid its eyes. It opened its great gawping mouth and roared while its lower jaw jutted out its great stubborn ridges. Madam Brunda had come out of the shadows of the Clarendon archway to call the others in when she saw it. Her one good eye opened in growing horror, while her hand instinctively went up to her eye patch. She simply whispered under her breath,
"Oh dear, Oh dear me."
Red helped the injured flee back up the great steps and hurried through the archway. Madam Brunda slumped slightly against the far wall. He was about to ask if she was alright when he saw it and let out a slight cry. This Ignor'n was even larger than the one they had seen near All Souls with Codrington.
It lumbered out of the hole, snapping at any Bods that were slower than the rest. Cynwise had reached the Clarendon then turned and realised that some of her Carrel were still down there with the thing. She spun around and before Red could stop her, she was running back towards it, trying to distract the huge beast as the others fled past her up into some kind of safety. Red grabbed a nearby glow staff and shot down to help his friend. They stood together trembling slightly as the terrible creature lumbered this way and that. It flicked its tongue in the air to find them. It had just to lick the air to work out where they were and move laboriously towards them. A giant, albino spider seemed to come out of nowhere and lock the vicious claw-like ends of its eight great legs into the side of the beast. The Ignor'n howled in pain. Its mighty roar was clearly heard above the gathering thunder as the rain began to lash the whole place. Cynwise and Red stood drenched and rooted to the spot as the two mighty denizens of UnderOxford rolled about, ripping at each other. the Bods couldn't tell which of the spiders it was.

Red turned to Cynwise to ask what they should do, but his friend had already started to run towards the two giants. By the time he realised what she was doing, Cynwise had leapt up high onto the Ignor'n's back and was battering it as hard as she could while the spider, whom she now could see was Major Gattling, carried on grabbing and biting the thing. He grinned at her.
"Well done young lady! Jolly good show."
 He took another chunk out of the bell of the blue and purple monster, but this brought him too close to the thing's great limb and it smashed a huge fist into the

Major's body, sending him reeling away. Cynwise held on as tightly as she could before smashing her glow staff hard into the Ignor'n's head. It flicked out its tongue to taste where she was then. Its massive lump-like tail-like end swung up with a terrible thump and flung her to the ground in front of it. Red ran for all his worth towards his friend. Everything seemed to slow down for a second as he stumbled. He watched as Cynwise knelt up and raised her broken staff. She shouted as loud as she could, but the wind swept her words to the corners of the city, and Red only just caught them.
"We are the People of The Republic of Lettered Men. You stand within the dominions of The Library of Sir Thomas Bodley, and you are most unwelcome here!"
The Ignor'n seemed to stall for a split second. Cynwise grasped the shattered staff between her two hands. Its vast and terrible jaws came crushing down upon the brave Bod and she was lost in its gaping maw. Lightning flew across the city as the monster arched its back and gave out a huge roar which seemed to challenge the storm itself. Even that did not quite drown out the cry of utter despair from Red as the True Spider scooped him up and, hobbling on its good six legs, dragged the Bod back towards safety.

***

Mr Simper sat in the dark in his little room, stroking the enormous book and giggling to himself slightly. He could feel the energy crackling and surging within it. Carefully, he lay his head upon the leather cover, covered in swirls of lettering. He whispered with his thin lips near the lock.
"Tell me everything. Tell me all of your secrets."
"It will tell you no secrets Simper (cough), for they are not its to tell (spit)," the voice was coarse and sneering

and came from near the door.

Mr Simper tried to sit up but found four large Mor'ns had sucked in the dust and grime of the room and so were very large indeed. They now pinned him down on the bed. The Gloob limped and scuffled its way over to the bed and clambered up a pile of books. The ones that had been stolen by Mr Simper over many years from many other libraries. He brought himself to head height with the human.

"It is ancient and (cough) foolish and knows not what it knows (spit). It was captured by its own attempts to hide and that, in the end, will be its destruction," The Gloob snarled.

Mr Simper tried to keep his still bandaged nose as far from spittle and phlegm that was staining and rotting his bedding as he struggled to free himself from the Mor'ns. "What do you mean destruction? It is mine now, you promised!" There was a frantic realisation in Mr Simper's voice that things were no longer going the way he had imagined they might.

The Gloob leaned in, the ancient, mouldy smell and rancid breath almost made the human sick. The evil, warped, little creature grinned all across the slash of his mouth. The nasty, sharp, pin-like teeth failing totally to shine in the stark light of the room's shadeless light bulb.

"I lied," its teeth did not glint, but its evil globe of an eye did as it leaned forward and jabbed Mr Simper in the centre of his damaged nose.

The human screamed, twisted and turned so much that he managed to unseat the Mor'ns. They rolled onto the floor in a ball of dirt and dust, before reforming and trying to remember where they were. Mr Simper grabbed the great book and fled the dingy room, leaping down the stairs and out into the street. The screams of The Gloob followed him all the way. At first, the rain obscured his

sight but then he began to focus and thought that the whole of Broad Street had been covered in candles. He imagined them to be in his honour as the new owner of The Bodleian. It was only when one of the glowing orbs was fired from the crowd of others by a small catapult and hit him, again in the nose, that he stopped and took stock of what confronted him.

Broad Street was full of Bods, each with their glow staff. Many had slingshots or manned the great engines. All of them let loose with glow orbs or pebbles and stones. One particularly clever device built very recently began firing volleys of drawing pins at him. He held up the Bibliolibrum in front of his head just in time and deflected most of the expertly targeted attacks. Thunder rolled through the purple and red sky above the City. The rain lashed Mr Simper's face, it seemed to him that it wasn't getting to the Bods quite as badly. Surely the Weather Mages weren't taking sides. He kicked out at the surge of Bods in front of him who were trying to get their climbing lines around his ankles. He sent them scattering backwards and badly injured many. He was about to take a swipe at a whole legion of them when two Mor'ns crashed into the back of his legs. The Gloob stood on the pavement outside the King's Arms and ranted into the storm.

"Give me that book!"

Mr Simper lost his balance and the Bibliolibrum went sailing over the whole multitude of Bods. It came crashing down into the middle of them as they scattered to get out of its path. The Herms who were watching from atop their pillars outside the Sheldonian Theatre watched as it arched through the air.

"That big book seemed to slow as it hit the floor so as not to hurt those beneath it." One of them noted.

Another blew the teeming rain off its nose and said "You haven't got the cone, so shut up."

As the Book crashed to the ground, so did Mr Simper. The surrounding Bods swarmed over him, beating him for all they were worth with their glow staffs. They were just getting the better of the situation when some began to scatter from his legs. The great Mor'ns were climbing up him and snatching Bods as they came, Their sharp teeth were click-clacking and the lifeless bodies were flung to the wet floor. Mr Simper screamed, the Bods retreated backwards as the Mor'ns cleared a path and The Gloob advanced. It hobbled forwards flinging sizzling balls of spit into the crowd of Bods who fled before it. As it stood high on Mr Simper's back, The Gloob stretched its arms from within its tattered layers of grimy coats and snarled and chanted. Its gnarled fingers wove patterns in the rain-drenched air.

The dirt and grime flowing down the gutters nearby seemed to begin to dance to the patterns The Gloob was making in the air. One after another after another, Mor'ns began to form out of the grime and filth. Five came, ten, then twenty. Some half merged and formed into bigger, even more terrifying creatures. The Gloob moved down from Simper, biting him on the way. He stood in front of his rapidly multiplying army. Beside him, from the gaping hole where once was, The New Bodleian Building came great and terrible roars as huge Ignor'ns lumbered out of the pit. Their tongues flicking and jaws snapping, they ranged out behind the Mor'ns. Row upon row, regiment upon regiment of stupidity and illiteracy, arrogance and scorn. They roared click-clacked, sniffed and grumbled behind The Gloob. The fiendish, filthy creature raised its claw-like hands and even the storm seemed to quieten as it shouted the length of Broad Street.

"Give me the book!"

The small Bod Scead, who stood drenched at the front of the rows of Bods cupped his shaking hands to his mouth

and shouted back one of the most ancient Bod replies to any threat.
"Come and have a go if you think you're hard enough!"
Many of the Bods around him started banging their glow staffs on the street. Those behind took up the shout. Soon, all of the ranks of Bods were banging and shouting. The Gloob didn't look quite as certain of himself as he had before.
Erasmus watched from the edge of the stone steps of the Clarendon building and squeezed Madam Brunda's arm.
"I believe, my good Lady, that The Battle of Broad Street has begun!"

Chapter Sixteen

Berga, Stan and Aedre hauled the great contraption up through the levels until they came to a ledge opening onto the pit which had held the bookstores. Thankfully, they heard the terrifying beast well before they saw it or it smelt them. Stan pressed Aedre against the wall and Berga began twisting her crutch handles to try and get them charged up. The Ignor'n lumbered up and past them. Only for a brief moment did it stop and flick its fat, slimy tongue in their direction. It carried on up then, using its huge, thorny limbs to drag itself out of the pit. Bods scattered as it roared at the rolling storm clouds above. Stan did his best to climb, though he had never really been any good at it. Fortunately, enough of the original platforms and bridges had survived on the edges of the pit. There was also the hasty but strong work of Bandinel Carrel building new rope walks, for them to make their way to the rim. The three were met by other Bods who had returned after the Ignor'n had dragged its way to join its master and his growing army on Broad Street. They managed to heave the equipment up and onto a nearby cart which they all pushed towards the Camera. Berga wiped her forehead and turned to Aedre.

"We'll head up to the top of the Camera, I need you to run and tell Cearo, Erasmus and the others that we have the balloon, and to meet us up there."
Aedre nodded and quickly made her way around the pit edge towards the Clarendon building.
It took Berga and Stan some time to get the whole set of pipes, vast, canvas boxes and tubes up to the top of the inside dome. The others got to them just as they reached Erasmus' rooms. He unlocked the door and let

them through. Stan gasped.
"You've been burgled!" Erasmus looked around his room and said nothing for a small moment, then he took off his hat and scratched his head.
"Oh no, it always looks like this. Now let us get you up to the very top."
Berga, with the help of Aedre, cleared an area and began to construct the tube and pipe system that would make the balloon airborne. Erasmus pottered about giving Stan instructions to pull this table over here and that bench, over there. Soon, a tower of old furniture reached the ceiling. Once again, Stan found himself climbing as he made his way rather carefully up the furniture mountain to the very top of the room. As he got higher, he saw that next to the central muddle of hooks and hoops that held the ropes from which the multitude of glow spheres hung, there was a trap door, bolted from the inside. Once at the very top of the pile, Stan could reach it easily. He pulled back the great brass bolt and pushed with all his strength. The wind and rain immediately swirled into the chamber, sending notes and stacks of papers swirling around the room. Erasmus clamped his hat back on his head and shouted above the indoor maelstrom.
"Oh good, a new filing system!"
Stan laughed and took the great swathe of canvas from those below. He began the long task of carefully shoving the balloon sack through the hatch and up onto the outer dome.
Once the whole canvas was onto the roof, Stan climbed out and tied himself to the round section beneath the orb at the pinnacle of the whole camera. The winds of the storm were fierce and more than once he had to grip tightly to the column to stop himself from slipping. The big Bod carefully edged his way around the column and knelt down. Very methodically, he began throwing

the folded sections out across the sloping dome as the rain lashed his face and the thunder boomed overhead. Once he had spread it out, he heaved himself up and finally looked out over the north of the city. Stan gasped and stared as he looked down at the vast hole where his beloved Library had stood for all of his life. Now there was but a great ugly pit. He could make out Bods moving across the newly constructed bridges and swing ways. Far off he could see, through the gap between the Clarendon Building and the Sheldonian Theatre, a great mass of glow staffs. Even above the raging storm, Stan could hear his comrades shouting and banging. He wanted to be up in the balloon more than anything in the world, but he wanted to be down there with his fellow Bods as quickly as he could too. He wasn't going to miss a good fight if he could help it. The others passed through the great length of tubes and pipes that connected down to a bizarre piece of apparatus that Berga had finally finished setting up in the study below. Stan hooked the harness around his shoulders and waist and stuck his head back into the room. Cearo climbed as high as she could and passed Stan the brass tube ornately carved with swirls and lettering. She smiled at the young Bod and then read from the surface of the tube.

"You just have to pull the rope that is in the hollow bit in the base it would seem. Good luck Aethelstan, may The Library look after you. Are you sure that you will be safe? It looks awfully dangerous!"

Stan grinned.

"Of course it's dangerous! That's why I'm doing it," he hauled himself back out into the storm. He sat with his knees in tight, gripping the beacon to his chest, not feeling overly safe at all.

Berga cranked the handle in the small box and a set of brass and leather bellows on the top heaved and spluttered

into life. She very carefully took a lead box out of her pocket and gently opened it The knobbly bit of glass inside glowed brightly and sent shadows swirling across the study. Erasmus lowered his glasses and stared at it.
"Where on earth did you get a Jericho Ember? They were all believed to be lost when the Inklings drove the Michaelmas Angel from Oxford. You are a very mysterious young Bod Aedelberga!"
Berga grinned and very carefully placed the Ember into the box, closing the little brass porthole door and screwing the clamps tight. Immediately the tubes and pipes tightened slightly as the vapours from the Ember pulsed through them, up and through the hatch. Stan watched as the canvas sack began to ripple and bellow out, filling with the mysterious force. The canvas sack slowly turned itself into a balloon and rose into the wind and rain-swept sky above Stan's head. He double-checked the thick cord of rope that lead down through the hatch. It was the only thing stopping him from floating off over Oxford. The big Bod felt the harness around his shoulders and waist tighten. His feet, very slowly, left the Radcliffe Camera below him.

"Oh well, here we go!"
Stan held the beacon for all he was worth as Berga's balloon rose into the rain above the wondrous City. He twisted and turned in the gales that buffeted from one building to another. He could see most of the great towers and spires of Oxford now. Looking down at the top of the Camera Stan laughed out loud. It looked just like the model in the Library shop. His voice caught in his throat as he rose high enough to see over the Clarendon Building. Hundreds upon hundreds of Bods were in Broad Street now, moving slowly forward towards masses and masses of Mor'ns and far too many Ignor'ns. He

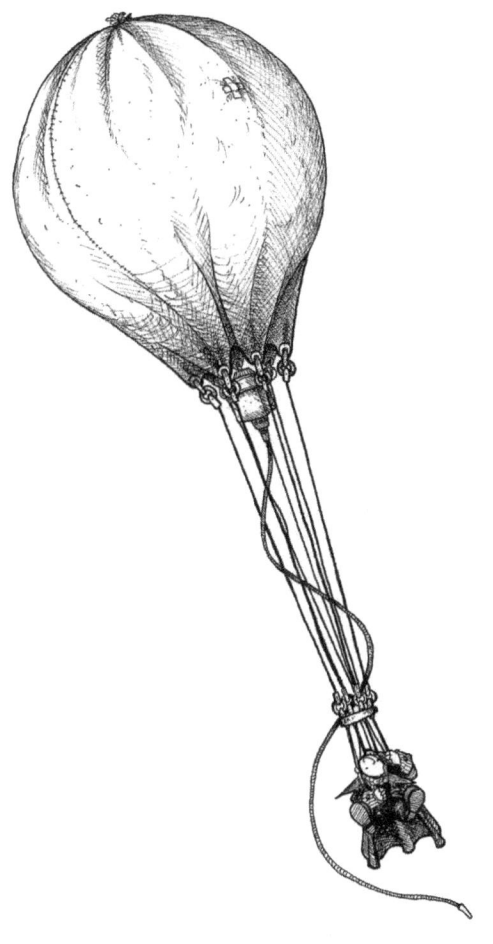

could just make out the vile Gloob standing next to a human who was lying in the street. The two sides seemed to have paused to consider their next important move. Stan had no idea who would win this battle, but he was certain that all of the Bods would do everything in their power to protect The Library, whatever form it was in. The rope jerked him to a halt as he came to the end of its length. He rocked slightly and spun round and round before stopping and simply hanging in his harness beneath Berga's amazing device high above the City. He struggled with the brass tube and held it high above his head, angling it outwards slightly. He really didn't think it was a good idea to shoot it into the balloon.

With all his considerable strength, Stan pulled on the rope cord under the tube. At first, nothing happened. Then, his arms nearly came out of their sockets as a great boom exploded from the top of the tube. A bright ball of green and red fire shot even higher into the sky. It flew up and up until, all of a sudden, it seemed to stop in mid-air as if ignoring the storm crashing around it. Stan thought it would start to drop, but it simply hung there for a moment before growing and growing and growing. The Bod had to shield his eyes as the small fireball became a huge shining sphere of light. It was as if one of the stars had descended to have a closer look at what was going on. Through the thunder and howling wind, there came a high-pitched note so pure and simple that it pierced all other noise. All of the Bods on the ground looked up and let out a mighty cheer as the beacon swelled and illuminated the whole of Broad Street and beyond. Even the Mor'ns and the Ignor'n looked up in some kind of awe as the note changed and danced across the city. Stan was transfixed as the orb flashed through the colours of the rainbow. The note sang out for some time longer before becoming louder. The great beacon shattered into the night sky, shooting tiny shards of light out in every direction. It took a while for the ringing in Stan's ears to stop.

"Well if that doesn't get everyone's attention, nothing will."

He tugged on the rope so that the others could start to pull him back in. It took him a moment to realise that he had tugged too hard and the knot had slipped loose. The amazing balloon began drifting higher. The rope coiled downwards towards the hatch where Cearo's horrified face could be seen staring wide-eyed as Stan began to float away. Stan looked around and scratched his chin.

"Oh dear. Well, here we go."

Chapter Seventeen

Red sat on the cold wet stone and cried. Madam Brunda tried to talk to him but he pushed her away. How did it come to this? They had been hatched, loved and looked after. They had lived in The Library all their lives and promised to look after it. In turn, it had nurtured them, fed them and loved them back. Now it was gone. Cynwise was gone, eaten all up by ignorance and hate. What was the point?
"Tell me," Red raised his head and looked up at the old Bod. "What's the point if they can take The Library away from us? What's the point if they can take my friends, take Cyn, from me?"
He began sobbing again and crumpled down onto the wet, stone step. A small hand touched his shoulder, he wiped his nose on his sleeve and looked around. Oswyn and Osric stood over him, side by side. Their eyes were red raw from crying, but there was anger there as well. They grabbed their friend and stood him up. Oswyn's face was like stone, grim, and stern. His brother ground his teeth together, scrawled on a piece of paper from his satchel and shoved it into Red's hand. Through his tears, Red focused on the one word written by the little Bod who had never hurt anything in his life 'VENGEANCE'.
He stared at the two brothers, standing as tall as they ever had and wiped his eyes. Red straightened himself up and nodded. He gathered up his bag and glow staff and looked out across the masses of Bods waiting all across the street. The storm whipped around them with thunder in the night and lightning in the sky. They stood as one. The Bibliolibrum lay deep within their ranks with old and young ready to die before anything would get close to it. This was their world and their society and no

nasty, greedy, little monster was going to tear it apart just because they wanted to own it all. The Gloob stood with its army of ignorance, greed and hate rallied behind it. Red stared down at the evil being and muttered under his breath.

"You can't kill us all."

Osric smiled then and nodded. He pointed to himself and his brother then gestured over the road towards Blackwell's bookshop and made the sign for 'book'. Red's eyes widened and then he smiled, it was a dark grin with no happiness, but a great deal of revenge in it.

"Go and get them. Bring them all to the fight," he turned and shouted into the wind, the rain mixed in with his tears as he held his glow staff high. "We are the People of The Republic of Lettered Men. You stand within the dominions of The Library of Sir Thomas Bodley and we will defeat you, or fall trying!"

As the words hurtled off into the storm, a great boom went up behind them all and a ball of fire shot up above the Radcliffe Camera and shone out across the city. It grew brighter and brighter and lit up the whole of Broad Street. The mass of Bods let out a great cheer that made Red's ears ring. The ball of fire grew into a vast sphere of light and a beautiful piercing note shot across the city, bouncing off the ancient Colleges, shopping arcades and council buildings. It rang out as the Beacon shone and the Bods shouted and cheered. Oswyn and Osric jumped up and down, grinning into the brightly lit night. They shook Red's hand, bowed low to Madam Brunda then ran down into the crowds below, off towards Blackwell's Bookshop. Madam Brunda looked down at the exhausted, angry little Bod in front of her,

"And you young Aethelred, what will you do now?"

Red looked up at the old Bod who had loved him from the moment he had hatched, as she had all of them across the years.

"I'm going to take our world back."

Alric had pushed through the crowds on the steps to get to his friend. He ran to his side and nodded, grabbing his own glow staff and readying himself to head off. Red clipped his backpack into place and turned back to look at The Gloob far along the street. He stood at the crossroad of Broad Street, Park Street, Catte Street and Holywell Street, here in the heart of their City.

The evil being stood there in the driving rain with his army behind him. The water running down his malformed head did nothing to wash away the grime and hatred. The wind whipped his tattered coats around him. His grotty blue neck scarf flapped like a banner in the storm. He swivelled his huge globular eye across the Bods reigned in front of him. He watched as the beacon shone across the city and followed the line of its accent downwards to behind the steps of the Clarendon Building. Through the rain, he saw the little Bod standing on the steps staring across the space between them. Just for the briefest moment, a shiver ran down The Gloob's spine.

***

Godwin brought some bread and soup over from the Camera to Brunda on the steps of the Clarendon. Most of the Bods were rushing through to Broad Street to meet their comrades for the battle. The storm sent leaves and rain swooping through the great gap where The Library had stood. He finally got to the edge of the steps where the old Bod stood, her robes and dress billowing out in the gale. This made Brunda look even more like a determined galleon than usual. She turned slightly and accepted the soup.

"Ah, thank you, Godwin. I was just thinking, it will be important to get food down to them all in the Street as quickly as possible before the battle truly begins. We seem to have come to some kind of blessed lull for just a moment."

Godwin smiled and wiped his hands on his apron and nodded.

"No fears Madam Brunda, us Bods of Creswick Carrel have already sorted that," he raised his hand.

At the sign, Masses of Bods loaded with bread and cheese, bottles and wrapped fruit began to pour past them and out into the crowds below, handing out provisions as they went. Madam Brunda smiled slightly and passed young Aethelred a piece of bread. His eyes were glassy as if he did not even recognise it but he took the food and began chewing on it. He was still staring off over the crowds. Brunda turned back to Godwin who had been joined by Yrre, one of The Quire and a member of The Old Guard. That dwindling group of Bods who had fought in the battles of times long gone and, in truth, had wished that the days of battles were far behind them all.

"Greetings, Yrre. How fare Hyde Carrel?"

The short elderly Bod looked up at Brunda with his tired eyes.

"We are battered and bruised Madam, that is the truth of it. We are given the task of protecting The Library with glyphs and wards and yet..." He swept his hand to take in the great pit and empty space where The Library should be.

"Only moments ago our best, Wuffa returned from the lair of the human traitor and now leads a group from James Carrel towards the great book," Brunda's eyes lit up at this news, for she had heard nothing of her old adversary and best friend Offa for some time. Wuffa was never very far away from his teacher and guide.

"Any news of Offa?"
The short old Bod glanced at Godwin, not wishing to meet Madam Brunda's enquiring eyes.
"Wuffa says he has fallen, Lady. He died a hero's death protecting Wuffa and some young Bods from the Mor'ns. Wuffa said the young ones fled like cowards while he and Offa tried to rescue one of them and were set upon by The Gloob."
"Liar!"
Red burst across at the old Bod, grabbing the lapels of his robes and shoving him backwards until Godwin grabbed him and held the young Bod. They were shouting and struggling whilst Madam Brunda helped Yrre to his feet. Red strained to get free, but Godwin was too big for him. He struggled to free himself and tears streamed down his face.
"We stood to fight. We wanted to fight. But, but Offa told us to get back here. To protect the Library. We didn't flee. We came back, but we weren't cowards!" He struggled even more until Godwin nearly lifted him off the ground to hold him firm. Red almost screamed in their faces.
"We had gone to get Cynwise. She was no coward. She fought the Ignor'n in the depths across the bridge. She fought the Ignor'n in the Street and gave her life to protect..." he broke down then and slumped down in Godwin's bear hug.
"We didn't leave him. He sent us back while he fought The Gloob. Wuffa was there, why would he..." Red's eyes widened and stared up at Madam Brunda, his memory clearing.
"Wuffa. He just stood there! He just stood as Offa sent us away. He didn't turn to fight!" The young Bod stretched his head to see across towards the Bibliolibrum towards the great book that Bods of James Carrel, led by Wuffa, were heading.

"He's turned against us! Can't you see?" Red stared up at Madam Brunda, whose eyes slowly widened.

"It is true these young Bods are no cowards Yrre. Godwin, let Aethelred go please," she placed her hand on the young Bod's shoulder. "If this is true, then the Bibliolibrum is in the gravest danger."

Red nodded to the great Lady and bent down to pick up her glow staff from where it had fallen. Yrre looked into his eyes,

"What are you going to do my boy?"

Red wiped the tears from his eyes,

"I'm going to do what I was born to do. I'm going to protect The Library from anyone or anything that wishes it harm," he stood and looked over the hundreds of Bods ranged across the street. "Just like all of them."

He jumped forward, followed by Alric, the two young Bods leapt down the great stone steps of the Clarendon Building and disappeared into the throng of Bods towards the Bibliolibrum, towards Wuffa.

***

Berga stared up out of the hatch at the very top of the Radcliffe Camera. She had clambered up using her strong arms. She had left her crutches on the floor next to the contraption as soon as the pipes had tumbled back down into the study. She watched helplessly as Stan floated off into the storm almost due south past the spire of the University Church of St. Mary. Stan saw the glint of her goggles as the lightning struck across the city and waved to her. He looked all around him and seemed to have the biggest smile on his face. Berga shook her head and couldn't help but laugh.

"He's mad. Totally mad," she ducked back in and scrambled as best she could down the chairs and tables to the floor

below. Erasmus looked up at the trap door in the ceiling. "There seems to be one Bod too few coming down from up there, yes? Yes."
Berga looked around at the startled faces of Aedre and Cearo.
"He's decided to go off on a bit of an adventure. The Beacon seemed to go off perfectly, so we really should get down to Broad Street and help the others."
They made their way down through the Camera. It was all but empty now. They pushed on through the driving rain over the makeshift bridges to the steps of the Clarendon Building. Madam Brunda bowed to Erasmus as he made his way forward and took in the whole scene before him. The armies of The Gloob had increased to an alarming quantity. Some of the Mor'ns had combined and built themselves up into vast, almost human-sized beasts. The filth and gunk of the drains were absorbed by their horrible bodies. The brave Bods of the front line were somehow holding their nerve and the standoff seemed to be continuing. The Bods were unwilling to advance to near the terrible things in front of them and The Gloob was unwilling to yet commit his troops against the raging force of The Library's protectors. They all stood in front of him shouting and stamping their feet. Erasmus smiled at their bravery.
"Makes you proud, doesn't it?"
Madam Brunda nodded but looked sternly over the heaving crowds.
"It cannot hold. The Gloob will not wait forever."
As the Bods talked, the True Spider Major Gattling, who had been lying further under the huge archway tending his wounds, gave out a painful sigh. The other True Spiders had joined him and stood in a circle around their injured friend. Marjorie stooped down and kissed his cheek,

"Come on old boy. We've had worse than this! Remember when you beat Lady Giltaleia, The Sandford Troll, at the bridge? She tried to pull your legs off!"
She smiled and the Major laughed, but this brought on a dreadful coughing fit and he sank back to the ground. the Bods came over and Madam Brunda made her way through the forest of high white legs to his side.
"Major Gattling, please hold on. We can get you into the Camera where it is warm."
He smiled at her but shook his head, his great fangs drooping as he spat green blood onto the floor.
"I fear, my good lady, that that damnable Ignor'n has had the better of me. Oh well, I say. There are worse ways for an old soldier like me to die than in a good fight!" He wheezed and the pain caused him to fold his remaining working legs beneath him.
"Promise me you'll beat these blasted things. We did it before Brunda, you and I! They must not win, The Library is too important to the City... to all of Oxford, for it to fall into the hands of the likes of those rascals!"
He raised himself up as he said this, but again a coughing fit overcame him, and the Major slumped back down. He sighed one last great sigh and the life went out of him, his great albino frame sinking to the ground. Madam Brunda patted his abdomen.
"I promise old friend," she whispered.
She moved away then as the other two Spiders stood in close around their fallen comrade and began singing a long and beautiful lament into the night sky as the rain teemed down and thunder shook the city.
Oswyn and Osric pushed their way through the masses of Bods across to the other side of Broad Street. They ran as fast as they could down along the wet pavement until they got to the railings to the side of Blackwell's Bookshop and the small air vent that would let them get in. The

shop was split into three large frontages, two sat together and were split from the third by the White Horse Pub. Many of the Bods had always thought this an excellent idea. If you must split up a bookshop, do it with a really

good pub. It was to the third, most western end that the brothers headed. They had never been into Blackwell's, but they knew the stories and knew where they should be heading, to the Norrington Room. Ever since they had been newly hatched there had been tales of Blackwell and Norrington, two of the maddest and strangest Fellow Travellers in the history of the Bods.
The tales said it was impossible to tell the two apart, for they were identical twins. This meant that they were able to get themselves into all sorts of mischief and blame the other, which had driven Madam Brunda and the other nursery Bods of the Jolliffe Carrel into a frenzy. Many of the older Bods who had been on the receiving end of the brothers' practical jokes were relieved when the twin brothers declared their wish to become Fellow Travellers. They took the red bowler hats and brass staffs at such a young age, making their way to the great bookshop across Broad Street. Here they had set up as guardians and protectors of the books held within. One brother took the name Blackwell, from the previous Fellow Traveller who had defended the place until her death at a grand old

age. Her red bowler and brass staff had returned to The Library, signifying that a new Fellow Traveller should make their way to take her place. The two had demanded to go together because all Bods can choose their own way, it was agreed that they both should go across the wide street. When they arrived there, they found that the Bookshop had grown beneath itself and out under the Trinity College quad next door. This was called the Norrington room and was a thing to behold in itself. The brothers decided to split their duties between the main bookshop and the new room, and so the second brother took the name, Norrington.

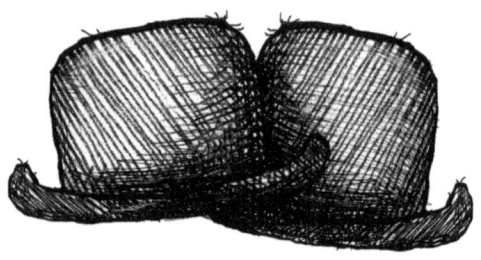

Every now and again, tales would come across to The Library of Blackwell and Norrington's latest adventure or disaster. No Bod had forgotten, least of all Oswyn and Osric, of the day word came across about 'Norrington's Underpants Disaster' or the tale of 'The Day Blackwell Bit The President'. Almost everybod's favourite was 'The Curious Incident of the Bum in the Fiction Section.
All of this meant that Oswyn and Osric worshipped the idea of the twin brothers, running around and having

adventures. They were more than excited as they climbed through the railings in front of the bookshop. They made their way through the slatted vent towards the vast basement that made up the Norrington Room. The brothers slipped off their rain hoods and cloaks as they moved onwards into the dry and silent tunnel beyond. This ended in a Bod door made to look like a heating grate. Oswyn pushed the latch up and swung it open from the bottom as his brother attached climbing lines and the two spun downwards towards a countertop below them. As they slowly lowered themselves down they took in the view of the biggest room that sold books in the whole wide world.

Even for two Bods used to The Library and its books, this room was something special. They managed to use the line to swing across from the wall to a tabletop that looked out across the vast expanse. Immediately in front of them was a sort of open area, in which were tables piled high with books. This was surrounded on all sides by bookshelves which ranged off into the darkness of the room, forming something similar to a maze. Indeed there were rumours that the Office of Imperial Curiosities had been chasing a Minotaur around the Norrington room for years. Far out beyond that, they could just make out rows and rows of pale pillars stretching into the dark and everywhere, of course, were more books.

Osric tapped his glow staff on the wooden countertop upon which they had landed, overlooking the expanse of books in front of them. The light gently beamed out into the darkness as Oswyn rummaged through his kit bag securing climbing lines for their descent onto the lower floor. They had really no idea how to find Norrington or Blackwell but the excitement of even trying was building up in both of them. It took no time at all for the experienced bookherders to get to the bottom and with a flick, unhook the line and let it fall to the ground. Oswyn coiled it back up and packed it carefully away. All of the stories about the two Fellow Travellers came flooding back to the two young Bods as they looked around them. This was the very room where Blackwell had cornered an Ignor'n which had somehow found its way from deep below. The Fellow Traveller had tricked it into eating its own tail and sat quietly as it proceeded to eat itself for the next half an hour or so. Across into the main bookshop was where Blackwell had sheltered several of the lesser gods. The Michaelmas Angel had stalked the streets of Oxford, causing havoc to all before it. The two small Bods smiled at each other and then sighed deeply. They both knew, of course, what the other was thinking. Cynwise would have loved it here, with the chance to actually meet the two heroes of all their favourite tales. Osric wiped a tear away as the anger of their loss welled up inside of him once again. He stood in the middle of the vast room and banged his glow staff on the floor three times. Each blow was accompanied by the staff bursting out a bright flash of light. From the corner of the room came a cough and the noise of shuffling feet.

"Enough. Enough already, I get the point that you're here. What do you want then, eh?"

Out of the dark came a Bod not much taller than the brothers stood there in the middle. He was bent over slightly and used the brass staff in his gnarled hand more as a walking stick than a sign of his great office. The red bowler hat sat on a thick thatch of white, matted hair. And his eyes were fogged and tired looking. He made his way unsteadily over to Oswyn and Osric and peered at them.

"I ask you again, what do you want here. I am charged with... what am I charged with, eh? Goodness me I should

know this bit."
Another voice, still shaky but more forceful than this one, shouted across the room from near the stairs.
"You are charged with protecting these books and all that dwell here you old fool!"
The Bod that hobbled slowly across towards them looked exactly like the first to appear. This one wore a brown heavy coat, whereas the first was wrapped up in a green one.
"You must forgive Norrington, he's past it I'm afraid. We are thinking of having him put down."
The first old Bod spluttered at this and banged his brass staff on the ground. This caused him to begin a prolonged fit of coughing and his red bowler hat to fall off and roll over to Osric's feet. The young Bod picked it up and handed it back to the old Fellow Traveller. Osric turned and looked at his brother, Oswyn simply shrugged. The old Bod who had just made his way over put his hand on Osric's shoulder.
"Something is wrong, isn't it? I can feel it in my very bones little Bod."
Oswyn nodded and pointed towards where The Library should stand.
The first older Bod, Norrington, scowled slightly.
"What's the matter? Why aren't you talking?"
Blackwell tutted at his brother then.
"They obviously feel there isn't anything worth saying out loud you old fool! I wish you would shut up sometimes!"
"How dare you! I have to sit here day in, day out listening to your rubbish! I think you should try a bit of silence for a while, it would be wonderful!"
They carried on like this for some time, as Osric and Oswyn looked at each other, shrugged and sat on the floor. They opened their packs and nibbled on some chocolate.

They watched their two heroes squabble until both old Bods had become quite tired and neither could remember what the argument was actually about. Oswyn banged his glow staff on the floor, which seemed to get their attention, even though Norrington had in fact nodded off for a moment. The two old Bods shuffled over and accepted chunks of the chocolate and sat down with the young brothers. Osric produced some scraps of paper and a chewed pencil stub from his pack and began writing down the whole terrible events that had engulfed them. The two old brothers sat in silence as they read the unfolding tale. Every now and again, one of them scratched their head in horror or asked for more knowledge. After some time, the Fellow Travellers understood the whole situation and a spark seemed to be glowing through their foggy eyes. Norrington stood up, this took him some considerable time and effort.

"Well little Bods, we must wake the shop. We must gather the books of Blackwell and join our brothers and sisters out in the street!"

Blackwell jumped to his feet excitedly and then spent several moments calming down from the dizziness this brought about.

"It has been some time since we went out into the City and caused trouble, my brother. I think it is about time Blackwell and Norrington rode forth again and reminded the world what mischief makers we can be!" He hobbled off towards the stairs and his section of the great shop.

His brother shouted after him,

"I agree, although I always thought Norrington and Blackwell had a better ring to it!"

Oswyn and Osric smiled at each other as the books of the huge shop began to awaken and shuffle on their shelves as their guardians called them to arms. Norrington grinned at the younger brothers as he jammed his red bowler hat down onto his head.

"Well then. Let us go from this place to another place. Onwards!"

Chapter Eighteen

Stan nibbled on a chunk of bread he had found in one of his many pockets as he floated through the rain south over the very heart of the City. Below he could easily make out The High as he passed over the long curving street that sliced right through Oxford from Magdalen Bridge to Carfax. He stared down at Oriel College as it passed beneath his dangling feet. As he approached the ancient buildings of Merton College, there was a distinct flapping of wings just above him. There were two Gargoyles or Grotesques. Stan could never remember the difference. They were taking a great interest in the balloon. They had large, stone-like heads with short, stumpy bodies. Their wings were elegant and huge, like those of a giant bat. They swooped and flapped to stay steady with the canvas bubble as it floated nearer to Merton, seemingly falling slowly towards the roof of the chapel. The two winged creatures managed to guide the balloon and its bread-munching passenger down onto the roof of Merton Chapel's tower. The balloon finally lost its buoyancy and sagged down onto the wet roof as Stan unhooked the harness and wiped down his soaked coat. As he rung out his hat and put it back on his head the rain seemed to slow and stop, the storm had finally raged itself out.
Stan stood and bowed to the creatures as they landed on the Chapel roof.
"Good day to you. I am Aethelstan, but my friends call me Stan. I am a Bod from The Library."
He grinned his best grin and bowed again. He knew from the Bodleian gargoyles that they could be sulky, dangerous things. Many Bods had come running into the Supper Room being chased by one of the great winged beasts.

Usually, it turned out that the Bod had been taunting it or not asked permission to be in the thing's domain. The two here on the roof turned their huge heads this way and that as they inspected first the balloon then Stan. He held out the remaining piece of bread.

"No thank you, we've already eaten," the smaller of the two stepped forward and shook Stan's free hand.

"I am Mr Bradwardine, and this," he gestured to his colleague, "This is Mr Heytesbury. I am a Grotesque of Merton, Mr Heytesbury is a Gargoyle of the same." He bowed slightly.

Stan smiled and nodded.

"I've never worked out the difference, I'm afraid."

Mr Heytesbury stepped forward and opened his mouth wide. A vast torrent of rainwater came shooting out of his mouth, hit Stan right in the chest and knocked him over. He sat on the cold roof and rang his hat out once again. Mr Bradwardine smiled.

"Gargoyles deal with rain water and the like. Grotesques, such as myself, do not."

"Oh, fair enough," said Stan as he stood up once again. Mr Heytesbury shot a massive stream of water over the side of the tower out into the street. Mr Bradwardine coughed slightly.

"There's been a storm."

Stan nodded and looked up at the sky which was clearing as the stars began to be visible once again.

Mr Heytesbury looked at the Balloon once again.

"Nice bit of kit there, Sir. You don't often get aeronautical Bods around here, not of late anyway."

Stan nodded once again. He had no idea what was going on, so did what he always did in moments of confusion. He took a piece of chocolate out of another pocket and began nibbling the corner. Another of their clan appeared over the crenulations of the tower and smiled a big, fang-filled smile at Stan.

"Oh, hello Mr Dumbleton, this is Stan, an air-born Bod. Stan, this is our good friend Mr Dumbleton.

Mr Dumbleton bowed slightly and shook the hand with the least food in it.

"Charmed, I'm sure." He turned to the other two. Have you seen Mr Swinehead? We are supposed to be meeting for coffee."

Mr Bradwardine shook his head.

"I haven't seen him for several hours. He did say he wanted to take a closer look at all the fuss in Broad Street and the great flare thing. Is that anything to do with your lot, Sir?"

They all turned and looked at Stan, who tried (and failed) to swallow the large chunk of chocolate he had just stuffed into his mouth. Stan looked up at the sky to try and gain some time to finish off the enormous glob of chocolate swirling around his cheeks.

"Erm... Well... Yes, actually, it is. Some nasty little ball of snot is trying to destroy The Library, and so (gulp) we, that is, the Bods, are going to stop him."

The two stone-like creatures flapped their wings and looked at each other. A third of the great, winged beings swooped onto the roof of the chapel to greet his friends and colleagues.

"Good evening Mr Bradwardine. Good evening Mr Dumbleton."

"Good evening Mr Swinehead," the other two replied, Mr Bradwardine scratched his long hook-like nose.

"What is the state of play in Broad Street?"

Mr Swinehead settled himself down and shook the last drops of rain from his vast, leathery wings.

"Well, The Bodleian is gone. All the little fellows are packed into the Street squaring up to a great mass of nasty-looking things that keeps coughing and spitting everywhere. It's all a bit of a muddle really. Oh, thank you Mr Bradwardine."

The other grotesque had poured a cup of tea from a flask and handed it to his colleague.

"We calculated this several seasons ago, just after we had deciphered the Paradise Street Cryptogram.

If you recall, we, unfortunately, dismissed it as one of the more outlandish possibilities."

Mr Dumbleton nodded.

"Indeed. Yet it appears to have occurred anyway. Slightly embarrassing for our reputation really."

Stan gratefully accepted a cup of hot tea from Mr Bradwardine but was completely confused as to what they were talking about.

"I'm Sorry, you predicted all of this? Are you psychics or something?"

Mr Swinehead looked as if his tea had suddenly turned into a cup of cold sick.

"Certainly not! We are mathematicians. We simply use slightly more... realities than most to calculate our findings."

"So you can see the future, different types of Oxford?"

Mr Dumbleton shook his rather bulbous head.

"No, you're thinking of the cats. We simply calculate."

"You calculate Oxfords?" Stan was still rather puzzled, he sipped his tea.

"Indeed we do. We calculate. We are the Oxford Calculators."

Stan still looked confused. Mr Swinehead looked rather annoyed that the Bod hadn't understood.

"We help the Trolls. They check the Trollomicus to make sure not too much of the City is wandering off. They do have a habit of meandering around you see. Oxford will insist on suddenly rearranging itself," Mr Swinehead pointed in various directions as if this all made perfect

sense, "It can all become tiresome for those that live and work here."

Stan grinned, suddenly understanding a bit of all of this. "The Trollomicus! That's the weird contraption that Berga has been working on for Madam Brunda."

"I have no idea what you are talking about."

"My friend Berga is an inventor. Madam Brunda asked her to repair a piece of this Trollomicus thing..."

"No, you misunderstand me. What I meant was that I neither have any idea what you are talking about nor do I care."

"Oh. Sorry," Stan looked at his boots.

Mr Dumbleton hopped forward.

"You must forgive Mr Swinehead, he can be a little waspish at times. We were not aware that the Bods were helping the Trolls in any of these matters."

Stan scowled at himself for perhaps telling something that Berga did not want too many others to know.

"Well, my friend is just helping somehow I think. I don't know really."

Mr Bradwardine finished his tea and replaced the screw cap back on the flask,

"Well, if a part of the Trollomicus is stuck within The Library as it is now, then we must help preserve it. I think the great Folly would not be overly amused if it was lost or destroyed."

Mr Swinehead nodded.

"Last time that happened, we lost ten days... Never did get the damned things back. The Gregorian Incident. Very embarrassing for all involved. The Trolls were furious!"

Mr Dumbleton unfurled his great wings and gave them a stretch, Stan had to duck.

"Well young Bod, it would seem that whether we like it or not, we are part of your fight now. Probably better for you that we are on your side. Now let's get you back to your comrades and finish this nonsense once and for all, eh?"

Stan grinned. He had begun to think he was going to miss it all.

Mr Swinehead moved forward on his great clawed feet.

"Come on then Bod. I take it from your balloon," the gargoyle nodded over to the great bundle of canvas and tubes which Mr Bradwardine was carefully folding up ready to carry. "That you have no great fear of flying?"

Stan stood as tall as he could.

"No sir. I appear to love flying!"

Mr Swinehead chuckled.

"Excellent. Well, let us go and join the battle and see if we can't cause some bother!"

He gently took up the limp chords of Stan's harness in his claws and beat his huge wings into the cold star-bright night. The other two Oxford Calculators followed close behind. Stan shouted into the sky as they swooped back towards Broad Street.

"Get ready Gloob! Here we come, ready or not!"

Chapter Nineteen

Red and Alric made their way through the great throng of Bods crushed together across Broad Street. Many shouted and cheered, buoyed up after the Beacon had shot so high above them sending out its message to the Fellow Travellers to come home. More waved to the two friends or shouted out and cheered. They wove through the crowds as the chants grew louder. Several of the Rouse Carrel struck up songs on their horns and mandolins. Others took the cue and drums started beating, flutes piercing the shouts further into the great mass of Bods. Each one was utterly determined to protect the great book that lay deep within their ranks. Red pushed his way through his comrades. He had lost sight of Wuffa but was certain that the traitor would be heading straight for the book. The young Bod knew they had to get to him before the turncoat could begin trying to move or even destroy the book. The rain seemed to be calming slightly, which made it a little easier to see through the crowds. Neither Red nor Alric were the tallest Bod in The Library, they could really do with Stan about now. All of their friends were scattered, Cynwise gone forever. He gulped and tried not to think about that too much. Were the others alright? Berga, Oswyn and Osric, Stan? All of them were somewhere in this nightmare. The panic and grief knotted in Red's stomach and he squeezed it into grim determination. He finally spotted Wuffa and three other Bods from James Carrel. They were nearly at the spot where the concentration of Bods was the strongest, right around the Bibliolibrum.

Alric had seen them too and tried to push through but the crowd was almost a solid defensive wall around the great leather-bound book. He struggled to get anywhere as Wuffa moved with calm authority towards his prey. Red tried to shout but was drowned out by the drums, chants, songs and whoops of the mass of excited Bods around him. He watched in horror as Wuffa finally made his way to the side of the book and began talking with one of the Old Guard who stood nearest to it. There were quite a few of the veterans standing in close defence. They were small and many had white whiskers, their hands gnarled as they gripped their staffs in the bitter wind. There was steel in their eyes, memories of battles fought and won before, thoughts of old friends lost and lives cut short. Each wore the armband that singled them out as members of the Old Guard. Red recognised most of them from sitting in the nursery when they wandered in from time to time, spinning tales of old fights, old victories. He wondered if he or his friends would tell such tales, or be remembered by the newly hatched Bods of times far from now. He spotted one of the Old Guards, Audrey of the Rouse Carrel who had valiantly tried and failed to teach Red to play the flute when he was little. She spotted him and waved. He pushed forwards to try to get to her and give his warning about Wuffa, but the crowd was simply too dense here. An old Bod standing squeezed in next to him looked down at the frantic little Bod.

"Are you well? There is no need to panic in the crowd. We are all safe," he smiled at Red,

"I am Drefen of Shakleton Carrel. I think our lines are holding pretty well really. Are you sure that you are fine?" Red took his hat off and wiped his forehead.

"I need to get to the Old Guard over there, but I can't get through! I have..." Red had always been rather good at making things up quickly in order to get his own way. "I have an urgent message from Madam Brunda for Wuffa," he tried his most innocent face as his rage and near panic battled to come to the surface. Drefen smiled and looked across the crowd.

"Well that should be easy enough," he cupped his hands and bellowed to those around him.

"Bod surfer coming over, if you please! Prepare for a Bod surf!"

To Red's surprise, Drefen then hoisted him up over the heads of all the others and laid him onto the outstretched waiting arms of all those surrounding them. Drefen shouted out again,

"To the Book please!"

Red found himself carried swiftly on a wave of arms over the top of the previously impenetrable crowd. Alric waved him onward and began pushing against the crowd to make his own way to the Book. They dropped Red onto his feet right next to Audrey, who smiled and patted him on the shoulder,

"Hello, Aethelred, nicely done there. I haven't Bod surfed for years! How are you?"

Red caught his breath and stared intently at the Old

Guard standing in front of him,
"Audrey, we have a problem."

***

Brec and Scead stood at the very front of the frontline of the Bods. They shouted, whooped, jumped and hammered their glow staffs on the ground as the vast hoard of Mor'ns and Ignor'ns. Who knew what else roared and howled along the Street before them. The two young Bods were too excited to realise just how frightened they truly were. They had been standing in the front ranks for what seemed like an eternity. Their fear had shrunk deep inside them when the Beacon had gone up and the terrible monsters facing them had stalled for just a moment. It had been a mere flicker of apprehension from The Gloob, but it was enough to see that it wasn't totally sure of itself. They had freed the Book from the awful human and now they stood ready for what must surely be the real battle.
"There's a lot of them, isn't there?" Brec said turning to his friend.
Scead grinned.
"Yep, but there's an awful lot of us too!"
One of Rouse Carrel Bods next to them began beating his drum and the others all around took it up by banging their staffs on the ground. Suddenly, the Mor'ns and Ignor'ns opposite them began roaring together in a terrible cacophony of noise and rage. The Bods became quiet as they waited for the great howls to die down. When they had done so, The Gloob moved forward and raised its gnarled withered hand up out of its many layers of coats and robes, and everything fell to silence. Even the rain faded to nothing as all eyes were turned towards the terrible creature. It gestured to several of the Mor'ns near it. They bowed to their master and somehow merged

into one another to form a much larger being. This great Mor'n scooped The Gloob up onto its shoulders so that he could see all across the great swathe of Bods before him. Mr Simper sat up, rubbing his head and scowling. The Gloob stretched out its arms and shouted, clear into the growing dawn light of Broad Street.

"You little people of The Library. You cannot win here. I am far older and far more powerful than any here today. This new morning will bring you nothing but death and fear. Hopeless destruction awaits you this day. Give me the Book and flee this place. Give me the book and I will let you live where ever you can find sanctuary in this miserable little city," it spat foul acid onto the tarmac which sizzled and cracked as it dissolved. The Bods nearest to him shuffled backwards and looked nervously at one another. The Gloob laughed a dark and nasty laugh.

"It was my Library long before you were ever thought of. They are my books and I shall have them back! You wish to share them all with everything that dwells in this cursed place? Well, sharing is for fools and idiots. What good is all of this knowledge? I tell you now, if you do not hand the book over to me I shall unleash such destruction upon you that none shall live to tell of it! Knowledge is for the elite. Power is for those born to it and I claim it all!" He paused then, this creature of hate and fury. Its great, putrid eye swivelled as it looked at the vast army of little Bods in its way.

The Gloob spat again, this time the great vile glob sizzled through the air and hit a young Bod on the side of their face. He screamed as the acid ate into his cheek, falling to the floor as those around him rushed to his aid. One of the nearest was of Myres Carrel, the healers and doctors for all the Bods. She quickly delved into her backpack and pulled out a cloth and ointment to try and stop any more of the acid from eating the young Bod's face. He

screamed again one last time before slumping dead in the arms of those trying to help him. The Myres Carrel Bod pulled his cap over his cold eyes. Those behind gently passed the limp little body backwards towards the Claringdon building. They turned to stare at the monster in front of them. Fear and rage danced in their eyes. The Gloob stood high on the shoulder of the great Mor'n and then bowed to them, sneering his revolting slimy smile.

"I do not want to hurt you. I only want the book. Give it to me and no more need die this day. I can be generous. Give me the book and leave this place. What do you say little Bods?"

There was silence across the ranks of tiny guardians of The Library. They were born to protect it but this enemy seemed too powerful to stop. The Mor'ns were multiplying and growing ever bigger before their eyes. The Ignor'ns strained under their master's hold to be let loose and wreak havoc amongst them. What were they meant to do in the face of such overwhelming hatred? Many Bods turned and looked into the eyes of their friends and comrades. How many would be lost today? Was any of this worth it? Many shuffled their feet and stood in the growing light of the day, uncertain of what to do next. From within the stunned silence there then came a small solitary reply, calling out from somewhere deep in the mass of Bods,

"Bugger off!"

The laughter grew across the whole army of them. Shouts followed, from all corners of their groups.

"Get lost!"

"Yeah, nobody likes you, you weird beggar!"

"Go and try your luck in Cambridge!"

The shouting grew and the stamping and drums began again. From somewhere deep in the ranks, a glowing globe hurled forwards in a beautiful arc, hitting The Gloob in

the eye. This caused a great cheer to burst from the Bods. Tens more flew over their heads and smashed against the Mor'ns, causing great damage to the hateful beasts. The Gloob howled into the growing light. Snarling and dribbling, he pointed out at the hundreds upon hundreds of Bods before him and screeched at his terrible forces.
"Destroy them all! Forwards into the dawn my creatures! Destroy them all!"
Brec watched as the Mor'ns rushed forwards towards them, all click-clacking teeth and boiling rage. He turned to his friend Scead and winked.
"Well, here we go then!"

***

Madam Brunda watched as the first wave of the monstrous Mor'ns crashed into the front ranks of her beloved little Bods. Ten or more fell immediately as the great beasts swiped claw-like hands into the mass of Bods before them. Close by, a large group of the little warriors had managed to topple a Mor'n. It writhed on the ground as glow staffs pummelled it and dissolved the filth and dust into nothing but a bad memory. The shout went up then, "Use your lights! Use the glow!"
More fell as three of the monsters tore their way into the crowd, throwing any in their path far across the street. The fearsome teeth wrenched arms from shoulders and screams went up as the beasts bit deep and hard.
Madam Brunda looked to Godwin and they both nodded to each other. She picked up her glow staff and roared into the growing morning.
 "Follow me! Come with me!"
The two old Bods raced down the ramps and ladders from the Clarendon Building through the throngs. Elswyth,

the cartographer of Craster Carrel joined with twenty or so younger Bods all carrying long poles with sharp nasty looking tips. Brunda smiled at them, and she drove forward with grim determination.
"Onwards!"

Several Mor'ns had moved to the outer sides of Broad Street. They were moving along the gutters attacking the sides of the main group of Bods. The guardians of the Library fought back with amazing ferocity, but again some of the Mor'ns began to merge. As one was brought down and destroyed, others formed larger creatures which smashed through the Bods' ranks. They were scattering the little defenders and leaving far too many dead in their hideous path. A small group of Bods rallied around a tiny little drummer who beat out a battle call for all she was worth. They crowded together as the shadow of a vast Ignor'n fell over them. They held up their glow staffs in trembling defiance as the monster reared up. Its vast jaws were dripping bile as it loomed in for the kill. Suddenly, a great albino blur smashed into the side of the Ignor'ns armoured body. Another leapt through the air and attached itself to the back of the giant beast.
"Nicely done Derek, now bite the foul thing!"
"Right oh, Marjorie" Derek opened his magnificent fangs and bit deep into the Ignor'ns neck.

Marjorie shot out length upon length of webbing that bound the beast's great arms together. The group of Bods rushed forwards and began smashing their glow staffs into the thing's exposed belly. It roared and thrashed about but could not stop itself from toppling over. As the True Spider's poison took hold, the last thing the dreadful monster saw was the little drummer running towards it, poking it in the eye with a drumstick.
On the far side of Broad Street, nearest the edge of the

gaping hole where the New Bodleian Building had stood, several Mor'ns were pushing forwards. They were trying to outflank the mass of Bods between them and the book. A small knot of the Old Guard had rallied many of the younger ones and were huddled together to block the way. The Mor'ns glared at the group as they held strong while those behind them manoeuvred a catapult into place. The engineer Bods of Craster Carrel had loaded it with sharp chunks of stone and glass. They heaved the mechanism into position and let fly a volley of debris into the main crowd of the Mor'ns. Several of the ignorant monsters exploded into dust clouds as lumps of glass and stone ripped through them. Others scattered and roared their frustration and anger. The beasts moved back slightly and the Bods braced themselves to advance. A great shadow suddenly fell upon the readied Bods. It was a human shadow that stretched far across the massed groups in the dawn light which flooded into the Street from Holywell Street. The King's Arms and History Faculty buildings cast great, long shadows with the long carpet of the new day's sunlight between them.

Mr Simper stood in a barely contained rage as he wiped the mud and filth from his knees. The Bods shuffled backwards slightly as he advanced towards them. The engineers frantically tried to reload the catapult. Mr Simper glared down and brought his left leg up high above them. They barely had time to scatter as the insanely angry human's foot came crashing down on the catapult, smashing it to pieces. Four or five of those bods nearest couldn't get out of his way. Those that did not fall beneath the devastating pounding of his feet were kicked, lifeless into the gutter or down through the darkness of the New Bodleian's pit.

Mr Simper could see the book through the throngs of horrid, little Bods, swarming around it, thinking they could keep it safe. What did they know? How could they possibly stop a human, especially one as clever as he?

He strode forward, Bods scattering in front of him, desperately trying to get out of the way of those murderous shoes. Glow orbs and stones, glass shards and pins flew at him from all directions, cutting him and slicing through his best suit, now muddy and torn. He didn't care. Very soon the book would be his. The Library would be his. He put his hand to his face to protect himself from the myriad of things being hurled at him. He shook off several Bods who were once again attempting to fix lines around his legs. He wouldn't fall for that again. Mr Simper laughed a loud manic laugh. This was his hour, his moment. Who could possibly stop him now?

"Oh, hello again!" said Stan, hanging in his harness from the claws of the gargoyle, Mr Swinehead.

He swung slightly in the dawn light, right in front of Mr Simper's face. The human stumbled back slightly as he tried to focus on whatever it was that had just appeared out of the sky. His eyes almost crossed as he glared at the Bod dangling in front of him. Then, Mr Simper whimpered slightly as he recognised his attacker from their previous painful encounter in his room. Too late, he tried to put his hand up before his face as Stan swung forwards and bit Mr Simper's nose even harder and deeper than he had the last time. The man squealed as he tried to wrench free, but the great gargoyle beat its huge wings and kept the whole merry dance from toppling over. To the Bods surrounding them, all the way to the Clarendon building, it looked like MrSwinehead was conducting a particularly odd and violent puppet show. Mr Simper howled and grasped at Stan, but the Bod was not letting go. All his anger and hatred pressed down into that snivelling nose. Flesh tore and blood oozed out as Mr Simper said a last goodbye to a good portion of his nose. Stan spat out the nasty, pointy gristle as Mr Swinehead gently lowered him to the ground.

"Yuck! Even I wouldn't eat that!"

Mr Simper stumbled further backwards and the Bods surrounding him renewed their bombardment with glow orbs, stones, glass and pins. The human's eyes were streaming and he screamed in pain. Then, he looked to the skies as the beating of great leathery wings seemed to fill his ears. Mr Bradwardine and Mr Dumbleton swooped down and each grabbed one of his shoulders, pulling up above the mass of the battle, A great cheer went up from the Bods below. Mr Swinehead dusted down his waistcoat and turned his bulbous head to Stan,

"We shall take the traitor to The Silent Brethren of the Sunken Cathedral of St. Giles. They will know what to do with such a wretch."

The gargoyle beat his wings and swooped up over the Street, still chaotic in the midst of the great battle and joined the two other Oxford Calculators. The dejected and beaten human was hanging by what remained of his best suit. They pushed higher into the sky and then began to glide westward over Trinity College and Balliol towards the Spire of the sunken Cathedral and whatever fate awaited Mr Simper there.

Chapter Twenty

Wuffa stood with the other three Bods of James Carrel and stroked the side of the Bibliolibrum. He was talking very quietly and calmly to the Old Guards who had surrounded the book. They were veterans of half-forgotten battles, long misremembered fights. These solid few would be the final line of defence if the rest fell and The Gloob made it to the Book. Wuffa sniggered into his scarf and tried to keep the utter contempt out of his voice.
"You have all done a marvellous job here, well done. We of the James and Hyde Carrels are charged with checking the protection of the great book so that it is ready for the evil before us."
The old Bods around the Book looked at the guardians with some caution. Bawdewyn stepped forward and put his hand on the shoulder of the nearest Old Guard, Aldfrith.
"Wuffa assures us that Offa himself has put these plans into order before his, erm, unfortunate meeting with The Gloob. We have no reason not to believe our dear comrade, and time is of the essence."
The Old Guard looked at one another and stood back slightly. They had no reason to doubt The James Carrel. They may be fairly pompous, but they were after all those charged with watching and guarding (though admittedly, this hadn't seemed to have gone so well recently).
Wuffa smiled his unctuous smile and stroked the book once again. He could barely keep himself from screaming out in triumph. The Gloob would be very pleased with him indeed.
"Thank you kind folk. Now, do any of you have the key to this rather large and curious lock?"
The great clasp that adorned the book was mighty indeed but there seemed to be no keyhole as such. Wuffa tilted

his head this way and that, trying to figure out how to get it open. Aldfrith looked confused at the other Bod's seeming indecision.

"There is no key. You are a Bod, sworn to protect Library, and therefore the book. Just put your hand on the lock and, as long as you mean the Bibliolibrum no ill will, it will open for you," he smiled and gestured towards the brass clasp.
Wuffa froze with a smile on his face and stuttered for a moment.
"Oh, I erm, well, it really is too great an honour. Yes, that's the point of it! It is too great an honour to be the one who opens the book. Arianrod, please, you do the deed," he bowed long and low as a rather startled Arianrod walked up to the book and gazed around at all those present.

"I am Arianrod of James Carrel. I am tasked with protecting the Library and all within it. I have never wished harm nor damage upon this great place and I hereby wish..." The Old Guards rolled their eyes at each other. They were more than used to the James Carrel Bods making long boring speeches about how important, yet humble they were. Wuffa shook with rage at the stupid fools before him.
"Just open the book you fool so that I... I mean, my good friends, time is passing. The Gloob draws ever closer, please, open the book!"
"Of course, dear Wuffa." The foolish and unsuspecting Arianrod placed her hand on the clasp and a deep humming grew from within it. Sparks fizzed around the edges as the lock rumbled and slowly opened. A great charge leapt from the corners of the yellowing pages and shot across at Wuffa, singeing his goatee beard. He let out a whelping cry as the blue shards crackled around him.
"Ow, ow, oh dear, ouch. I seem to have, I seem to be having a slight problem with the static in my scarf. Quickly Arianrod, if you please, open up the Book!"
The others around him stared at the strange dancing Bod and then turned back to the Book. A wind seemed to grow up around it and it slowly heaved its great leather cover open. Its ancient-looking pages flicked this way and that. There were words, sentences and letters within, but they all swarmed around and around. Every possible style and font, pages of formula and scribbled pictures broiled around the thousands and thousands of pages. Every book of The Library mingled, swooped, dove in and leapt about the pages. It was a literary ballet of all the publications held safe within it. The patterns were mesmerising. All of the surrounding Bods could feel the power from within. The pages flickered and flapped. The

letters and words seemed to spiral down into their own inner world of ideas, notions and wonder. The pages were merely the rolling surface of a great deep churning ocean of knowledge.

Wuffa staggered forward and pushed Arianrod out of the way. He leapt up onto the edge of the pages, peering down into the maelstrom before him. The Old Guard was too mesmerised by the swirling might of the book to realize what he was doing. Great bolts of blue fire danced around Wuffa singeing and burning him. He seemed too manic to either notice or care. The traitorous Bod screamed into the air.

"Master! Mighty Gloob! I have it, I have the book! Come and take what is rightfully yours!" He turned then, arms stretched triumphantly into the air and began screeching a terrible laugh into the growing morning light.

This was immediately cut off as Red smashed straight into his stomach, knocking the air from his lungs. The two teetered on the edge of the swirling power of the Bibliolibrum as Wuffa scrambled to regain his balance. Red untangled himself from the nasty, little traitor and threw a wide punch at the side of his head. Wuffa let out a great howl and fell backwards into the book. As he dropped he grabbed Red's arm and tugged him down into the whirlpool of the whole Library. The great cover of the book slammed shut just as Alric pushed his way through the dazed crowd around it. The Old Guard, Audrey, who had pushed through with Red, grabbed Aldfrith and shook him,

"What has happened here, why did you let Wuffa near the book?"

Aldfrith looked stunned.

"But he is a Bod. A Bod would never harm..." His voice drifted off as his eyes widened at the reality of what had just happened. Arianrod, Bawdewyn and Wilda stared in horror at each other as it dawned on them that Wuffa had betrayed them all. Alric tried to prise the book open but it seemed firmly locked once again. Arianrod placed her hand on the lock, but nothing happened. Wuffa and Red were sealed within. A great and terrible roar went up nearby as several Bods came pushing through, battered and bloodied.

"The Mor'ns are coming, The Mor'ns are coming for the Book!"

All those around it moved forward. Audrey grabbed Alric's arm as he gripped his glow staff and went to advance with the others.

"No, little Bod, you must stay right here and wait for Aethelred. He will need you I fear if he returns."

Alric scowled at the idea of not standing with the others as their foe approached, but he nodded and stood firm up against the edge of the great tome.

The wave of Mor'ns hit the main body of the Bods with a mighty crash. Ignor'ns swept great swathes of the brave little defenders out of their path, the lifeless bodies crashing to the floor. At the very front of the Bod line, Brec and Scead smashed and pushed for all they were worth. Madam Brunda and Godwin had moved forward and were ranged at the front. The great block of pike-wielding Bods formed a long spiny wall against the dreadful beasts lumbering towards them. Few of them could tell which way they were actually facing. The dust of exploding Mor'ns and the glaring swarms of launched glow orbs disorientated everything into a great fog of confusion.

Alric climbed atop the Book better to see what was happening. It still flickered with strange lights and rumbled beneath his boots. Far towards the back of the enemy lines, he could make out Mor'ns climbing on one another, again moulding and merging into vast, human-sized beings. They staggered and swayed as the growing beasts tried to get their footing. His eyes widened as they became more confident. They were huge, what were the Bods meant to do against these things?

Another wave of Mor'ns and Ignor'ns crashed into the line of pikes and flattened many. Others rushed forward and took their place, grabbing the long, sharp poles and readying themselves once again. Other Bods shot out from behind the ranks and made darting attacks on the closest beast to them. Brec and Scead pushed deep into the mass of Mor'ns, bashing any and all with their glow staffs Then they scurried back, shouting and laughing; half in delight, half in terror.

The Mor'ns which had manoeuvred down the flank of the Bods in front of the Clarendon Building were met with the full force of the engines. They were ranged along the vantage point of the steps. Berga moved as quickly as her crutches would allow from one machine to another.

She was shouting orders or making adjustments so that the great heaving engines were more powerful, more accurate, anything to give them a chance. The Mor'ns rumbled forwards as the shards of glass, stones and sharp pins tore into them. Some disintegrated in howls of pain and fury. Those that avoided destruction there found themselves faced with the might of the True Spiders. They were charging into the enemy lines, clawing, binding and biting into the beasts which were left thrashing in their silken prisons. A single Ignor'n somehow evaded the Albino warriors and lumbered over the cobbled pavement and up the great stone steps of the Clarendon Building. It swung a huge thorny arm at the nearest engine, sending it crashing back into the gap between the vast high pillars. It advanced and threw several Bods down the steps into the chaos below. It devoured one who desperately tried to ignite his glow staff before disappearing into its deadly maw. The terrible beast turned and flailed around. Engines smashed and collided with each other as its stunted tail swung back and forth. Berga braced against one of the pillars as it seemed to pause in front of her, sniffing the air. It caught her scent and gave a triumphant roar as it raised its head to come crashing downwards. The roar quickly turned to a dreadful scream as the True Spiders Cynthia and Petunia launched at either side of its head. They stabbed deeply into its tough hide with their claw-tipped legs whilst biting ferociously with their poisonous fangs. Berga desperately twisted the arms of her crutches, but at first, they refused to charge. The ends finally sparked up and energy flowed between them. The young Bod rammed them forward into the underbelly of the Ignor'n, pushing as hard as she could, shouting at the top of her lungs.

"For Cynwise!"

The enormous beast writhed and shuddered before collapsing in a great, fetid heap on the stone paving. The True Spiders detached themselves and swiftly bound the dying creature with their unbreakable silk. They rushed then to Berga, as she slid down to the floor, trying to regain her breath. Petunia smiled (or as near as the Truer Spiders came to a smile between their gaping fangs).

"Well done old girl! Top shot there, when all this is sorted and tickety boo, we really must do lunch."

Cynthia tapped her fellow Spider on one of her shoulders. "Come on my dear, duty calls," they swiftly bound into the crowds below, navigating their way over the Bods towards ever larger enemies beyond.

The gigantic Mor'ns had begun to move forward, almost hesitantly at first. It was as if the many creatures that made it up were unsure as to how to work as one being. Slowly, they staggered forward and overtook the great Ignor'ns still held in reserve by The Gloob. He stood towards the rear of his army pointing and directing the whole battle, almost tasting the book as his forces grew closer to it. The drums and horns of the mass of Bods, which had been banging and blasting as their comrades repelled wave after wave of attack slowly fell silent as the gigantic beings came crashing into view. The front line of Bods almost shivered as one. Brec and Scead and the others who had been shooting forward, fell back, almost dropping their staffs. Great volleys of glow orbs, glass and stone flew forth as the engineers of Craster Carrel adjusted the engines to attack the giants coming towards them. It seemed to have little effect on the towering beasts.

The front ranks held firm with their pikes and their shouts until the first of the Mor'ns smashed a vast foot down amongst them. They scattered and the whole line broke. Madam Brunda managed to grab a tiny messenger Bod out of the path of destruction and crashed down into the high curb of the street. As it roared onwards, the Bods tried to pull together but many were terribly injured or gone forever. There was chaos and confusion everywhere.

Brunda pushed back into the mass of terrified defenders. It took only moments to find Godwin's body, crushed and lifeless on the ground. She hauled him to the side and covered his head with his cap, extinguishing his glow staff and placing it in his arms. Gently kissing his forehead, she took up her own staff and shouted to all those around her as she eyed the great gaps in the line,

"To me! To me!"

A little drummer close by took up the beat of her words and they were joined by horns, flutes, fiddles and mandolins. The mass of the broken line began to reform as the Mor'ns, huge and truly terrifying, began to bare down on them. Madam Brunda glared her one good eye at the mindless obedience of the evil before her. Brec and Scead stood beside her as the numbers grew and grew.

Any and all that could walk or stumble grabbed a staff, pike or rock. Others simply curled their fist into tight balls. The noise of her troops grew and grew as she looked at The Gloob in the distance. Madam Brunda lifted her glow staff high above her head and roared with defiance.

"Coming to get you!!"

The Bods surged forward with a roar.

Chapter Twenty One

Stan wiped the blood from his smashed and swollen cheek as he pushed through the crowds to get to Alric on top of the book. He had managed to help take down two Mor'ns and push forward against a great Ignor'n before he had spotted his friend. In the chaotic madness surrounding the Bibliolibrum, Stan shoved forwards. He watched as a single Mor'n broke through the near flank and stumbled, murderously towards Alric and the book. Audrey and Aldfrith regrouped with the other Old Guards before it, jabbing and shoving to try and push it back. It swung its mighty arms to and fro, missing Aldfrith but smashing Audrey with such force that she flew backwards, crashing silent into the edge of the book. Alric stared down at the stunned Old Guard. His eyes widened as the terrifying thing pushed closer. He gulped down his fear and gripped his glow staff ever tighter.
"We are the People of The Republic of Lettered Men. We are the People of The Republic of Lettered Men!" his whole body trembled as the Mor'n smashed its way towards him. He could smell the hatred, ignorance and blind obedience to orders almost steaming off it. There was no reasoning with a thing that did not question anything about what it had been instructed to do.
As it reared up right in front of Alric, the Bod felt very small indeed. Aldfrith rammed his glow staff into the Mor'ns gut causing the monster to roar in pain. It managed to raise a great, filthy foot and stamp down on the old Bod who fell then on the cold wet street, lifeless. The terrifying beast reared up once more and roared at Alric. He staggered back but just managed to hold his footing. The creature seemed to stop, confused for a moment then Stan clambered into Alric's view scrambling

up the back of the thing. He was kicking and hitting it as it tried to shake him off. Alric took full advantage of the pause in the attack and leapt forwards at the Mor'n bringing his glow staff down on the thing's mushy, filthy head as hard as he could. He grinned at his friend as they pummelled the beast.

"What kept you, Stan? I've had to do everything around here."

The bigger Bod laughed as he twisted the great arm of the creature nearly off its body.

"I had a dinner appointment, you know how it is."

The two friends continued to beat the Mor'n until it finally stumbled to the ground. Instantly, a great swarm of Bods descended on it. They were smashing and kicking until it disintegrated with a violent howl. A great cheer went up but just as quickly, one of the Old Guard nearby shouted.

"More are coming! Get ready for the charge!"

Madam Brunda and the great Bod front ranks had taken down three Mor'ns before the greater beasts were upon them. The old Bod knew better than to try to tackle them and called for the others to regroup further back.

"To the Book! Defend the Book!"

The whole mass of Bods began to swarm towards and around the Bibliolibrum. Madam Brunda joined the other Old Guards. She turned to Audrey who was gasping and wounded, leaning on her own glow staff.

"Aldfrith?"

The other Bod looked down and shook her head. Madam Brunda cursed to herself.

"I've had quite enough of this, thank you very much."

She raised her glow staff as the enemy loomed towards them all and shouted across the ranks.

"All Equal!"

The Bods took up the cry, little ones in the middle of it

all banged on their drums as the roar of the great Mor'ns grew louder and closer, but the Bods shouted louder still.
"All Equal! All Equal!"
Stan turned to Alric.
"Come on, last one in is an un-hatched!" Alric stopped and shook his head.
"I can't. I have to stay by the Book, Red's in there somewhere," Stan stopped and his eyes grew wide. He looked at the huge book, brimming with power and glowing from red to green, yellow to purple as its sealed pages seemed to ripple. He stood there in the middle of the chaos, unable to decide what to do.
At that moment an Ignor'n plunged its way in from near the kerb and crashed into the mass of Bods between it and the book. Another one smashed its way nearer from the other side of the Street. Whilst the giant, staggering Mor'ns lumbered ever closer, the Bods were being pushed backwards. The front lines did not break yet could not stop the evil beasts from advancing and so fell backwards bit by bit. Eventually, the mass of Bods was packed tightly around the book. Alric and Stan watched as one of the greater Mor'ns made a rush forwards, crushing tens of Bods and causing many more to scatter. Several of Bandinel Carrel desperately tried to get climb lines around its gargantuan feet, but they were flung far across the Street. Other of the more usual-sized Mor'ns came in its wake, thrashing and tearing with their click-clacking teeth. Ten or more Ignor'ns came behind and around their fellow beasts. They were roaring and clawing towards the Bods as the little guardians of The Library tried desperately to reorder themselves. Many grabbed fallen pikes and formed a front row of spines against the coming onslaught, whilst others shouted and banged their glow staffs. They did their best to convince themselves that they were ready for whatever was to come next.

The Bods once again fell silent as the giant Mor'ns came nearer. Many other Mor'ns were massed around their giant brethren. Ignor'ns roared and stumbled on stunted arms nearer and nearer. In the midst of them all, The Gloob shuffled ever closer to his goal. Spittle dripped from the slash of his twisted mouth. He gathered great globs of it and flung it forward, burning and scarring any that were unfortunate enough to be in its path. He could see the Book now. Two Bods stood foolishly brave on top of it. There was no sign of his pet, Wuffa. Perhaps it had fled along with the pathetic human. It would all be his very soon. He had waited so very long, now it was all coming together. He signalled to a Mor'n close by who shambled over and hoisted its master onto its shoulders. The Gloob shouted into the morning air, surveying the terrified Bods before him.

"I gave you a chance and you have thrown it away. I will destroy you all now, and then I will destroy your beloved Library. When it was all stone and millions of books I had no chance, but a single book, now that is easy to destroy!" His great bulbous eye swivelled and the spittle dripped down his stained and ripped coats.

"I will have my revenge! I will destroy that book!" His outstretched claw-like finger pointed towards the Bibliolibrum. The Ignor'ns and Mor'ns roared and howled until silence fell once again.

From within the ranks of the Bods, a single shout rang over Broad Street.

"I told you before, Bugger off!"

The Gloob shook with rage and lifted both hands to the sky.

"Forward! Destroy them all!"

The mass army of blind obedience and ignorance began to move indestructibly towards the tired but determined Bods. The greater Mor'ns began to roar, a terrible noise that bounced from the building along the street that was suddenly cut short by a vast and beautiful humming, and the sound of a mighty organ playing.

The sound came from further down Broad Street, beyond the back of the Bods' lines. The Gloob strained to see as vague shapes began to come into view. They were huge, and the sun glinted off each one's tiny glasses. They wore leather overalls and their huge steel toe-capped boots boomed as they marched towards the battle. In their vast digging hands each carried a shovel or a great hammer. Their whiskers twitched from the sides of their stubby noses as they squinted to see in the daylight.

Alric turned when he heard the humming and almost jumped for joy as he saw them come into view. There were dozens of them marching up Broad Street towards the Book.

"It's the Ashmoles! The Ashmoles have come!"

Many Bods strained their necks to see as the huge guardians of Tradescant's Ark came ever closer.

Stan shouted then and pointed down near the Ashmoles' feet. Almost lost in front of the giants came twenty or thirty Bods. The light was shining off their brass staffs. Their red bowler hats were almost glowing in the rising sunlight. Stan let out a great laugh.

"The Fellow Travellers are with them. They saw the Beacon, they've come home!"

A huge cheer went up from the Bods. Drums beat and horns sounded. The Bods parted as the Ashmoles moved through their ranks, pushing towards the giant Mor'ns with grim determination. The Fellow Travellers banged their brass staffs on the ground as they joined the mass of Bods now all turned to face The Gloob and his dreadful army. Stan spotted Codrington of All Souls, bowed to Alric and jumped down to join her as she marched forward.

She smiled at him.

"Oh, hello, fancy seeing you here!"

Stan grinned back and wiped his chin.

"Hello! I don't suppose you've brought a picnic with you, have you? I'm remarkably hungry."

"Let's get this spot of bother out of the way and I'll see what I can do."

The two of them joined Madam Brunda at the Front Line. The Mor'ns and Ignor'ns had once more begun to roar, but it didn't seem so certain this time. The noise of the Bods was almost as loud. Erasmus, from the steps of the Claringdon building, looked over the battle site in front of him, his long scarf blowing in the chill morning wind.

"This is it, yes? Yes," he said, as much to himself as to anyone else. "This is when we stand or where we fall."

Madam Brunda stood at the head of the lines. She raised her glow staff high and called out above the beating of the drums.

"For The Library! Onwards!"

***

The first clash was horrifying. The wave of Bods rushed forwards with their great sharp pikes and hit the Mor'ns head-on. The Mor'ns in their turn swooped deep within the ranks of the little fighters, slashing and tearing with their teeth and sharpened claws. The greater Mor'ns stood still at first, allowing those in front to clear a murderous path. The Ignor'ns smashed and punched at the dense edges of the Bods to try and break them. The True Spiders came then, hurtling over the heads of their comrades. Petunia dived forwards and knocked a Mor'n down to the ground, a mass of Bods instantly fell upon it and it exploded into dust and filth. The Gloob pointed and shook his hands, directing his blindly obedient forces further towards the

Book. Alric swung his glow staff as a Mor'n grabbed at the edge of the Bibliolibrum, smashing it into its nasty little eyes. It fell backwards and the remaining Old Guard finished it off. The Ashmoles surged forwards and took their hammers and shovels to the Ignor'ns in their path. One of the horrendous beasts leapt forward and toppled one of the great honourable guardians of Tradescant's Ark. It fell fighting to the end as the evil thing crushed its skull between its massive jaws.

More of the Ashmoles fell, but Mor'ns and Ignor'ns fell with them. The Gloob slowly began to get nearer to his goal.

The Bods rallied to the horns around madam Brunda and regrouped, once again darting out and hitting the enemy, before cunningly coming back into the protection of their friends. Alric, from atop the book could see that the Ignor'ns were moving down the sides of the Bods, trying to contain them into an ever smaller area, the easier to control and overpower them. He shouted down to the Old Guard beneath him to try and warn them that they were now in real danger of being surrounded. His voice left him though, as a greater Mor'n, built from ever more of the mindless creatures, suddenly towered high over him. It loomed there for a moment swaying and roaring into the clear blue morning sky. Alric stood on top of the book which held the one thing he had promised to defend with his life. He didn't tremble at all as the beast raised its huge arm high above it preparing to swing down. the Bods immediately around the book smashed into the giant, but it shook them off. The True Spider Cynthia leapt high and attached herself to the thing's neck, biting and clawing. It grabbed her and crushed her in its vast fist, dropping her crumpled dead body to the floor far below. It shook its head as some of the spider venom got into it, but it was so enormous that there seemed to be little real effect. It raised its arm high over the little Bod on top of the book and then something seemed to catch its attention. It turned slightly as a copy of the Shorter Oxford English Dictionary (volume one A to M) with Oswyn riding on its spine, flew straight at it and smashed into the side of its head. Osric followed swiftly behind on volume two (N to Z), he leaned in tight as the book conducted an expert turn and hit the giant monster deep in its gut. The whole of the bookshop's books came flying out then, great squadrons swooping out above the Street. They shot out at the Mor'ns and the Ignor'ns. Blackwell and Norrington shot into daylight. They were both mounted on a copy of Absolute Sandman (volume four). Its huge leather cover flew low as the two mad, old Fellow Travellers hurled glow orbs down onto the enemy below. The Bods cheered, banged their glow staffs and rallied once more for another, perhaps final push against their enemies. Madam Brunda drew in her breath. Whichever side came out of this attack standing would almost certainly hold the Book.

Alric shouted and cheered as his friends swooped past on the dictionaries. He was about to call out to them when the book below him shuddered and suddenly heaved open. A vast wind shot up from within it, power and light spilt out as Alric leapt to the ground. The Bods immediately around the book dived out of the way as the great cover toppled open. The pages inside still surged and broiled in a beautiful but terrifying maelstrom of all the words, knowledge and wonder held inside. The Library, inside the Bibliolibrum. The chaos of the battle still raged around them, many were too busy fighting for their lives and their beloved Library to notice what it was doing. Berga and Erasmus stood on the Clarendon Steps as the young Bod directed the engines against the nearest Ignor'ns. From here, she could clearly see the Book glowing in a myriad of wondrous colours. From within it, she just made out two small figures clawing their way out, still kicking and punching at each other. Alric was much closer as Wuffa came piling from within the book. At least the little Bod thought it was Wuffa, it looked like him except his hair and skin had gone completely white. His eyes were glassy, ivory-like orbs and his clothes were ripped and torn yet also bleached of colour. Red came hurtling after him, grabbing the traitor by the head and smashing it as hard as he could into the edge of the pages still swirling around them. Red was battered and bruised. At first, Alric thought his friend was one great bruise. He soon realised that just as Wuffa had been turned completely white, Red had turned, well, red.

As the two enemies punched and kicked at each other, Alric saw that what he had taken for cuts all over their bodies were in fact words, sigils, sentences and emblems from within the pages. What, in the name of The Library, had happened in there?

Red managed to hook his arms under Wuffa's elbows and flung him out of the book onto the street. He staggered up and lashed out at the Bods nearest to him. Red stumbled out of the book and fell into Alric's arms. Wuffa shoved and pushed his way through the chaos before him into the confusion of the battle. The traitor stumbled backwards, pale, cream blood streaming from his nose. He did what he was most skilled at, he fled. As he shoved his way through the crowd he ranted back at Red,

"You're too late little Bod! He's coming. The Gloob is coming for the book."

Around them, in the chaos greater Mor'n after greater Mor'n crumbled into their smaller beasts under attack from Berga's engines and the True Spiders. They were immediately surrounded and attacked by the Bods who quickly swarmed over them. The Ignor'ns who had attempted to come around the back were set upon by the surviving Ashmoles as the two groups of giants from UnderOxford fell upon each other.

The book lay swirling in its own pages as the noise grew around them. Red held onto Alric and tried to stand, looking across the crowds before him. A large group of Mor'ns were clearing a path in the distance. They were getting ever closer as the Bods tried bravely to stop them. In the creatures' wake came The Gloob, spitting out acid and bile and slashing at any Bods still left in his way. Red could just make out Wuffa who let out a sneering laugh from the distance but then disappeared into the madness. The advancing Mor'ns suddenly came under attack from Madam Brunda and the Fellow Travellers, who fell upon them with all their remaining energy. Many fell to the terrible teeth and claws of the beasts but the Mor'ns tried in vain to push forward. Madam Brunda turned in the midst of it all as Stan shouted a warning from nearby. She twisted but was too late to avoid the vast fist of the Ignor'n that had come crashing through the crowds. The old Bod was thrown sideways by the force, right into the path of The Gloob. He stood over her sneering and dribbling in equal measure. Madam Brunda made a grab for her glow staff, but the evil thing looming over her kicked it away. She lunged out at him and caught the side of his leg causing him to trip and fall next to her. She heaved her magnificent self up and glared into his bulbous eye, her one good eye holding enough hatred for a thousand. She regained her breath, unaware of what was happening directly behind her.
"You have failed Gloob, you will always fail."
She spat into his eye as he lay on the damp street.
He grinned that horrible, slashed grin then, wiping the spittle from his eye, hissed his words at her.

"Not bad. But I can do much much better!"
He spat out a vile sizzling glob then which hit Madam Brunda right in the face. She screamed and stumbled backwards, right into the giant brutish arms of the Ignor'n. Stan howled in rage and ran at the great thing, smashing and beating at it as it crushed the old Bod in its merciless fists. Her body dropped from its maw as Stan rammed his glow staff into its under chin. The creature shrieked and fell backwards whilst Stan picked up Madam Brunda's limp body and dragged himself near the kerb to a quieter spot amongst the chaos. He crumpled down gently holding the old Bod who had nursed and fed him from his smallest of days. He wiped her smashed forehead with great care as the tears poured down his big face.
The Ashmoles were too preoccupied with the Ignor'ns and Mor'ns on the outer fringes to realise what was going on towards the centre. The Fellow Travellers were busy taking out the last of the greater Mor'ns to understand what was happening at the Book. Berga and Erasmus could only watch from afar as The Gloob got closer and closer. The Old Guard held out for some time as three Ignor'ns pushed forward. The Gloob was now on one of their backs as he pushed to within a touching distance of the Bibliolibrum. They fought and they fell bravely as the books swooped and tried to get to The Gloob. This was in vain as he was too low for them to strike. The great, stupid, obedient beasts shoved forward as The Gloob grinned in victorious glee. Alric pulled the exhausted Red out of the way as the last few Bods stood their ground. Brec and Scead stood fiercely at each other's side as The Gloob came within striking distance. Each pounced forward but was smashed aside by one of the advancing Mor'ns, rolling away into the fearful crowd of Bods. Finally. The Gloob was placed by his loyal troops on the edge of the pages of the thing he had craved after for so very very

long The Library.

Chapter Twenty Two

The battle seemed to stall as an eerie silence flowed out from the epicentre where the Bibliolibrum lay. The Ignor'ns and Mor'ns stopped fighting and shuffled back, then let out triumphant roars and howls. The Bods slumped as they realised that The Gloob had reached the Book. Many fell where they stood, exhausted and battered. Others shouted but the heart had gone out of it. Others simply stood and cried. The wind blew the detritus of the battle across the street. The Gloob stood on top of his great prize and gazed in a kind of madness into the swirling patterns of all he craved, all he despised.

The victorious creature's grimy, soiled coats flapped in the wind as he motioned to one of his Mor'ns. The beast loomed over Alric and grabbed Red. The exhausted, little Bod put up no defence as the monster hoisted him up and shoved him onto the edge of the open Book. Alric lunged forward, but the Mor'n lashed out and the exhausted Bod crumpled to the floor, dazed and bloodied.

The Gloob grabbed Red's arm and roughly pulled him near. Droplets of the thing's spittle flicked and splattered onto Red's torn coat, burning and eating away at it. The evil creature held onto the Bod tightly as he slumped in defeat. Turning to the whole battlefield of Broad Street, The Gloob raised his free hand in a high salute and shouted out across the silent, broken troops.

"You are lost! You are nothing! I have everything!" His great, swivelling eye met the gaze of Erasmus far across the street. His crumpled old frame was shaking. It took The Gloob a few moments to realise not from fear or despair. The old enemy was actually laughing. Berga and the other Bods stood staring at him. Had he finally gone completely mad? Erasmus turned to Berga and winked.

"Watch little Bod, watch the bravery and cleverness of your friend."

The Gloob had no time for the old fool's last acts of lunacy. He grasped the broken Red even closer and showed him to the crowds.

They looked away or at each other as their comrade slumped on the high edge of the Book.

The Gloob laughed again and spat down onto the floor.

"See your defenders Bodley? This fool thought to warn them against me. This idiot thought to stop me! My great mistake was not to destroy him much earlier!"

Red coughed through the blood.

"No."

The Gloob sneered at him.

"Too late little Bod."

Red raised himself and whispered into The Gloob's ear, "Your mistake was letting me get this close."

With that, the little Bod shoved The Gloob backwards, forcing him to swing his arms to keep balance on the edge of the maelstrom of images and words within the Book.

"You have no idea what I've seen in there. You have no idea what I know now." Red raised himself to his full height. The swirls and arcane lettering all over his body seemed to glow through his scarlet skin. He grabbed the greasy lapels of one of The Gloob's jackets and stared into the great swivelling eye. His own now piercing deep red eyes glared at the evil quivering thing.

"Now, you nasty, fat-headed, pointless little creature, get out of our City!" Red pulled back his own head and smashed it into The Gloob's own, horrified face. At exactly the same moment, the little Bod let go of the lapels and sent The Gloob hurtling into the heaving, swirling pages of the Bibliolibrum. The scream seemed to descend into it forever.

The Book convulsed and shuddered, slamming itself shut

as Red somersaulted backwards. He landed by his injured friend then leant down and winked,

"You didn't think I was going to let him win did you?"

At that, the Bibliolibrum burst open. A great light flew out from within, containing every book, every manuscript, every page, everything that made The Library what it was. The huge mass of it swarmed into the air above Broad Street, spinning and whooshing around and around. The wind was fantastic as a great storm of wondrous words and knowledge, information and learning sped back into its rightful places. The Ignor'ns tried to flee down into the deep pits, some escaped, but most were caught by the flying books and cut to ribbons in the growing storm.

The Bods and the Ashmoles and the True Spiders watched in wonder as the Library span back into being above and around them. The remaining Mor'ns were caught up within the gale and splintered into thousands of insignificant pieces. They had finally been shown for the pointless, obedient servants of a nasty, selfish mind that they had been.

When the great mass of knowledge finally stopped its great dance in the air, the Bods looked around them and exhausted and battered though they were, let out a great cheer. The Library was back in its correct and noble place. Of the Bibliolibrum and The Gloob, there was no sign at all, all the stone and bricks, shelves and millions of books were right where they should be, home. The New Bodleian and the grand Old buildings stood gleaming in the morning sunlight. Those that could, gathered the others together and made their way up towards the Clarendon Building and into the Old School Quadrangle where they helped the injured and tried to identify those that had been lost. As Red tended to Alric, the Bods of Myres Carrel took his friend in their arms as they fanned out to do what they could for the injured. Many other

Bods came and began helping, so he lifted himself up and hugged his friend, then went running to find the others.

***

It took him some time to find his friend in the mass of Bods all trying to help the injured or, much worse, move the fallen from the street. When Red did finally spot Stan, he almost wished he had missed him. The bigger Bod sat, slumped against the kerb. The vast bulk of the New Bodleian loomed up behind him as if nothing out of the ordinary had happened to it at all. The large shape cradled in Stan's arms showed that nothing was very ordinary at all. Madam Brunda's limp body lay there as Stan gently wiped her bloody and bruised face. He looked up as his greatest friend approached, fear and anguish in his eyes.
"You've gone all red, Red."
Red managed a half smile.
"I've been away Stan."
Madam Brunda coughed and blood dribbled down her badly injured chin. Her magnificent robes were dark and stained and her hands hung lifelessly onto the still-damp street. Red knelt down and wiped her forehead. The old Bod's eyes flickered open then and tried to focus on his face. She recognised him after a while. She smiled slightly at the mischievous young Bod whom she had scolded more often than she had praised.
"Did we...?" She managed a whisper before coughing again and wincing in pain. Red nodded.
"We won. The Library is safe and back, you can come and check that everything is as it should be."
He sobbed slightly then, he couldn't help it. The old Bod smiled slightly and tried to sit up but coughed blood again and slumped back against Stan. The two younger

Bods simply looked at each other, unsure of what to do. Red sat down next to his friend as three of the healers of Myers Carrel came rushing over and gently took Madam Brunda from Stan's arms. He started to protest but Red held him back.
"Let them do what they can Stan."

Berga found them still slumped against the kerb when she made it across from the Clarendon Building steps. The Fellow Traveller Codrington had found them a little before and true to her word, had somehow found some food for them to eat. Neither had quite realised how hungry they were. Stan was devouring a large chunk of crusty bread as Berga swept through the crowds on her crutches.
"Thank Goodness that you're alright!" She lowered herself down next to Red and gave him the biggest hug of his life.
"I thought I'd lost you too!" Tears came then, rolling and rolling down her battle-weary face. Red hugged her and handed her some chocolate from Codrington's bag.
"Have you seen Erasmus? Is he..."
"He's fine. He's organising getting everyone back into The Library. Most of Craster Carrel is getting all of our stuff back inside. Thank goodness human students sleep late, can you imagine if any of them had walked into the middle of all of this?"
Stan wiped crumbs from his chin.
"They probably wouldn't have noticed! The humans in Oxford have an amazing ability to ignore anything too strange for them to think about."
The others smiled and nodded at this. Red stood up and wiped his hands on his coat, it was only then that he realised that all of his clothes had turned various dark shades of red as well. This was all very odd.

"Come on, let's get ourselves inside and try to work out what to do next."

Chapter Twenty Three

Alric was waiting for them as they made their way into the Old Schools Quadrangle amid the organised chaos around them. His coat was ripped, torn and splattered with who knew what stains and strange splashes. His usually proud knot of hair was drooped into lank and tired dreadlocks down his face. But there was a fire in his eyes, the despair at losing so many friends not quite able to dispel the triumph of finally beating The Gloob. Bods were everywhere, making sure the injured were getting to the exhibition room, where the majority of Myres Carrel had set up. Erasmus had managed to climb onto the back of Marjorie and was shouting across the square, coordinating as much as he could. Most of Red's Carrel, Bandinel, was busy doing a rather less enjoyable type of herding than that of the books. They were bringing home the fallen. Too, too many limp and lifeless bodies were carefully brought into the Library. They took them all below, into the chambers beneath the main buildings of the Old Library. They were to be washed and prepared for the ceremony each Bod was given at the end of all their days, The Great Goodbye.
Red smiled wearily as he caught Erasmus' eye across the Quadrangle. He raised his tired and aching arm into a wave. Erasmus smiled with relief to see them back safe, although he was still anxious, as Brunda had not yet returned. His eyes widened in amazement when he realized that Red had actually turned red. The words and patterns were quite visible across his face and arms. The old teacher's eyes narrowed as to what that actually meant had happened inside the Book. the Bods had quickly formed into small groups to help any who needed it. Even

though so many had been lost, there was a great sense of relief and victory throughout the Library. They had won. the Bods of Creswick Carrel had swiftly resumed cooking and getting food to everyone. The Rouse Carrel had formed into groups of singers, drummers and other musicians to begin what looked like was going to be a huge party. Red shook hands and bowed with many who came to wish him well. Berga was slowly being surrounded by others of Craster Carrel who wanted to know how she had fought the Ignor'ns with only her crutches. Alric went and got them some more food. Stan insisted on helping him in case he had trouble carrying it all.
Suddenly a huge cheer went up as the Fellow Travellers all came into the Quadrangle, smiling and waving. Some

of them were back home for the first time in many, many years. Right at the front was Norrington, exhausted from his air battle but still waving and bowing to all who greeted him. From within the crowd of Fellow Travellers burst Oswyn and Osric. The two small brothers were battered and bruised from their own encounters but both were bursting with pride. They ran over to their friends and hugged one another. The two smallest were laughing and gesturing with their hands to tell of their amazing views of the battle. They all sat down where they were as Alric and Stan returned with plenty of cheese, bread, chocolate and dandelion and burdock. Stan's pockets seemed somewhat fuller than when he had left. Berga turned to Red and placed her hand on his dark, scarlet shoulder.
"What happened in there Red? What did it do to you?"
Red looked down at the floor as his friends all went quiet. "I... I don't think I'm quite ready to talk about it. It wouldn't make much sense I don't think. Not really," the others looked at each other and silently agreed to leave the whole thing alone, at least until curiosity got the better of them anyway.
They sat quietly for a few moments eating and trying not to think about the space between them where Cynwise should be sitting. Eventually, they began to fill in the bits each had missed from the others' tales. By the end of their meal, they pretty much knew all of what each had got up to (except, of course, the bit in the Book). As they finished their stories, a large group from Myres Carrel carried Madam Brunda into the Quadrangle on a long wide trolley. Leof and Odelyn from Madam Brunda's own Jolliffe Carrel ran straight over when it entered. Others quickly joined them as word went around that Madam Brunda was alive but very weak.
Red and the others pushed their way through, no one

dared stop the small bright red Bod as he hauled himself up to kneel beside their old Nursery teacher. Her eye fluttered open as he closed his hand around hers and he leaned in close to hear her words.
"What is it Madam Brunda? You should rest."
She shook her head and pulled him closer.
"Remember Aethelred, remember that The Library is not what we truly protect. The old thing can look after itself, I think." She coughed then and slumped a little. The young Bod looked confused.
"I don't understand. If we don't protect The Library, what do we protect?"
The Old Bod smiled slightly, even in her pain.
"The buildings and all of the books are important, of course, they are. But they are not everything... Neither are the stones, the glass, the roofs above nor the chambers below. We are the people of The Library. We matter too. We fought, Aethelred and we won. The Library did not protect us, we saved it. We are The Library. The stories spun about us will not be about paper and card, brick and stone. They will be about all of us," Red nodded but wasn't sure if he understood it all or not.
"But what about the books?"
"The books matter, yes they do, but the stories matter much, much more. Never forget, books are just stories dressed in smart jackets."
She squeezed his hand and smiled before her good eye flickered slightly and slowly closed for the very last time. Red buried his head into her shoulder, as he had done, as they all had done, many times when they were tiny and newly hatched. Leof let out a great wailing sob as Odelyn comforted him. As was the custom, Red picked up Madam Brunda's glow staff and placed it in her arms. He gently kissed her head and climbed down to be with the friends that were still there, they were the important ones now.

Erasmus clapped his hands and held his stick in the air atop the True Spider Marjorie.

"Bods! You must remember the fallen, that is right and proper, but we all must celebrate their lives, not wallow in dark memories. You have won! You have defeated ignorance and greed. You all came together and nothing could beat you. We must prepare The Great Goodbye for our friends and comrades, but we should also celebrate our freedom and victory as well!"

A great cheer went up and the music once again began to spill forth from the different groups around the Quadrangle. Erasmus smiled. These little creatures never failed to amaze him.

"Get some rest, all of you, for this night shall be remembered forever. A great feast will be gathered and we shall eat and drink to our fallen and our triumph!"

***

At sunset, they came from every corner of The Library, rested and less exhausted from their sleep. Still, a few had carried on through the day, preparing and setting up the two great events that would dominate the evening and through the night. The Great Goodbye, and the Joyful Feast. They entered the Divinity School in small quiet groups. Many had never been to a Great Goodbye and even those Old Guard who were still alive to tell their latest tales, and remembered far too many goodbyes, had never seen anything like this.

From the majestic fan-vaulted ceiling hung hundreds and hundreds of glow lamps all at different heights, casting warm light across the vast floor. The banners of every Carrel stood battered but proud, high on the table in front of the great door at the end of the vast room. The Fellow Travellers stood as honour guards all around the edges of the hall. Their red bowler hats and brass staffs held low as they paid their respects to all, the fallen and those that remembered them. Norrington stood alone, quietly sobbing, and holding two hats, two staffs and quietly thinking of what on earth he would do without Blackwell, his brother. Norrington had always told him that he was no good at flying with the books. Blackwell hadn't time to swerve when the Ignor'n raised itself up and lashed out for a final attack.

The Cowley Carrel – those who prepare the dead for their last goodbye had had a busy day. The hall was full of every fallen Bod that could be found, each laid out gently on one of the Library's books. The books had floated over to the School one by one as the fallen Bods had been brought in. Many more books lay there empty, for even if Bods could not be found, The Library knew they had gone. Friends stood around each of the books, remembering. Meghan and Brec, the latter with his smashed arm in a sling, stood over the calm silent body of Scead. The little warrior had fallen at the last attack, kicking and punching a Mor'n that had dared try to get past him to the Book. Many of the cooks and brewers of Creswick Carrel stood around the shrouded body of Godwin. They were remembering good times as he had cooked and brewed throughout the day to make sure his beloved Bods had full bellies before they each went about their work.

Around one of the empty books there stood six friends, heads bowed in thought and loss. Red stared off into the distance whilst Berga tried to keep Oswyn and Osric standing as they began to crumble into sobs. Stan stroked the book gently, trying to think how any of them would cope without Cynwise talking sense to them. Alric glared at the floor, surely victory was meant to taste better than this.

At the centre of it all stood a great pile of books, all covered in a long purple velvet cloth save the top one, on which lay Madam Brunda. A glow staff stood at each corner of the base, whilst a member of the Nursery Carrel, Jolliffe, stood guard on each of the four corners. In life and after it, the Bods were all equal, but Madam Brunda had hatched almost all of them and nursed them through the early days of their faltering steps in The Library. They raised her high because they loved her. Odelyn, Leof and the others from Jolliffe Carrel held the tiny hands of the smallest Bods from the Nursery, some of them hatched not so long ago.

They made a great circle around the pile and hummed and swayed slightly, though truth to tell, few of them knew exactly what was goingon.

In front of Madam Brunda there lay a great old book, ancient even by The Library's reckoning. Upon it lay Offa, for whilst many had slept, the True Spiders had searched through the day to find him and bring him home. His broken glow staff had been repaired and lay on top of the plain green sheet that covered him.

Many were lost in their own thoughts when the singing began. At first, it was a quiet hum, but soon built into a beautiful surge of sorrow and remembering. The AshMoles entered the hall as they sang. The wondrous sound of Tradescant's Ark floated up and around the great beings as if they carried it into the hall with them. The True Spiders followed, carrying the silken bundles of their fallen friends into the hall to lie with their comrades. The song grew and grew. It seemed to envelop the whole of the hall as each Bod slowly left their place and walked to the banners in front of the great door. Each took a small glow globe from one of the attending Cowley Carrel Bods and kissed it before releasing the shining orb to float high into the high space above them. Slowly, the vaulted ceiling filled with tiny stars as each said goodbye and let their sorrow go. The AshMoles continued to sing as each orb ascended to join the ever-growing constellation above their heads.

Red and the others kissed the empty book and moved forward to collect their glow orb. Erasmus joined them from the edge where he had been watching, remembering many more fallen than he would have liked. He thanked the Cowley Carrel Bod and took a glow orb, touched it to his head and let it go. As it floated up, Red smiled at him, "Who do you say goodbye to?"

The old teacher looked over his green glass spectacles and sighed.

"I say goodbye to Comatus," Red tried to recall anyone with that name, he shook his head and Erasmus smiled at him. You called him The Gloob, my boy."

Red's eyes widened in horror.

"But... Why?" He was almost shaking with rage at the thoughtlessness of the mad, old teacher's actions. Erasmus placed a hand on the small Bod's shoulder.

"For all that he did, he was my brother once and to lose a brother is a terrible thing," he patted Red on the shoulder and sighed once more before moving away so that others could say their goodbyes.

Berga kissed the glow orb in her hand, which brought it to life. She hurled it high at the ceiling remembering the bravery of her friend before any of the rest of them had realised they had to be brave. Red, Stan and Alric sent their glow orbs and their goodbyes sailing into the expanse of stars floating above, now crowding the fan-vaulted ceiling. Oswyn and Osric walked forth and each took two orbs. They kissed the orbs for Cynwise and, tears running free down their tiny faces sent them up and said, finally, goodbye. The other orb they knocked together and whispered their goodbyes to Blackwell. They had not known him very long. Norrington and he had shown the two tiny brothers what they really wanted to do with their lives.

The orbs joined all the others above them until the air was full of glowing spheres, bathing the hall in gentle light. The AshMoles grew silent, as did the whole of the Divinity School as the last goodbyes were said. the Bods and the True Spiders, the Ashmoles and Erasmus moved to join the Fellow Travellers around the outside of the wall. The glow globes began to grow much brighter as The Cowley Carrel led the Bods in the chant of The Great Goodbye.

"Now is the time to say goodbye!"

The rest of the Bods quickly joined in, "Goodbye!"

"Now is the time to yield a sigh!"

A great shout rang out, with even Red calling out as loud as he could.

"Yield it! Yield it!"

Many of the Bods punched the air as they roared the words of The Great Goodbye.

"Now is the time to wend our waaaaaay!" This seemed to take over the whole mass of Bods who started jumping up and down shouting the words and almost dancing as the hall was slowly enveloped in the ever-brightening glow of the orbs. Each of the orbs had begun a single note, slowly growing and flowing over each other, beginning to overtake the shouting Bods. Erasmus, along with many others, shielded his eyes, as he whispered,

"Until we meet again, some sunny day."

The Bods could not even see their own hands as the light overtook them all, yet they sang on,

"Goodbye, Goodbye. We're leaving you! Goodbye...." The rest of the song was lost to the beautiful choral songs of the many hundreds of tiny orbs.

As the song of the orbs faded away, the blinding light

also dimmed until the hall was lit once again by the glow lamps hanging from the vaulted ceiling. The Bods and True Spiders, Ashmoles and Erasmus all blinked and rubbed their eyes, the AshMoles more than most. Across the whole hall, the books lay empty. Where their fallen friends had lain, there were empty shrouds. Where a glow staff had lain in place of a lost Bod, nothing lay there now. the Bods bowed their heads for one last goodbye and slowly made their way out of the Divinity School, some of them still singing.

"Fatattata, Fatattata....."

The Great Goodbye was over, it was time to celebrate Life.

Chapter Twenty Four

Most Bod feasts took place in the Supper Room at the top of the Tower of the Five Orders. The victory of the Battle of Broad Street called for something a little larger. The sheer number of Bods also made the only sensible place to have the feast and celebrations was outside, in the Quadrangle itself. Great glow lamps had been set up. Much to Berga's delight (and slight embarrassment), her balloon had been salvaged from the battlefield and re-inflated by other members of Craster Carrel to make a magnificent centrepiece. It floated at about the same height as the top of the tower, with a multitude of glow lamps hanging from it. The whole square had light bouncing from every surface.

Creswick Carrel had set themselves (and their food tables, groaning under the feast and barrels of dandelion and burdock) up around the base of the tall statue of Billy Herbert on the opposite side of the square to the Tower. Every type of food a Bod could hope for was available. The Creswick Carrel were determined to put on a feast that Godwin would have been proud of. His apron fluttered over the tables, raised high on a tall pike as a banner. The whole of the Quadrangle was full of all of the Bods. They had hung flags and ribbons across the whole length of the place, whilst the edges of the square had great swathes of canvas connected to pikes and rope. These formed long tent-like coverings with glow staffs hung from their tops. Everyone could come and sit lazily on great sacks and cushions which were thrown together in a long comfortable train of colours and patterns.

The middle of the Quadrangle had groups of friends sitting on blankets and cushions together laughing and drinking. Each had tales to tell of the battle and their part in it. Tiny Bods ran in and out of the groups whilst Fellow Travellers caught up with old companions or made new ones.

Many of the smallest Bods had gathered around the Ashmoles, who hoisted them up onto their shoulders. This resulted in much shrieking and laughter. The Bods of Rouse Carrel had quickly found their instruments and were huddled in trios and quartets within the other groups playing old Bod folk songs, or quickly making new ones about the night before. The Storytellers had already begun weaving the events into legends and great stories and Alric smiled as he passed one, surrounded by other Bods. The teller was spinning the story of Cynwise the Brave, who had defeated the King of the Ignor'ns. A great book came then, for though Bods hate Ignor'ns, they hate Kings even more. He shielded his eyes a little and scanned the growing crowds, looking for his friends. Many groups had put up tall poles with flags and banners, ribbons and small kites in the shape of gargoyles or the Michaelmas Angel so that friends could easily wander off and find them again. He spotted Stan first, of course. He was carefully trying to persuade Derek, the True Spider that he didn't really want the great chunk of chocolate in his jaws, and that he should really give it to Stan for safekeeping. Alric laughed and made his way through the crowds towards them.

Red was sitting near Stan, on a cloth of woven green, nibbling on a crust of bread. The cloth was covered in bread, cheese, chocolate and bottles of dandelion and burdock. He was talking to Berga and Norrington, who had stuck close to Oswyn and Osric since losing his brother. The two small Bods were huddled together on the other side of the cloth, deep in hand-built conversation. Alric crashed down onto the cloth and ripped off a chunk of bread, only then realising just how hungry he was. He grinned at all of his friends.

"Well, here we are then. What do we do now?"
Red smiled a small smile and took a swig from one of the several bottles scattered around him. The light from the myriad of glow lamps shone back from the markings all over his body. He had changed his clothes when they had all tried to get some sleep through the day. He wasn't sure if it happened suddenly, or more slowly, but he had looked down at his coat as he made his way up to see Erasmus in his rooms at the top of Radcliffe Camera. The coat had turned a deep scarlet. The rest of his fresh clothes had also transformed into various shades of red. He stood there looking at himself with a mix of confusion and curiosity. Eventually, he shrugged and carried on up to see the old teacher.

***

"Come in Aethelred, I'm, erm, tidying up I think. Yes? Yes."

"My name is Red," the young Bod seemed to be standing a little taller than he had in the past. He stood in the middle of the general chaos of Erasmus' study, still covered in books, notes, charts and maps. The removal of Berga's balloon inflation contraption in order to get the thing up in the Quadrangle had not really improved anything. Erasmus looked up at his visitor.

"I liked that book! Oh, I see. Red it is then. So, Red, what can I do for you?"

Red held out his arms and allowed the symbols and patterns to shimmer in the light of the high glow lamps.

"What happened to me in there? What have I become?"

"I rather think only you know what went on in the time you spent inside the Bibliolibrum my young Bod. You and Wuffa of course."

Red scowled slightly.

"I didn't mean that. I meant what are these things, why does everything I wear turn red?"

Erasmus was furkling about under one of his sofas and delighted himself by finding a missing teapot.

"What? Oh, erm, I have absolutely no idea! But I fear we will one day find out my boy. Tea?"

Red had laughed then, the first time in a long while and took a cup from the mad old teacher. He was, the young Bod thought, possibly not as mad as he liked people to think.

"What do we do now? Offa is gone. Madam Brunda is gone. How do we carry on?"

Erasmus sipped his tea and stared around him at all of the maps and charts pinned to the wall. Which way would their Oxford go, he wondered.

"The Bods will carry on my boy, you always do. When

the Scriblerus Club finally defeated the Samhain Angel, it was the Bods who lost the most, but they survived. You folk are remarkable tough."

"I suppose so. Everything changes now, doesn't it?"

"Of course, it does my boy. Everything always changes. It would be awfully dull otherwise, don't you think?"

Red smiled again and finished his tea.

"It's just that, The Library seems smaller now somehow. When I was tiny, I thought that this was my whole world. Now, I'm not so sure. Madam Brunda used to say I would be a wanderer. I thought she meant that I would decide to be a Fellow Traveller, now I think she meant something very different."

Erasmus sipped his tea and watched the young Bod over the top of his green glass spectacles.

"The words that you heard when you were young will always stay."

Red stood and gave Erasmus the teacup back.

"I suppose we should head down to the Quadrangle, time to dance and eat and laugh with good friends."

Erasmus nodded, "What a splendid idea!"

Stan shoved Red on the shoulder, causing him to fall backwards,

"You're daydreaming again. Here, have some chocolate,"

Red reached out to take the chunk, but instead grabbed his friend and brought the big Bod crashing down into the middle of the cloth, sending bottles and food everywhere. Berga laughed and dived into the middle of the scrum. It took very little time for the whole lot of them to be tumbling around shrieking and laughing. Norrington was standing to one side shouting encouragement and suggesting certain neck holds to whichever one stuck their head out as the friends rolled together. The music of the feast grew louder and different songs could be heard across the great Quadrangle. The sounds and smells of the night drifted on and up into the clear sky, full of beautiful stars. The Bods feasted, sang, danced and laughed through the long night. They were still spinning tales and hugging friends as the new dawn light spilt across the City once again. The sunlight began glowing from the high walls and windows of The Library as it had done each morn for many, many years, and would do for many more. the Bods would make sure of that.

Chapter Twenty Five

Time had passed, as it had a habit of doing. Alric was starting to get a little fidgety. Most of the Bods had settled back into their routines or had begun new ones within The Library. He thought it was about time that he was heading back down into UnderOxford. There were many tunnels and chambers still unmapped, and he had seen things during recent days that needed to be explored further. He had been meeting with Erasmus again, and the teacher had pointed out that great areas of the Old Quarter were totally unmapped. He had mentioned this almost casually as he was rolling up various maps and handing them to Alric, but there had been a smile on his face and a glint in his eye. It was true that the west of the City carried many stories within it. The Paradise Street Irregulars, the Wyrm Vespasian who slept a fitful sleep under Castle Mound, the Sisterhood of the Brewery Gate. All lay out there, waiting for some adventurous Bod to find them and write it all down. Alric nodded to himself; perhaps it was time to head down and out again.

Things were returning to normal or as normal as anywhere quite as mystical and mad as The Library could ever really be. Meghan and Brec wandered through some of the lower corridors, heading for the one final room on their list. Brec absent-mindedly scratched his dead arm. The healers of Myres Carrel had done their best, but the thing was useless now. He had unsuccessfully attempted to get them to chop it off so he could get Berga to build him a new one, with a hook, he'd always wanted a hook. They had patted him on the head and moved on to the next injured Bod. Meghan checked the list again and stared up at the tall door in front of them.

"I think we are here, Brec."

There was a small Bod door in the base of the frame and they squeezed through into the storeroom behind. Brec stamped his glow staff on the floor and the warm light slowly filled the room. At first, they couldn't make it out, but then a slight rustling noise came from near the ceiling. Meghan took a glow orb from her pack and blew on it. It rose from her hand and floated up, bobbing in the air as it hit the bottom of the comic which was floating next to the air vent in the ceiling.

"Well, there it is, the last of The Nine. Thank goodness for that, I thought we'd be on this forever!"

Brec grinned and took out a small flute from his own backpack. He gently put it to his lips and blew a soft melody into the air. At first, it seemed that the comic was deliberately ignoring them but soon the music got to it and it glided slowly downwards. Meghan stroked it and smiled,

"You can't wander about, you are much too important for that kind of thing. Off to the store please."

The comic flapped slightly then rose to its allotted place within the stacks. Detective Comics number twenty-seven, from May 1939, settled into place and the whole Library seemed to sigh with relief.

Brec smiled.

"Job done, let's get back to the Supper Room and cause some trouble!"

Meghan laughed as the two friends sprinted back up through the labyrinth of rooms and passageways, corridors and chambers of The Library, their home.

Much of Berga's time was spent supervising the move from her deep cramped little workshop to the much more grand chambers that had been cleared and made ready for her by the other members of Craster Carrel. At first, she had been most uneasy about moving into the high vaulted set of rooms for they had been Offa's since before most Bods could remember. Audrey, one of the few remaining Old Guard had brought her down here and suggested to the rest of Craster Carrel that Berga should have them, in order to carry on her work. Audrey had been especially impressed and a little envious of the balloon. It had taken days to move everything over. Berga had personally supervised the moving of the section of the great Trollomicus which she had been working on for Madam Brunda. She had no idea how she was going to contact the Trolls in order to find out what they wanted to do with it. Perhaps the gargoyles would take a message? She heaved herself across her new grand room on her crutches and stared at the plans that lay scattered across the vast table at its centre. Schematic drawings of gliders, new glow lamps and maps of areas of The Library that Red seemed convinced were in different places than they had been before the coming of The Gloob. Berga would have laughed at him once. Everyone tended to take Red a little more seriously since it had turned out that he had been right about everything. The young Bod ran her hand through her thick, ginger dreadlocks and picked up a pencil and a large sheet of graph paper. There was a lot to do and an awful lot of time to do it.

"What do we do now?" The three black-clad Bods had been sitting at the table in the middle of their hall for quite some time. It was Arianrod who had broken the silence.

Bawdewyn looked up and sighed.

"Well, Offa is gone. Wuffa is gone thank goodness. I think we should simply gather the rest of James Carrel together and start again. We are the guardians of The Library..."

Wilda banged her hand on the table.

"And we failed!"

Bawdewyn nodded.

"Yes, we failed, and Wuffa betrayed us and his own Carrel, everyone in fact, but we must rise through this. The Library is still weak from all that has happened, we can feel it. Hyde Carrel is doing all they can weaving new protections but we must rise to our duty."

The other two looked at each other and nodded. Arianrod stood and took up her glow staff. She headed into the main chamber where all the others of their Carrel waited. Bawdewyn and Wilda followed.

"Let us do Offa's memory justice here, and hope we never hear of Wuffa again."

Bawdewyn nodded but had a bad feeling that they had not seen the last of the little traitor.

Stan Stared down at the note in his hand while he chewed on a particularly good piece of Battenberg cake. The messenger, a small Bod named Kendra, smiled up at him whilst she waited for a reply to take back to the surviving members of The Quire.

"There seems," Stan swallowed the (regrettably last) bit of cake before continuing. "There seems to be some kind of terrible mistake."

The little Bod looked up at him, her arms crossed.

"I don't make mistakes. They said to find Aethelstan the greedy and give him this note."

"Oh, well that's... Wait a moment, Aethelstan the GREEDY!?"

She grinned at him.

"I may have made that last bit up, but they said to find you and give you the note. And I have. Now, can I please have an answer so that I can go and get on with the rest of my life?"

Stan looked down at the messenger, the younger ones were definitely getting ruder. They had no respect. He

folded up the note and handed it back to her.
"Tell the grumpy old duffers that I'll be there as soon as I've found the Jaffa Cakes that I seem to have misplaced." He wandered off with a solid determination that only came over him when he hadn't eaten for the last few moments. Kendra shook her head and began the journey through The Library back to the Quire.
The Ashmoles had left at the end of the feast, returning through the tunnels and chambers to their home in the west of the City. The True Spiders had lingered a little longer, saying their goodbyes and agreeing to meet for a variety of lunches and teas. They had spent a good deal of their time towards the end of their visit talking to the smallest and newest of the Bods' Carrels, Thomas. There was only a handful who had joined, as was the way when a new group formed. They had been members of Hyde, the ward makers, and James, the guardians and watchers, but in time, they had come together and formed. Eventually, the newest of the Carrels, Thomas. Their interest and delight were in the strange devices that had begun to appear in The Library some while ago. These had begun as great big things, humming away in rooms all of their own but recently had become no bigger than the books on the stacks. The humans called them computers and Thomas Carrel loved them. These things seemed to get smaller and smaller all the time, which excited the Bods even more. Some of the more helpful humans had taken to 'accidentally' leaving a computer switched on somewhere in The Library, and it took Thomas Carrel no time at all to hunt one of these down. The group had sent word to the Quire that a new Carrel was forming. It had found a great deal of support from their old groups, now both rather weakened by the recent events and slightly more eager to please. It was Marjorie who had started to get interested when she had taken lunch with one of the

younger Bods of Thomas Carrel, Rowenna.
"This all sounds utterly delightful young lady, tell me more. I especially like this idea of a world wide web...."
It had taken quite some time to coax several of the older books to head back to their rightful places. Oswyn and Osric had supervised the more belligerent ones themselves. Most of Bandinel Carrel had been working nonstop since the return of The Library to get everything back to where it should be. The two brothers had just finished herding a particularly stubborn copy of the Rubaiyat of Omar Khayyam back into Duke Humphrey's Library and had headed back to their own room to get some rest.
Norrington was sitting waiting for them, grinning. He sat on one of their camp beds and seemed to be trying (quite unsuccessfully) to hide two boxes behind his back.
Osric raised an eyebrow and signed to Norrington. The old Bod looked shocked,
"Me? Up to something? The very thought, I merely came to say hello and give you two rapscallions a little present." He produced the boxes from behind him and handed them to the brothers. They looked at each other and began to unwrap them.
"You see my young friends, I have made a decision. It was not an easy one, but it is nevertheless made. I am far too old to look after Blackwell's on my own now that..." His voice broke slightly and trailed off. The old Bod coughed.
"Anyhow, I have decided to return to The Library and make myself useful here. I have a mind to make a study of the different smells of the inks. I like the smell of the inks. All different you know. Some are..." It was Oswyn's turn to cough.
"Oh yes. Well, anyhow, I'm staying put, so I thought that you two might like..."
The brothers had opened the boxes and were staring inside. Their eyes widened as they realised what lay within.

Oswyn and Osric turned to each other and grinned.

***

It had been some time since the group of friends had managed to find any time to spend together and it was, now Cynwise was gone, Berga who sorted things out. She had suggested the picnic on the roof of The Library for sunset, one warm day after they had all agreed to meet up.
Stan arrived first, in order, he said, to make sure there was enough to eat. There seemed to be quite a lot less to eat just after he got there, however. Berga had left others working on various projects in the workshops and sat down on one of the huge cushions scattered around.
"It's all different isn't it Stan?"
"Yep. But that's what it's all about Berg. If everything always stayed the same, what would be the point in living?"
Alric arrived next, carrying his pack which was brimming with maps, charts, notepads and glow orbs.
"I can't stay long, I'm heading down into the deep areas. I think I might try and find one of the tunnels towards Boswell's and then head out from there."
Berga handed him a bottle.
"That's far, Al. Have you got any maps to go on?"
"Erasmus has given me a few, and I've found several journals from past Bods of Shakleton Carrel, so I should be able to figure out some direction or other. But don't forget, it's impossible to get lost if you don't mind where you are going."
"That's very true, mister," Red wandered over and sat himself down on the vast rug that covered this part of the roof. He ripped a chunk of bread from the loaf in the middle of the food pile and smiled at his friends.
"Where are Oswyn and Osric?"

Berga shrugged.

"I sent word, oh, wait a minute..."

The two brothers appeared from one of the tiny doors in the crenelations. Each wore a brand new, red bowler hat and carried a brass staff. They hugged their friends and joined them on the rug, eating and drinking as the sun went down.

The glow lamps had been lit for a while when Berga turned to Stan,

"So, what have you been doing lately? I've heard some disturbing rumours."

Stan looked over in mock outrage.

"How dare you! I'll have you know I'm very very important. I'm on The Quire you know!" He stood up and bowed as his friend clapped and bowed even lower, laughing and then throwing bread at him.

Red grinned as his piece bounced off Stan's forehead.

"Things must be bad. I hadn't realised The Gloob had destroyed so much! They must be desperate!"

"I am a well-respected member of our glorious committee. I have influence!" He smiled at his friend and ate the bread.

Alric laughed.

"You have wind Stan, and that is not the same thing at all."

"I'll have you scoundrels know that I have raised several important points in our endless, mind-numbingly serious meetings."

Oswyn and Osric clapped and bowed again, swooping their bowler hats off as they did so. Stan stuck his tongue out at them.

"Only yesterday, or was it the day before? Anyway, I have brought to the notice of The Quire... good grief, I'm starting to talk like them... a very serious problem. I am convinced that the portions at supper are much too small

and I am of a mind to..."
The rest of his speech was curtailed in a barrage of bread and at least one bottle of Dandelion and burdock which narrowly missed him as it sailed past his head.

They fell about laughing as Stan dismissed them all with a wave of his hand, before spotting a chunk of chocolate in the pile and diving in. Berga turned to Red, the swirls and words on his skin almost glowing as the full moon rose in the night.

"And what about you sir? Each of us is settled on our own course, for now. I am too busy for words, and today they tell me that the Trolls are coming. The Trolls! Our little brothers here are Fellow Travellers no less and off to Blackwell's Bookshop. Stan thinks he's become some kind of Prime Minister and Alric is heading back into UnderOxford, determined to find St Frideswide's lost Banjo or some such." Alric grinned and nodded enthusiastically.

"But you Red, what is to be done about you?"

Red stood up and dusted the crumbs from his scarlet coat and crimson boots. He stood and smiled at his friends and stared up into the sky. The stars were bright in some places, though the full moon cast its light far, like the world's own glow staff. He wandered over to the edge of the roof and climbed up the ladders and ropes onto the high stones so he could look out across the city. He could see it all from here, every mysterious arcane bit. What wonders were happening in Oxford right then? What old gods sat playing cards in late-night coffee shops? Who watched for the beasts from deep, deep down, and protected the College Sorcerers as they span cantrips to keep the world at bay? What beings strolled in University Parks, making pacts or selling wishes? It was all there somewhere in this amazing, strange, marvellous City. Red stared out into the night, the words and patterns glowing

across him. Stan shouted up to him.
"So, What shall you do my friend?"
Red smiled,
"I'll think of something."

'Tis Done

Curious Art for Curious People....

www.greenspike-art.com

www.ingramcontent.com/pod-product-compliance
Lightning Source LLC
LaVergne TN
LVHW061608070526
838199LV00078B/7205